DEADLIGHT HALL

DEADLIGHT HALL

Sarah Rayne

This first world edition published 2014
in Great Britain and 2015 in the USA by
SEVERN HOUSE PUBLISHERS LTD of
19 Cedar Road, Sutton, Surrey, England, SM2 5DA.
Trade paperback edition first published
in Great Britain and the USA 2015 by
SEVERN HOUSE PUBLISHERS LTD.

British Library Cataloguing in Publication Data

Rayne, Sarah author.
  Deadlight Hall.
  1. West, Nell (Fictitious character)–Fiction. 2. Flint,
  Michael (Fictitious character)–Fiction. 3. Missing
  children–Fiction. 4. Twins–Fiction. 5. Haunted houses–
  Fiction. 6. Horror tales.
  I. Title
  823.9'2-dc23

ISBN-13: 978-0-7278-8471-8 (cased)
ISBN-13: 978-1-84751-574-2 (trade paper)
ISBN-13: 978-1-78010-620-5 (e-book)

All Severn House titles are printed on acid-free paper.

Severn House Publishers support the Forest Stewardship Council™ [FSC™],
the leading international forest certification organisation. All our titles that
are printed on FSC certified paper carry the FSC logo.

Typeset by Palimpsest Book Production Ltd.,
Falkirk, Stirlingshire, Scotland.
Printed and bound in Great Britain by
TJ International, Padstow, Cornwall.

ONE

'I don't mean to imply the house is haunted,' said Professor Rosendale firmly. 'And it's probably nothing more than childhood memories that have become distorted with the years. I really do think that's all it is, Dr Flint.' He waited for Michael to tip Wilberforce off the most comfortable chair, on which Wilberforce had shed cat hairs before going to sleep on a wodge of Michael's lecture notes, then sat down.

Michael Flint, whom the professor had approached midway through one of Oriel College's more somnolent autumn afternoons, said childhood memories could be strange things, and asked where the house was.

'It's just this side of Wolvercote. Only a few miles out of Oxford. It's an early Victorian mansion and it's been derelict for years. But now it's being renovated – turned into apartments. Six or eight of them. It sounds as if they'll be very smart,' said the professor, rather wistfully.

'Professor, I'll help in any way I can,' said Michael, 'but I hardly know a roof joist from a window frame. I'm the last person to advise anyone about property purchase.'

'Oh, I'm not buying,' said Professor Rosendale at once. 'It's the house itself. I'm concerned about people going to live there. I knew it for a while when I was a child, and there's a strangeness – a darkness to it. Now you'll think I'm strange myself,' he said, apologetically.

'I don't think that,' said Michael at once. 'Houses can be odd things.'

'And childhood memories can play odd tricks.'

'Well, yes. But events – tragedies, perhaps – can sometimes leave an imprint on a building. And an impressionable child witnessing something traumatic—'

'But that's the difficulty,' said Leo Rosendale. 'I don't know if I'm remembering actual events, or if it's all in my imagination. And I don't know how reliable my memory is either. Not,' he said, rather wryly, 'after so many years. So I thought if somebody could go in there and take an objective look round – someone who understands that houses sometimes possess—'

'Darknesses?' Michael deliberately repeated the professor's own word.

'Yes. I don't mean to sound melodramatic, and I'm fairly sure I'm not succumbing to some weird illness. But I believe you've had one or two strange experiences with old houses. Dr Bracegirdle from the History Faculty was talking about it the other day in the SCR. Somewhere in the Fens, I think he said.'

Michael silently cursed Owen Bracegirdle, who was a good friend, but also the liveliest gossip in College. He said carefully that he had stayed recently in a couple of places that had slightly macabre histories.

'I really would be most grateful if you could spare an hour or so,' said the professor. 'I thought you might be the one person in College who might understand.'

'How would I get in?' asked Michael.

The professor's face lit up. 'The builders are working there during the week,' he said, 'so you'd be able to go inside quite openly.'

Michael was becoming intrigued. He said, 'I've got a free morning tomorrow. I could take a look then.'

'Could you? I'm sure I'm making much out of very little, but it would put my mind at rest.'

'Of course. What's the address?'

'It's called Deadlight Hall,' said Rosendale, and Michael had the curious impression that by saying the house's name aloud, an invisible hand had scribbled the words on to the air in black, greasy letters. It was absurd to imagine the black scribble remained there for the rest of the afternoon.

It had taken Leo Rosendale a long time to decide to approach Dr Flint. He did not know Michael very well – his own faculty and the English Literature department did not have particularly close contact – but there had been one or two vaguely friendly meetings in the SCR or in Hall.

English literature was hardly a subject that qualified someone to grapple with Deadlight Hall. No matter how learned Michael Flint was about the Romantic poets, and no matter how many odd experiences he had had, what lay at Deadlight Hall's dark core was worlds away from elegies in graveyards and cobwebbed mausoleums. But after today's meeting Leo felt he had done the right thing. Dr Flint was said to be trustworthy and generally well liked by his colleagues and his students. The fact that he bore that strong resemblance to the English romantic poets – Keats before he succumbed to consumption or even Byron before he succumbed to debauchery – would have helped Flint's popularity, of course. The professor had occasionally wished he had been given the gift of good looks himself, although good looks probably only brought trouble with the opposite sex. He sometimes thought it might be nice to have got married and had children, but these were things that had never come his way and he had not really missed them. There had been Sophie, of course, but she had been lost to him a very long time ago.

He let himself into his own rooms, and sat down to read the advertisement for Deadlight Hall's new apartments again. There was a photograph of the Hall, which appeared to have been taken either at midnight or in the middle of a thunderstorm, and which made the old house look more like a gothic ghost setting than any house had a right to look. Leo read the description of the proposed flats again, and the comments from the builder, one Jack Hurst, whose firm were doing the work.

'Unusual old place,' Hurst had said. 'But we're hoping to retain the character of it – although we're having to rip out some of the original features and fittings, of course.'

The original features and fittings . . . Such as what lay behind the iron door deep in the basement . . .? Leo frowned, and threw the cutting into the bin. Too many memories, and most of them so dark.

Or were the memories what nowadays were called false memories – memories that seemed real, but that had never happened? But some of the memories *are* real, he thought.

During all the years when Deadlight Hall had been empty and derelict and more or less forgotten, he had been able to keep the memories – real, imaginary or simply just exaggerated – banked down; to enjoy his modest, rather quiet life at Oxford. Then, a few months ago, had come this advertisement about the Hall's renovations. At first, Leo had wondered if he could go along to the house, even present himself as a potential buyer. Would that lay the ghosts and the memories once and for all? But immediately the fear had come scudding in. To go back there, to enter that place again . . .

Had the builders working there – Jack Hurst and his workmen – sensed anything wrong about the house? Would Michael Flint? Or would Dr Flint return to say he had not heard or seen anything in the least peculiar, and remark what a splendid job the builders were making of the renovations?

Leo got up, opened the locked cupboard on one side of the fireplace of his study, and sat for a long time looking at what lay inside it. The trouble with old possessions was that memories clung to them, and those memories were not always good or happy. Could he discard this particular memory after so many years? Sophie was part of the memory, of course, but he did not need physical possessions to remember Sophie.

He snapped the box shut, replaced it in the cupboard, and with decision reached for the phone to dial Michael Flint's number.

'Professor Rosendale phoned after the meeting to say he's decided to sell what he calls an old memory,' said Michael to Nell West, later that evening over supper in the little house behind her Quire Court shop. 'He wondered if you might be interested in helping with the sale of it, so I said I'd ask. I have no idea what it is, this memory.'

'Does he need the money? I thought professors were quite well paid.'

'He just said he was shaking off the past. I don't know if that's true or if he needs the money. I don't know him very well, but I think he's rather unworldly.'

'What is he? I mean, what's his subject?'

'Philosophy and Theology. The Joint School thereof. He's supposed to be brilliant when it comes to all those philosophy questions – logic and perception and free will and all the rest. He's Czechoslovakian or Polish, I'm not sure which, and he's been at Oriel since anyone can remember.'

'I suppose he came here after the war?' Nell spooned chilli con carne on to the plates, and accepted the glass of wine Michael had poured.

'No idea. He's well into his seventies, I should think, but he never talks about his childhood or his family. Actually, he doesn't seem to have any family. If he comes into the shop, you'll do what you can for him, won't you?'

'Yes, of course.'

'He's a nice old boy,' said Michael, rather absently.

Nell looked at him. 'There's something worrying you, though. Is it to do with Professor Rosendale and the old memory? Or is the chilli too hot?'

'The chilli's fine.'

Nell was usually hesitant to press Michael – he was unfailingly courteous, but he had a way of occasionally putting up a barrier which it was difficult to penetrate. But she said, 'Are you worried by the prospect of grappling with an eerie old house? Yet again.'

'Since I met you,' said Michael, 'I think I've encountered more eerie old houses than Wilberforce has caught mice.'

The barrier appeared to have come down slightly. Nell said, 'How will you get in?'

'There's a firm of builders working on it. Apparently they're perfectly used to people wandering in at random to look at the flats.'

'Would you like me to come with you? Oh wait, I've got that Italian couple coming to look at the rosewood table tomorrow.'

'Then I'll have to ghost-hunt alone,' said Michael.

Nell spent the first half of the following morning applying Danish oil to the rosewood table, then setting it in the shop where it would display to the best advantage. She had bought it quite cheaply because it had been in a very neglected state, and had spent hours restoring it. If the Italian customers bought it, she would probably buy Beth the piano she wanted from the proceeds. It was nice that Beth was enjoying her music lessons so much; Beth's father had loved music, and Nell was trying to encourage Beth without over-kill. Enthusiasms at the age of ten did not necessarily last, of course, but there was room in the little house for a cottage piano at least.

She was just putting away the oil and the cloths when the shop door opened somewhat tentatively, and a tallish, rather elderly gentleman came in. He was wearing a long overcoat, and he had dark eyes and strongly marked cheekbones. Professor Rosendale, thought Nell. Or if it isn't, I'll drink the rest of the Danish oil.

But it was the professor, of course. He introduced himself with careful courtesy, and although he did not quite have an accent, there was something about the phrasing of his speech that was not quite English. Nell found this rather attractive.

He explained that Michael had suggested she might take care of the selling of something for him.

'Of course I will. Michael said you might look in. I'll be very happy to help if I can.'

'I'm having a kind of mental Spring cleaning,' said the professor confidingly, and with extreme care placed on the desk a small wrapped object. As he unfolded the soft dark cloth around it, Nell felt a sudden prickling of anticipation. This is going to be something good. Something really unusual. He folded back the wrappings, and there it was. A figure fashioned in what looked like solid silver – a chunky man-shaped outline about eight or nine inches high. There was a rudimentary face with a markedly benign appearance.

Nell lifted it from its cocoon, and turned it over in her hands, loving the smooth, cool feel of the surface.

'It's what is called a golem,' said Professor Rosendale.

'I've heard of them, but only in a very general way, and I've never seen one. I'm not very knowledgeable in this area, but it's from Jewish mythology, isn't it?'

'Yes. The Hebrew word *gôlem* means formless. So a golem is a figure supposedly created from inanimate matter – you can see how this one has been crafted to represent the legend of the being hewn from clay or fashioned from mud. The legend tells how at times it could be activated by mystical force. It's usually regarded as a force for good, but some of the tales relate times when it was harnessed for malevolence.' He smiled. 'People will always find a darker side to any story, won't they?'

'Sadly, yes.' Nell went on studying the figure, which was attractive and endearing.

'All the stories about golem figures animating are myth, of course. But interesting to hear and pass down – and analyse. There's said to have been a sixteenth-century figure – the Golem of Prague – created by a rabbi of the day to protect the Jewish people. It's supposed to have been stored in an attic or entombed in a graveyard in Prague's Zizkov district. All good tales, but no provenance for any of them.'

'Is there any kind of provenance for this figure?' asked Nell.

'I'm afraid not. Nothing written down, that is. It's also said to be from Prague, but I suspect that's said of all golems, in homage to the famous one. What I do know is that this figure came from the synagogue in my home – it was there for a great many years. I used to see it as a boy. It's one of the few things I brought with me to England.'

Nell reached for a magnifying glass to inspect the figure in more detail, and the professor waited, leaving her to concentrate. After a few moments, Nell said, 'I think this is very valuable, and I think that, offered in the right way, it might attract a good deal of interest. But I'm not an expert in this kind of antique. There's a hallmark just here under the feet which should identify where it was made, although I'd need to look in the reference books on that.'

'Would that mean leaving the figure with you, though?'

He sounded unsure, so Nell said, 'Not if you'd rather not. I could take some photos right away. Some close-ups of the hallmark, particularly. Then you can keep the figure until we know a bit more about it.'

'That would be very acceptable. And you could arrange its sale?'

'Yes, certainly I could, in fact I'd love to handle the selling of something so unusual and beautiful, but, Professor, are you sure you want to part with this? It's such a wonderful heirloom, and it's obviously part of your family's history – and of your religion.'

She hoped this was not a tactless remark, but Rosendale only said, 'I am quite sure. It's very nice of you to ask, though.' He smiled at her.

It was a strange thing, thought Nell, that Leo Rosendale was not a particularly good-looking man, apart from his eyes, which were very nearly mesmerizing. But when he smiled, such extraordinary sweetness touched his face that you wanted to keep looking at him.

He said, 'It has, you see, rather mixed memories for me, and sometimes one can carry memories around for too long. I believe it's time to put those memories away for good.'

'Then I'll very happily deal with it for you. I think, though, that it would do better at auction. Would you be all right with that?' He nodded. 'Good. Then what I'd like to do is sound out an auction house where I've got a couple of good contacts. They're called Ashby's. They aren't quite Christie's or Sotheby's, but I think they'd do a good job of selling and their commission is very reasonable.'

'I regard you as my agent,' he said, and the smile came again.

TWO

Michael spent the first half of the morning with a first-year student who was wrestling with the intricacies of prosody, and the second half rescuing Wilberforce from an attic. Investigation indicated that Wilberforce had got into the attic by means of a decorator's ladder, from which he had prowled curiously through a hatch inadvertently left open by them. He appeared to have spent a pleasant interval diligently ripping some roofing felt to shreds, most of which fell on still-wet paintwork, then discovered, to his indignation, that the ladder had been carried away, by a tidily inclined painter.

It was unfortunate that Wilberforce's vociferous demands for assistance reached the ears of the Bursar who had looked in to check the progress of the painting, and who investigated the banshee-like caterwauling. Michael, abruptly dragged out of the world of Elizabethan word-rhythms, reinstated the ladder, and spent ten minutes coaxing an indignant Wilberforce down. He then spent a further fifteen minutes placating the ruffled Bursar, who said Michael should remember that decorators were (a) expensive, (b) booked up for months ahead, and (c) apt to take umbrage if their handiwork was plastered with roofing detritus. He added crossly that the entire wall would have to be sanded down and done again, and demanded to know what use *Wet Paint* signs were if people paid them no attention.

Michael cursed Wilberforce, bundled him into his own rooms, and offered to foot the bill for the extra painting, to which the Bursar said, well, perhaps they did not need to be quite as penny-pinching as that, but please see it doesn't happen again, Dr Flint. By this time it was midday and the first-year student had gone off to keep a pressing appointment in the Turf Tavern. Michael went along to Professor Rosendale's rooms to tell him he was heading for Deadlight Hall and would call back when he returned.

'And Nell is finding out about an auction sale,' said the professor. 'What a delightful lady – so knowledgeable and helpful. I'm very grateful to you both.' He paused, then said, 'I'm glad you're going out to the house. A firm called Hurst & Sons are dealing with the renovations. They're an old local family firm, I think.' He hesitated. 'What will you say if they ask about your visit?'

'That an acquaintance mentioned the renovations, and I'd be interested to have a quick look round,' said Michael.

'Yes, that's exactly right.'

'And truthful,' said Michael, with a grin.

The Hall was, as the professor had said, only about fifteen minutes' drive from Oxford, on the outskirts of a village, which Michael found after taking only one wrong turning. It was a tiny place, with a little straggle of shops in the main street – including a greengrocer's and a pharmacist's, all of them with pleasingly old-fashioned frontages. There was a small square with a green and a stone cross war memorial.

And there, a mile out of the village, was an estate agent's board with arrows pointing the way, and tempting suggestions about mortgages and part-exchange deals on existing properties. The asking prices for the flats made Michael blink.

Beyond the For Sale board was a short drive, churned up by builders' lorries and dotted with slumbering cement-mixers. The house was framed by ancient-looking trees, and Michael switched off the engine, and sat looking at it.

Even in bright sunshine, Deadlight Hall would have looked grim, and there was no sunshine today – in fact huge storm clouds like purple bruises were massing, as if the gods had decided to provide a traditional gothic backdrop. Michael studied the harsh dark stonework and the frowning eaves. The renovations looked as if they were well under way, but they had not quite managed to dilute the Hall's sinister appearance. Approaching the front door, he thought that although any ghosts had probably long since left, an overlooked shade might remain: a leftover spirit who still wrung its hands and clanked its chains in hopeful, but futile, competition with the twenty-first century sounds invading its territory – stereos and iPads and the constant trill of mobile phones.

Several of the windows were circular – thick-glassed and rather unpleasantly suggestive of single lidless eyes. Were they the deadlights of the house's name? Michael had a vague idea that a deadlight was a small window or a skylight intended never to be opened and therefore ensuring permanent darkness.

Four shallow stone steps led up to large double doors at the house's centre, and as he pushed open the doors, the first faint growl of thunder reached him. The big hall beyond the doors was filled with the scents of paint and sawdust, and with the sounds of cheerful voices from somewhere outside, along with the tinny musical crackle of a radio. And yet just beneath all this were other scents and sounds. The sensation of a fetid darkness, of air old and stale, of extreme loneliness . . . And a far-off voice, echoing slightly, calling for something or someone . . . Were they real sensations, or was Deadlight Hall's past seeping through, like charred bones?

As Michael looked about him, a chubbily built man wearing overalls and wielding a chisel came in, and enquired amiably if he could be of any help.

'A colleague mentioned the renovations here,' said Michael. 'And since I was passing, I thought I'd like to take a look at the flats. I hope that's all right. I haven't spoken to the agents or anything.'

'No, that's all right,' said the man. 'I'm Jack Hurst, and my firm's doing the work here. No reason why you can't take a look inside. We haven't finished the flats by a long chalk, but the first floor ones'd give you a reasonable idea of what they'll eventually be. Up the stairs and to your left. I'll leave you to find your own way, if you don't mind. I need to sort out some of the electrics, before the storm arrives.' He looked through one of the narrow windows. 'Coming in from the east, if I'm any judge, and it's difficult to work in a thunderstorm. Feel free to look round the whole house if you want – although I'll ask you to avoid the basement. There's not much to see there anyway, but we're ripping out pipes and an old furnace, so it's a bit of a mess. Health and Safety stuff – it'd be easy to trip over something.'

'I'll remember. Thank you very much.'

The stairs were wide and shallow, and there seemed to be four flats on the first floor, one on each corner of the house. Michael ventured into the first one. It was strewn with builders' implements and dust sheets and coils of electrical cable, and he picked his way carefully through these. The flat was larger than he had expected, and the windows had views over trees and fields, apart from a side window which was one of the circular thick-glassed settings.

He came back to the main landing and started down the stairs to the hall. Jack Hurst had said amiably that he was welcome to explore the place, with the exception of the basement. Michael tried not to think that there was a faint sinister echo there of Bluebeard's chamber.

'You can have the keys to all these rooms in the castle, my dear,

except this one, and that you must never enter . . .' And as if the warning was a trigger, the ingenuous bride-heroine or the gallant knight must then yield to the sinister treacherous temptation, and instantly open the forbidden door by hook or by crook, by picklock or jemmy, to find the room did not contain priceless treasure or the elixir of life at all, but something far more macabre . . .

Michael paused on the half-landing to look through the narrow windows, which were slightly open. It looked as if Jack Hurst was right about the storm. Huge clouds like purple bruises were gathering in the east, and a faint growl of thunder rippled the sky. From the ground he could hear the rap of hammering and cheerful voices. Someone was calling out to Darren to make a brew, they were all spitting feathers, and someone else wanted to know had anyone thought about a bit of a fry-up before the storm got going.

Storm rain was starting to spatter the windows, and Michael, who often suffered from a severe headache in a thunderstorm, was aware of needle-points of pain starting to jab at his temples. He thought he would make a quick tour of the rest of the house, then beat it back to College and take a couple of paracetamol. He closed the window against the rain, and he was about to go down to the hall when he heard footsteps behind him, and then laboured breathing, as if someone was carrying something heavy. He turned, expecting to see one of Jack Hurst's men, but there was no one there. Had the sound been simply an echo? No, there it was again. Footsteps – slow, rather uncertain ones, coming from a second, narrower flight of stairs at the far end of the landing. Second floor? Yes, of course. And muffled thudding or hammering from up there.

Then a voice called softly, 'Are you here?'

The words were ordinary, the words of someone looking for somebody, but Michael found them extremely sinister. He took a step towards the second stair.

'Hello? Are you looking for someone?' His words echoed in the empty space, and although he could still hear the difficult breathing, there was no response.

Two, then three flickers of lightning tore into the house, and in those split-second flares of brilliance, Michael saw a figure standing on the narrow stairs – a small figure, not exactly deformed, but hunched over . . .

A child? Frightened by the storm? Maybe it was the child sought

by the owner of that voice he had heard. There was a blur of movement, and the sound of the footsteps again – this time going away,
back up the stairs, not exactly running, but scuttling away. Michael
hesitated, then started forwards.

'Don't be frightened,' he called. 'It's only a thunderstorm. Wait
for me and we'll go downstairs – I think someone's looking for
you, anyway.'

The stairs wound sharply to the right, decamping on to a second
landing, strewn with more builders' rubble and tools. It looked as
if two smaller flats were being created up here. A sullen light came
in through the windows, but there was no sign of the figure. The
thudding was still going on – it sounded as if someone might
be hammering somewhere under the roof, but Michael's headache
was throbbing against one side of his head, and his vision was
blurring slightly, as if he was seeing underwater.

But he was sure he had seen a figure, and he was equally sure
it could not have gone back downstairs without passing him. It must
still be somewhere here, perhaps hiding fearfully from the thunder,
or even from Michael himself. Nell's small daughter, Beth, hated
thunderstorms, and always shut herself into a narrow storeroom at
the back of the shop.

He looked into the partially built flats, finding nothing, and began
to have the feeling of having fallen into the kind of nightmare where
the dreamer embarks on a panic-stricken chase for something he
never reaches. Was there anywhere else he ought to check? Yes, a
further flight of stairs at the end of this landing, small, half-hidden,
dusty-looking. Attic floor? It seemed to be where the thudding was
coming from.

The movement came again, no more than a blurred outline, but
more substantial than the shadows that clustered there. It was small
enough to be a child, but there was something about it that was not
entirely childlike. Michael hesitated, then went up the stairs, which
swayed slightly, and creaked like the crack of doom. They had not
done so when the small figure went up them.

The attic floor was dim and warm and there were huge pools of
shadows and a thick smell of dirt. Michael had the sensation of the
immense old roof pressing down on him.

Massive beams spanned the open space overhead; stringy cobwebs
dripped from them, and thick swathes of roofing felt hung down in
tatters. Shreds of light trickled through in those places. It was to be

hoped that Jack Hurst and his men would make the roof sound before the flats were actually sold.

Items of discarded household junk lay around – old bits of broken furniture including several dismantled iron bed-frames. They were small beds – children's beds?

The attic looked as if it had once been split into two or three separate rooms; there were vague outlines of door posts and of a couple of piles of rubble that might be a collapsed wall. At the far end a door looked as if it opened on to an inner room that must be situated on the corner of the house, almost under the eaves. Servants' rooms, thought Michael. Cramped and airless. Cold in winter and stiflingly hot in summer. There was an unhappy feel to the place, but there was no sign of the small figure, and the strange hammering had stopped. He would go back downstairs and find one of the workmen to ask if a child was known to be in the house.

But to make sure there was no one here, he went over to the door in the corner and tried the handle. It resisted, but the second time he tried, a soft voice from the other side of the door – a voice that was within inches of him – said, 'Are you there?'

Michael leapt back from the door, as if it had burned him, then took a deep breath and called out, as he had done earlier: 'Hello? Is someone there? Are you trapped?' His voice sounded strange in the enclosed space. 'Is someone there?' he said again, a little louder.

The lightning flickered again, showing up the worn joists and the crumbling floorboards, and thunder growled again. Then silence and blackness closed down once more. Michael, his vision still fuzzy, was momentarily dazzled by the flickers of light. But he waited, and after a moment the voice came again.

'Children, are you here? I shall find you, you know . . .'

Prickles of unease tinged with fear scraped across Michael's skin, but he tried the handle again, this time pushing harder. It protested and creaked like the crack of doom, then it opened.

The lightning tore through the attic again, showing up the small, sad room beyond. At the far end was a pallid figure, its head bowed over, the shoulders hunched. It moved slightly, and Michael gasped. The flare came a second, then a third time, and he let out a deep breath of relief, because after all it was only a swathe of old, pale curtain, tattered and almost in shreds, that had caught in the old roof timbers.

There was no one here. Anything he had seen or heard had been his imagination – tricks played by the storm and the house's strange atmosphere, and by his thudding headache. With the idea of proving this, he stepped into the room and looked around. It was not too dark to see that it was much the same as the outer attic. The floor was worn and uneven, with what might be burn marks in a line across one corner. There was a dismantled bed and a small table, and an old-fashioned, marble-topped washstand. Beyond the bed was a little stack of books, leaning against one of the roof supports. Michael knelt down to examine them. The livid crackles of lightning and his headache were still blurring his vision, but he was able to make out a row of titles, some of which were vaguely familiar, others which were not. At one end were a couple of battered-looking volumes with rubbed leather covers. He ran a finger lightly along the spines. It did not seem very likely that there would be any valuable first editions amidst this dereliction, but he would mention the books to Nell, who might want to speak to Godfrey Purbles, the antique bookseller at Quire Court.

The lightning sizzled again, briefly turning the thin old curtain into a drooping figure once more. Michael closed the door on it and went down to the second floor, and then the first. He was thankful to see that the oblongs of sky through the windows looked lighter. The thunder seemed to have growled into the distance, and he stood on the first-floor landing for a moment, leaning against the cool window pane, feeling fresh air coming in through the small opening at the top. His headache was starting to recede, and in another ten minutes he would be fine to drive home.

Below him were the cheerful voices of Jack Hurst's men. Somebody was being told to pick up a takeaway order, and never mind about driving through a bit of rain, and somebody else was compiling a list of what was wanted, making the ribald most of the choice of pork balls, and lugubriously wondering how long Darren would take to fetch the food, because they were all starving. The normality of this made Michael feel better.

Several rooms led off the big hall, all of them large with high ceilings and ornate fireplaces. Most were in various stages of renovation, with high stepladders and tubs of paint or cement lying around. If they were intended to eventually form more flats, they would be rather grand ones.

But there was one room that caught Michael's attention. It led off what he thought must have been the main drawing room, which had got as far as the redecoration stage of its renovation. The smaller room beyond it had not yet received much attention. A squat old stove, probably originally for heating, crouched in one corner, its flue corroded and leprous-looking. The plasterwork around it was dry and flaking, but near to the floor was something that caught Michael's eye. A sketch? A date? He bent down to examine it, briefly curious. It was not a sketch; it looked as if it had been carved very precisely into the plaster itself. It might be an initial, or a date. Or was it more than that? He moved round, so that the light from the narrow window fell more directly on to the wall, and saw it was an apparently meaningless pattern, perhaps slightly abstract, but not seeming to signify anything. It looked like something a child would draw, without having much regard to its meaning.

He went back to the hall. Sunlight was coming in through the windows, laying diamond-shaped patterns on the floor from the latticed glass. There were window seats in each of the window recesses, and Michael thought the house was almost pleasant, seen like this.

But he would be glad to be driving back to Oxford, although before he left, he would find Jack Hurst or one of his workmen, and mention seeing or hearing someone on the upper floors.

As he went out through the main doors, Jack Hurst himself came around the side of the house, carrying a coil of electrical cable.

'Everything all right?'

'Yes, thank you. I had a good look round – the flats are going to be lovely. You're making a very nice job of everything. But there was just something . . .'

'Yes?'

'I thought I saw someone roaming around the top floors,' said Michael. 'And I thought I heard someone calling for a child.'

Hurst's eyes flickered. 'Did you see anyone?'

Impossible to say that all he had seen had been a shadow and a fall of old silk in an attic. 'No,' said Michael. 'I did think there was someone up there, though – I heard a kind of thudding sound. It seemed to be in the attics.'

'Pipes,' said Hurst at once. 'Water hammer – major airlock some-where. It can be remarkably loud at times. We keep hearing it, and we're trying to track it down, but in a place this size . . .' He made a rueful gesture. 'As for the children, well, I dare say it was just local kids. They get in here and think it's a great place to play. Kids' paradise, this place. I'll take a good look round later.'

Michael did not think children had ever played in Deadlight Hall, but he said, 'Thanks,' and went back to his car.

THREE

B ack in Oriel, Michael prowled around his study, and tried to read an essay from a promising second year on the influence of mental instability on Charles and Mary Lamb's work.

But the image of the hunched figure he had seen in the attics and again in the hall would not leave him. Jack Hurst had said it would be a child or children, playing in the house, but Michael was not sure that what he had seen had been a child at all. And yet what else could it have been? And where had it – or they – gone? The impression he had received had been of fear. Fear of what? Of an eerie old house? That was very likely, of course. But what else might a child have feared so much that it ran away and hid itself – hiding so thoroughly it could not be found?

Jack Hurst had not seemed a likely candidate for the role of any kind of villain, but there had been that unmistakable flicker of unease when Michael had mentioned seeing a child in the house. And most villains must appear normal to the world for the majority of the time. They had to do ordinary things like the rest of the population; they had to go to the dentist and collect the dry-cleaning, and they had to earn a living – to pursue ordinary jobs.

After half an hour, he abandoned his attempt to read the second year's essay, and phoned the local police, to ask if any children had been reported missing.

It seemed they had not. Was Dr Flint sure he had actually seen a child inside the house?

'I'm not sure,' said Michael. 'And when I searched I didn't find anything.'

'You did say Deadlight Hall, sir?'

'Yes.'

'Ah. I see. Well, it's an odd old place, that one,' said the police sergeant. 'You wouldn't believe some of the reports we've had about that house. Myself, I put it down to peculiar bits of brickwork casting shadows.'

Shadows, thought Michael. But the shadow I saw moved.

'We'll take a look though,' the sergeant went on. 'And we'll make a few discreet enquiries. Social workers and the like, you know. You can trust us to follow it up, but I don't think you need worry, Dr Flint. We'd certainly know if any children were missing, and I'd hope we'd be aware of anything . . . well, anything wrong anywhere. Good of you to take the trouble to call us, though. Can't be too careful. I'll give you a reference number to quote if you need to come back to us. There'll be a log of this call anyway.'

Michael wrote down the reference number, replaced the phone, and returned to his second year's essay. This time his concentration was interrupted by the arrival of the head decorator into his room, who reported with indignation that Wilberforce, clearly still sulking from the attic incident, had dabbled his paws in a pot of paint which the decorators had left ready for the ceiling. He had then stomped white paw prints across most of Oriel's stairways, and you never saw such a mess in your life – the decorator did not know how they were ever going to get it properly clean.

Michael pacified the aggrieved decorator, who was annoyed at having a twenty-litre can of paint ruined, managed not to point out that it would have been better not to leave the lid off in the first place, agreed to foot the bill for a fresh can of paint, together with what seemed like an unreasonably large amount of turpentine, tipped his scout to help them clean everything, then hauled Wilberforce off to the vet to have his paint-spattered paws dealt with.

'Poor Wilberforce,' said Nell that evening in Quire Court. 'He'll smell of turps for ages and his dignity will be severely damaged, never mind his street cred.'

'If the Bursar finds out it'll be Wilberforce who'll be severely damaged,' said Michael. 'He's already furious about having to get Wilberforce out of the attics.'

'Yes, but I bet you get a chapter out of it for the new book.'

'Well, I might.' Michael had in fact already emailed his editor at the children's book publishers about the idea as soon as he returned from the vet's. He had received a cordial response, together with a reminder that they had a publication date of February and a first draft by the end of September would be greatly appreciated by the illustrator. She supposed that would not be a problem, however. There was not quite a question mark at the end of this last sentence, but Michael heard it anyway.

'And,' he said to Nell, 'she apparently thinks it would be "rather fun" to have some publicity shots of the real Wilberforce for the new book and what do I think?'

'Well, what do you think? And are you staying to supper? I made a huge lasagne this afternoon, so there's plenty.'

'Anyone who can keep Wilberforce still for long enough to photograph him – never mind finding him in the first place – is welcome to shoot an entire album of photographs,' said Michael wrathfully. 'And yes, I'd like to stay to supper, please. Where's Beth?'

'Bashing out scales with her music teacher. She hates scales, but she loves the second part of the lesson when she's allowed to try one of the simpler Mozart pieces. She'll be back by eight. We'll save her some lasagne.'

Later, over the lasagne, she said, 'How was the professor's haunted house?'

'A bit odd.' Michael had been looking forward to being with Nell – to the familiar comfort of the little house behind her shop – but he discovered he did not want to talk about the small strange shadow he had seen. Instead he said, 'I might see if I can unearth any details about it. It'd be interesting to research its history.'

'I've been doing some researching,' said Nell.

'The professor's silver golem?' Michael was instantly interested.

'Yes. I've had a discussion with Henry Jessel at Silver Edges. He's got dozens of books on hallmarks – it took ages to track the golem's markings down, and even then Henry couldn't be absolutely sure about its place of origin. Apparently hallmarks struck in Central Europe – Bavaria, Czechoslovakia, Hungary – Bohemia, if you like – can be confusing. There were so many wars and the borders kept changing, so extra marks were sometimes struck on items from other countries. That means you often get a plurality of marks, and it's not always easy to know which one to trust. That's what seems to have happened with the golem. Henry says we'll probably have to take the professor's word that it was made in Prague.'

'Could you tell when it was actually made?'

'It's stamped as 1780, and there's a figure of fifteen over the top, which indicates it's a very pure silver.'

'Valuable, then.'

'Yes, I think so, but I'm waiting for Ashby's pronouncement on that. They'd be more than happy to include it in their next sale, by the way.'

'Of course they would. Did you say you'd taken photographs? Can I see them?'

'Yes, of course,' said Nell, pleased at his interest.

'It's an extraordinary object,' said Michael, as she laid the photos on the table. 'But it's rather attractive.'

'I think it's quite endearing. A bit like a silver version of a child's teddy bear. But,' said Nell, 'here's one rather curious thing. The professor told me about a legendary golem crafted in Prague in the sixteenth century. Ashby's knew about that. They said quite a number of figures were later made in Prague – I think as a kind of echo, or even homage, to the sixteenth-century tale. But there were two in particular – an exact pair – made in Prague in the late 1700s, said to have been valuable.' She paused to drink the wine Michael had poured. 'Both those figures vanished in the early 1940s. Ashby's won't commit themselves until they see Professor Rosendale's figure, but they think it might be one of that vanished pair. They've got some correspondence on it – they're going to send me copies.'

Michael said, 'That date's significant, isn't it? Could the figures have been smuggled out during the Second World War? Or even looted by the Nazis? No, that's not very likely is it? The Nazis wouldn't be likely to seize such a very Jewish symbol. Or would they?'

'The Nazis squirrelled away a huge amount of paintings and silver and whatnot. I wouldn't discount anything. But don't you see that it begs the question—'

'If Leo Rosendale owns one of the vanished pair, how does he come to own it?'

'Exactly. I do like not having to spell things out to you,' said Nell. 'And the other question, of course, is what happened to the second figure.'

'I wonder if the professor knows.' Michael was still studying the photographs. 'Is this the hallmark?'

'Yes, I took several close-ups. That's the date, as you can see, and a figure fifteen indicating the purity of the silver. And—'

'What's that?' Michael interrupted, indicating a small symbol on the side of the main hallmark, set a little apart. 'It doesn't look as if it's part of the hallmark.'

'No, in fact it looks as if it was added much later – a bit amateurishly, as well. I thought about asking Professor Rosendale if he knew what it was, but—'

'He's a bit defensive about the figure?' said Michael.

'You noticed that, too? Yes. But Henry didn't know what it was and we couldn't find it in any of the reference books. I'm hoping Ashby's will recognize it.'

'I recognize it,' said Michael. He was staring at the small symbol, which was a little like three vertical branches jutting up from a horizontal line.

'You do? What is it?'

'I don't know. But the exact same symbol is carved on a wall inside Deadlight Hall.'

*

The Village School House, Nr Warsaw
Autumn, 1942
My dear M.B.

We agreed that, in the British expression, there would be 'no names, no pack drill' in these messages, so I address you by your initials only, and sign in the same way. Forgive the discourtesy, my good friend.

With great reluctance, we have agreed that despite the emotional cost to their families, the children in our village may need to be removed to safety. You mentioned a possible escape plan from the man we both know as Schönbrunn. Does such a plan actually exist? Can you give me information about it? And can it – and Schönbrunn himself – be trusted?

Affectionately,
J.W.

Prague, 1942
Dear J.W.

I have spoken with Schönbrunn (through the usual sources) and he has given me details of his plan. I do not dare commit those details to paper, but I can assure you the plan is a simple one and should work. It will be an enormous wrench for the families, but in the end we will have saved the children, and we can only hope they will be reunited with their parents before too long.

Schönbrunn can be trusted completely. Remember how many of our people he has smuggled to safe countries already. I suppose someone somewhere knows his real name, but I certainly do not and I don't suppose you do, either, which probably is safer for both of us. I shall never forget the first time I met him – just outside Buchenwald, it was. He has the eyes of a poet and a dreamer, but in his hands is a machine gun.

Your friend and one-time colleague,

M.B.

School House, 1942

My dear M.B.

If Schönbrunn can save our children, we do not care if he is one of the seven princes of hell.

J.W.

School House

Winter 1942

Dear M.B.

It is being whispered that the march towards our village will soon begin, and a terrible dread is pervading every house.

We hear that Dr Josef Mengele is being called the *Todesengel* – the Angel of Death – and that he is particularly focusing on experiments on twins. We therefore have great concern for the Reiss girls – you will remember them, I dare say, from your time here teaching at the school. If so, you will certainly recall that very unusual gift they seemed to have. I think special arrangements may need to be made for those two.

If our village is invaded, we plan to hide in the crypt of an old Christian church on the village outskirts – the last place we will be sought, we hope!

J.W.

Prague,

January, 1943

Dear J.W.

Schönbrunn's agents have told us that an order has gone out from the High Command that *7,000 of our people per day* are to be 'resettled in the East'. Once, we would have accepted this at face value; now we know that these deportations end in mass extermination.

Exact details of the plan for the children should by now have reached you. Schönbrunn has contacts in the country to which the children will be taken – safe homes can be provided for all, and I believe there is some kind of secret list of people who have indicated they are prepared to give shelter. I do not enquire, but I think it is information that can be trusted and all the parents can feel reassured. Siblings will be kept together if at all possible.

I do indeed remember the Reiss twins who undoubtedly possessed that extraordinary gift – it was occasionally somewhat disconcerting in the schoolroom! I have told Schönbrunn about them, and he agrees that we must have particular concern for them. Josef Mengele's spies are in the most unexpected places.

Schönbrunn advises most strongly that you do not alert any of the children until the very last minute. You must not risk them inadvertently letting something slip, or being too afraid to obey the requirements of the plan when the time comes. They should take only the minimum of possessions, and the journey itself will cost nothing, but I think none of their families will want to be dependent on charity of any kind. So it is my suggestion that each child is given several small but valuable items. Actual money might pose problems, but jewellery is always sellable.

M.B.

School House, 1943
My dear M.B.

Even amidst the fear and desperation, I smiled at your suggestion to provide the children with sellable valuables. It is so like you to have an eye to the practicalities and the finances.

J.W.

Prague, 1943
Dear J.W.

We think your situation has suddenly worsened. Late last night one of our people sent word that residents in a village thirty kilometres from yours were taken away. This happened just two days ago, and we believe your village will be next.

Schönbrunn is putting the plan into action at once. Tonight, as soon as it is dark, you must take the children, and hide out in the old church you mentioned. There is an irony, isn't there, in making use of a Christian sanctuary to shelter Jews? But if you can be safe there, it does not matter what it is.

Most worrying of all is that we believe within the detachment of soldiers are two of Mengele's agents. As you know, we always feared this particular menace – there is a general order that any twins, boys or girls, are taken to him. But we now have information that one of his spies has heard about the Reiss girls and their exceptional telepathic gift (we do not yet know how such information could have got out), and we fear that the march to your village is not a general one as the others have been. We are afraid that Mengele's orders are to take Sophie and Susannah Reiss to Auschwitz. You must make it very clear to those two – to all the children, of course – that during the days ahead, they must never trust strangers.

I would like to think that along with the Reiss twins, the intelligent little Leo Rosendale will be safe. He was such a delight in the infant class I taught for you last summer – such a bright, enquiring mind. But all of the children must be made safe, of course.

Hold firm and fast, as I do – as we all do – to the belief that one day this nightmare will end and we will all live together again in peace and safety and harmony.

M.B.

FOUR

Leo Rosendale had listened to Michael Flint's account of what he had seen and heard inside Deadlight Hall with dismay. Dr Flint had been deliberately casual – even vague – about the shadowy figure and the voice calling for the children, but it was clear to Leo that Michael had heard and seen the things Leo himself had heard and seen all those years ago. The strange misshapen shadow that walked through the old house, calling for the children . . .

He had expressed his thanks, and said something about going out to take a look for himself. Flint had offered to accompany him, to which Leo said, carefully, that he was going to think it over first.

But after Michael had gone, Leo sat for a very long time, staring out of his study window. Was he reading too much into this? Was it possible that Michael had encountered nothing more sinister than some local children playing some game? Hide-and-seek, perhaps – did children still play that? He had played it all those years ago in the village where he had lived for the first five and a half years of his life. There had been a little group of them, all good friends. The Reiss twins had been part of the group, Sophie and Susannah. They had been Leo's particular friends – they had been pretty and clever, and he had loved them both with uncritical devotion. But then there had come a night just after his sixth birthday when they – when all of his friends – had played what had become a macabre game of hide-and-seek. That had been when the nightmare began.

It had seemed an ordinary evening at first. Leo had his supper as usual, Mother washed up the dishes, and Father worked on some school papers – Leo thought they were exercises from pupils in his father's class at the school. Leo did not yet go to his father's classes, which were for learning French and English, but his father had taught him a few phrases of both, because he said it was important to know about other lands and the way people in other countries spoke. That night, as he sat over his pupils' homework, occasionally making tsk-ing sounds if he came across a mistake, Mother read a story to Leo, and it should have been an ordinary night, exactly like all the others. But it was not. There was something different, something frightening. Nothing you could see or hear, but a feeling that something was spinning a huge black spider's web, and as if the threads were being spun closer and closer . . . As if the spider at the heart of the web had turned all of its eyes on to Leo and his parents and all their friends. When Leo thought about it afterwards, he realized the fear had been in his house – in everyone's house – for a very long while. Once – no, it was more than once – he heard the grownups whispering and looking worried. One of them said something about ovens, and some of the women turned away, trying to hide that they were crying. People at school talked about the ovens, as well, doing so in a scared, whispering way, but Leo did not think anyone really knew what they were. Sophie Reiss said they might be like the oven in Hansel and Gretel, which the bad old witch had made roaring hot in order to roast children for her dinner, but Susannah, who was inclined to be more practical, said that was stupid, that people did not roast children and it was just a fairy story.

Leo knew Susannah was right, but he also knew that the grown-ups were very frightened indeed. Once, when his parents thought he was busy with his school work, his father said, 'The ovens are being fed with thousands every day now.' And Leo's mother said, in a voice Leo had never heard her use before, 'How long until they come for us?'

It was two nights after that when Leo's father woke him up in the middle of the night and said he must get dressed in his warmest things, because they had to go on a journey, but Leo was not to be afraid, and everything was going to be quite all right.

Leo had never been woken up in the middle of the night and told he was going on a journey, and he although he was a bit afraid, he was also a lot excited, because this could be the start of an adventure, the kind of thing people did in books.

They had gone along to the church on the edge of the village, Leo holding tightly to his father's hand on one side and his mother's on the other. He was still a bit frightened, but this was starting to be an adventure all by itself, because he had never been inside the church – he had never been inside any church – but one of his friends at school knew someone who had, and he said churches were a bit like synagogues where you had to chant things and there was a priest, and music.

When they got to the church, Leo's friends were all there. Sophie and Susannah came straight over to him; they were wearing their scarlet coats and mittens, and their cheeks were pink with excitement and apprehension. They had known he would come, said Susannah. They had felt his fear in their minds when he set off from his house.

This was the kind of thing the twins often said, so Leo did not bother to question it. He asked what was happening.

'We don't know,' said Susannah. 'Sophie thinks it might be something to do with the Ovens.'

'What about the Ovens?' asked Leo, but neither of the twins knew any more than Leo did about the Ovens, except that the grown-ups talked about them a lot and always seemed frightened of them.

A register was called, as it was in school, and they had to answer to their names, then go down some crumbly stairs to a long dark room under the church. Leo would have liked to stay in the real church and look round – there were carved bits of stones and beautiful tall windows with sparkly colours in them – but it seemed there was no time to do that, and anyway it was all in shadow and they must not put on any lights. Sophie and Susannah did not think there were any lights, on account of it being an old, old church where hardly anyone ever went.

The room under the church was cold and there were huge stone boxes with carvings on them, and stone figures lying on their lids. It smelled damp and musty, and the twins put their scarves over their mouths so they would not have to breathe in the smell.

'Dead people,' said Sophie. 'But a long time ago.'

But then Leo's mother, who was dreadfully pale, brought them all hot soup, and after that they did not notice the smell, and drinking soup in the middle of the night inside a church seemed part of the adventure.

They sat on the ground, on blankets and cushions, and waited to see what would happen next. Leo's mother gave him a small canvas bag which, when he looked inside, he found had his best sweater, pyjamas, socks, toothbrush, and some pieces of jewellery and a silver box that had belonged to his grandmother. He had only the haziest memories of her, but he knew she was one of the people who had vanished, along with his grandfather. His mother had never talked about them, but once Leo had found her sitting on her bed, clutching their photographs and sobbing.

She was not exactly sobbing now, but her face had a white, hurt look. She hugged him and said he was to be a good and brave boy, to do whatever was asked of him, and to never forget that they loved him very much and always would. His father gave him a small package – something wrapped in layers of cloth. Leo unwrapped a bit of the cloth and saw it was one of the silver golems from the synagogue. He looked questioningly at his father, because the two golems at the synagogue were special things, even a bit magical, and no one was ever allowed to touch them.

'Keep it safe and it will protect you,' said Leo's father, and although he was not exactly crying, his eyes were shiny and his voice was husky as if he might be getting a sore throat.

It was Sophie who suddenly sat up and looked towards the crumbly stairs as if she had heard something. Susannah looked as well, at exactly the same moment. They've heard something, thought Leo, his heart starting to thump. Or they've felt that something's about to happen. Whatever it is, it isn't good. As this thought formed, Sophie looked across at him, and shook her head. *No, it isn't good.*

Moments later, Leo heard marching feet, and voices sounding sharp and angry, calling out. The grown-ups made signs to the children to be very quiet. 'Like a game,' said one of them, softly, but Leo thought they all knew it was not a game. He whispered to his father to ask if it was something to do with the Ovens, and his father looked at him in a startled way, then said, very quietly, 'Pray it is not.' The twins' mother said something about the Angel of Death, and her face twisted as if she was going to cry. But she did not; she put her arms round Sophie and Susannah and hugged them very tightly to her.

Leo reached for the golem tucked inside his bag, and curled his hand firmly around it. It felt friendly and reassuring, and he fixed his eyes on the stair leading up to the church. The footsteps were louder now; they rang out sharply and in exact rhythm, like a fast-beating heart, and the voices were louder. Leo could not understand what they were saying, but some of the grown-ups pressed back into the shadowy corners as if wanting to hide. Leo discovered he was shivering, but he sat up very straight so no one would know.

It seemed a very long time before the marching footsteps and the voices faded, but eventually they did, and the adults looked at one another and smiled a bit shakily.

The twins' mother was just pouring coffee for everyone from two large flasks, when the sound of new footsteps reached them – not the hard, frightening ones they had heard earlier, but soft, light steps. Before anyone realized it, a man was standing at the foot of the stairs, a faint shaft of silver moonlight falling over him like a thin cloak. Leo's father said, 'Schönbrunn. Oh, thanks be that you've reached us,' and went forward to shake the stranger's hand.

The man called Schönbrunn was thin-faced and dark-haired, and although he was somehow very quiet-looking, once he stepped into the room, the clogging fear seemed to vanish, and everyone sat up and smiled and nodded. It's going to be all right, thought Leo. Whatever was wrong is going to be put right. He'll put it right.

Schönbrunn knelt down in front of Leo and the twins, and the other children, and held out his hand. There were still flecks of silver moonlight in his hair and his eyes.

'Hello,' said Schönbrunn. 'I'm glad to meet you all.' He smiled at Leo. 'You're the young man who can speak a little English,' he said and, when Leo nodded, Schönbrunn said, 'That's very good indeed. That will be a great help to us.' He looked at Sophie and Susannah then. 'And you're the Reiss twins.' Leo thought he frowned slightly, as if somebody had suddenly given him a very difficult task, but he only said, 'I'm particularly glad to find you here.' He sat back on his heels, and looked at the other children, all huddled into a fearful little group. 'We're going away,' he said. 'It's a bit of an adventure and you must promise to do everything I tell you. But it'll just be ourselves – you'll have to leave your parents for a time.'

Leo felt a surge of panic, because he knew that people sometimes vanished. You never saw them again, and no one ever said what had happened to them.

Then Schönbrunn said, 'But one day you'll see your parents and your friends here again, and for the moment I'm going to keep you safe.' His eyes went to Sophie and Susannah again. 'You must promise to do what I tell you,' he said again, and Leo had the impression that he was talking solely to the twins now.

'We promise,' said the twins, speaking exactly together.

'Leo?'

'I promise as well.'

'Good. Now, listen, after tonight, you must never trust anyone you don't know,' said Schönbrunn. 'You are going to be looked after by people you can trust. But if anyone else – any grown-up you don't know – should try to talk to you, or offer you a treat, or perhaps a ride in a car, you must refuse. Do you understand all that?'

'Yes,' said the twins, staring at him solemnly, and the other children nodded.

Schönbrunn smiled. 'Don't look so scared,' he said. 'It will be all right. I'm going to keep all of you safe.' He moved slightly and the silver moonlight moved with him. 'I always keep people safe,' he said.

The time that followed was blurred, but even across the years, Leo could still see and feel the jolting of the carts that had taken them across land, and then the boats that had crossed a river, until finally they came to the sea. He would have found this exciting because he had never seen the sea before, but everything was confusing and frightening, and some of the others were crying and some were sick from the swell of the waves. Leo did not cry and he did not feel sick, and he did not let anyone know how frightened he was, because he thought his father would not have wanted that. And Sophie and Susannah were with him, which made things almost bearable. He thought Schönbrunn watched Sophie and Susannah a lot of the time.

Somewhere during that dark, confusing journey, Leo found out that the twins had been given the second silver golem from the synagogue. As Sophie said, it was like having a tiny piece of home with them.

'And we've got one each.'

Both golems had been marked on the underside with the children's initials. There was the Jewish *S* symbol on the twins' – the horizontal line with three branches, and on Leo's was the *Lamed*, the thick horizontal stroke with the upjutting line on the left and the downward tail on the right, for *L*.

It was Sophie who said, very softly, 'Let's swap.'

'Should we?' The golems were immensely special, and had to be treated with huge respect.

'Yes, then it'll link us forever,' said Sophie.

'We'd like that,' said Susannah.

Leo said, 'But you'll always be linked to each other anyway.'

'Yes, but we like to be linked to you, as well.'

'Um, all right.'

Solemnly they unwrapped the two figures, and switched them over. As Leo carefully stowed the twins' figure in his pocket, Susannah said, 'It doesn't need the golems to link us at all, really. We'll always know if you're not all right, or if you're in trouble.'

'And you'll always know if we are, as well,' said Sophie.

FIVE

Prague,
April 1943
Dear J.W.

I am deeply relieved that I can tell you the children have
all reached England safely and are presently being cared for
by various trustworthy organizations. Homes will be found
for them with English people, and perhaps one day they can
be reunited with their families.

We have lost too many of our people to the gas chambers
and I'm afraid we shall continue to do so, but at least we are
saving some of our children.

M.B.

The School House,
April 1943
Dear M.B.

Your message brought more joy and relief to everyone here
than I can convey. We can never be sufficiently grateful to
Schönbrunn.

If you are able to let us know where the children are, it
would give all the parents so much comfort.

J.W.

When the children reached England, they had to separate
and go to different places. Several of them cried, but
Leo and the twins managed not to. They clung to one
another though, and Sophie said they would not say goodbye,
because it was a forever kind of word. Susannah said they would
all soon be going home anyway. Schönbrunn had promised that.

'And we'll always know if there's anything wrong,' said Sophie.

'I'll know, as well,' said Leo, and hoped this was true.

Leo was taken to a place called Willow Bank Farm in England,
which was owned by a brother and sister called Hurst. Simeon Hurst
and Miss Mildred Hurst.

'They're good people,' Schönbrunn said. 'They're one of a number of families who are prepared to give a home to children like you. I think you'll be all right here, Leo.' He knelt down and took Leo's hands in his. 'And you'll be safe,' he said. 'That's why your parents wanted you to come here. To be safe.'

'From the Ovens.'

Schönbrunn's eyes flickered, but he said, 'Yes, you're quite safe from those, Leo.' He stood up. 'I think your friends, the twins, will be living quite near, so you'll most likely see them. Will that help?'

'Oh yes.' Leo would put up with a good deal if Sophie and Susannah were nearby.

Willow Bank Farm was not like anywhere he had ever known. There were fields and animals, and the farmhouse smelled of cabbage and carbolic. The chairs were not very comfortable and the table where they ate their meals was a bare, scrubbed one, not like the glossy one at home, which Leo's mother polished every week. Each night, after supper, Mr Hurst read the Bible to them, Miss Hurst nodding in approval over her mending basket. Leo had never seen a Bible before and he did not understand many of the words in it.

His room was at the top of the house, looking across fields and trees. There was a place to hang the few things he had been able to bring with him, and a shelf for books. A kind of picture with words in sewing hung over his bed. He knelt on his bed and traced the words with one finger, trying to understand them, but his English was not enough.

At first he put the silver golem on the window ledge by his bed, because it would look after him and he liked to wake up in the morning and see it there. But the Hursts were horrified; they said it was a heathen image and not something that could be on display. Leo managed to understand most of this, although he had no idea what a heathen image was. He explained, as well as he could, that the golem was a piece of home – of his family – and he must keep it. He was allowed to put it in a drawer in his room, but each night, after the Hursts had gone to bed, he set it on the window ledge, so that it would not feel shut away, and so that Leo would know it was looking after him. He always made sure to put it back in the drawer before breakfast, and he supposed this was a bit deceitful, but he could not help it. He wondered if the twins were allowed to have their silver golem in their bedroom, or if they, too, had been told it was a heathen image.

On Sundays the farmhouse smelled of boiled mutton – occasionally roast lamb, although that was rare and was generally accompanied by Farmer Hurst's talks about how sacrifices to the Lord must be without blemish. This precept, however, did not appear to apply to the more elderly sheep of Willow Bank's flock, whose flesh found its stringy way on to the dinner table more frequently than any other dish. Leo, obediently eating whatever was put in front of him, thought that when he was home he would never eat mutton again.

Mr Hurst tilled the land and saw to the sheep and oversaw the labourers who worked for him. Miss Hurst looked after the house and cooked and cleaned, which she did very thoroughly, because cleanliness was next to godliness. When she was not cooking or cleaning, she was at church.

Leo was taken to church and to something called Sunday School. He was made to learn prayers and told to always speak English, and he was pulled into a culture he had not previously known existed. It was bewildering and desperately lonely, but his father had said he must do whatever he was told, and Schönbrunn had said it would not be for very long. Leo trusted his father and he trusted Schönbrunn, so he tried to do all the things expected of him, and he did his best to learn English. He seemed to be quite good at this, and he discovered that he liked learning new words and trying them out.

He thought there might be letters from his parents, but Miss Hurst said there was a war going on, an evil, wicked war it was, and it meant letters were very difficult to send. Leo might write to his parents, of course, and they would post the letters, and trust in the Lord that they were delivered safely. Leo was given paper and a pencil, and he wrote very careful letters every week. He did not know if his parents received them, but he told himself they did, and he imagined them opening the letters and reading them and being pleased that he was safe and working hard and being looked after.

After a while he found he was becoming interested in the stories about Jesus Christ that the Hursts told him, and he found he was also starting to look forward to the music played in the church. Listening to the massive velvet of the organ chords, he could almost forget the aching misery for his parents and his friends at home. He thought the men who had written this music had known about being lonely and fearful and this made a link for him with the music. He was allowed to join the choir, which he liked and which was friendly.

Each day he was sent off to school, which was quite difficult at first because of not knowing very much English. But Sophie and Susannah were there as well, because they were living nearby, exactly as Schönbrunn had said. They were with people called Mr and Mrs Battersby.

When the grown-ups were not around, Leo and the twins talked about their homes and their families, and the people they were living with now. Once Sophie was worried because there had been a man near their house; he had been in the street, and he had come up to them and talked to them in their own language. They had not answered him; they had run to their house and slammed the door hard. Susannah thought they should tell somebody, but it did not seem anything very much, so they decided not to.

They talked about the man for a while, then they talked about Schönbrunn. When Mr Hurst and his sister told Leo about Our Lord Jesus, Leo thought Jesus had probably looked exactly like Schönbrunn. He told the twins this, and they agreed. Sophie said she would like to marry Schönbrunn when she grew up.

They did not talk about the Ovens or the Angel of Death. Leo did not think they dared.

Christmas was not something Leo had known much about at home, except as something other people did, but the Hursts said it had to be celebrated, because it was the birth of Our Lord. Leo tried to explain about Hanukkah, the wonderful Festival of Lights, which they had at home and which all the children had loved, but Mr Hurst said they were not having any of that Jewishry in their house, and Miss Hurst sniffed disapprovingly at the very idea.

She said they would have to ask a few neighbours to eat Christmas dinner with them, because it was expected. Mr Hurst supposed they would have to ask that Mr Porringer again, but he gave his sister fair warning that if he started his airs and graces like last year, not to mention his suggestive remarks, he, personally, would show Mr Porringer the door. He was nothing but a shopkeeper, said Mr Hurst with a rare display of uncharitable feeling towards his neighbour.

'A dispenser,' said Miss Hurst. 'It's a chemist's shop, Simeon. An old family firm.'

'Lot of nonsense.'

There was a special church service, which they all attended, and the neighbours came to eat the dinner Miss Hurst had cooked, including the vicar and his sister. Mr Porringer came as well. He did not say very much, but he ate a great deal. The guests were still there by teatime, and Leo had been allowed to invite the twins for this part of the day. There were turkey sandwiches, a cream trifle and mince pies. Farmer Hurst was watchful that they did not eat too much and make themselves ill, but Miss Hurst, who had been drinking elderflower wine with the vicar all through dinner, was more indulgent and said they could have as much as they wanted.

After her fourth glass of wine, Miss Hurst told Leo that sin was everywhere and it was necessary to always be on guard against it. There had been sin in their own family, said Miss Hurst in a very solemn voice. Her face was red and her eyes were blurry, and once she slopped some of the elderflower wine on the table, which Leo found deeply embarrassing. After the wine had been mopped up, she began to tell the vicar about her family. There had been someone who had been wild and godless – a black sinner, said Miss Hurst, oh yes he was, they had proof of it, here in this very house. It had been their own great-uncle, or maybe it was great-great, she was not exactly sure.

Mr Porringer, who had a doughy face and small eyes like a watchful pig, said that would be Mr John Hurst would it, ah yes, he thought so, the man had been a byword in the area, there was no other term for it. Folk still remembered John Hurst – why, his own grandfather, that had started the family chemist's business, used to speak of John Hurst, and in no flattering way, said Mr Porringer, tucking his chins righteously into his stiff Sunday collar.

'It's the shame of it that hurts,' said Miss Hurst. 'Simeon and I have worked all our lives to atone for the wickedness of that man. For the sins of the fathers visit on the children, even unto the third and fourth generation. That's so, isn't it, Vicar?'

The vicar, who appeared to be having some difficulty in focusing on Miss Hurst or, in fact, on anything else, mumbled that it was necessary to be vigilant about sin. He had three attempts to say the word vigilant, and gave it up in favour of watchful.

Miss Hurst said she would not dream of criticizing the Bible or saying this particular text was unfair, but it made you think. After this pronouncement she succumbed to a fit of hiccups, and the vicar's sister finally helped her up to her bed. Mr Porringer wandered round the house looking at things and once Leo saw him open the sideboard drawer, but he closed it when he realized Leo had seen him. He told Leo he had a nephew about Leo's age, but Leo did not think this could be right, because nobody at school had an uncle called Porringer. It was not a name you would forget. Sophie said Porringer Pigface was just making an excuse to snoop around. Susannah thought he might really be a burglar, whether he had a nephew or not.

Left to their own devices, Leo and the twins finished up the mince pies and carried plates and cups out to the scullery, which was what Leo had been taught to do at home, and which the Hursts liked him to do here. The twins came out to help so as to avoid Mr Porringer, and then Sophie discovered there was still some elderflower wine in the bottle, so they tried it before going back to the sitting room. Susannah said it was awful, like drinking turpentine, and spat it out in the sink, but Sophie and Leo drank an entire glass each. It did not really taste like turpentine, but it tasted peculiar, and it gave Leo a headache.

It snowed hard all night, and when Leo woke up his room was filled with white light. He still had the headache from yesterday, and by this time it was a very bad headache, but he thought it might be from the white glare of the snow rather than the elderflower wine. It was making him feel quite sick, so he could not eat any breakfast, but Miss Hurst, who appeared to have got over her hiccups and blurred eyes, said that was because he had eaten too much yesterday. It was a pity that everywhere was snowbound, or she would have suggested a good brisk walk in the fresh air, she said. But the road was practically impassable already, and the wireless had said more snow was on the way. Still, Leo could help Mr Hurst to clear the paths, which ought to blow the cobwebs away, and then they would have cold turkey and vegetable soup for lunch.

The snow-clearing did not cure Leo's headache at all, and by the middle of the afternoon he had started to be very ill indeed. There was a throbbing pain in his head, a red mist kept coming down over his eyes, and sudden uncontrollable sickness sent him running blindly to the privy just outside the scullery to be painfully sick.

He began to think he was inside a nightmare, because everything was starting to seem distorted. Miss Hurst and the farmer stood at his bedside, and their faces seemed to swell then shrink, and their voices came booming down a long tunnel, so that Leo was not sure what they were saying. But there seemed to be some kind of argument going on – something to do with Miss Hurst wanting to ask somebody to come to the farm, to which the farmer was objecting, saying something about God's will, and snow chains. But in the end Miss Hurst stumped angrily down the stairs and Leo heard the ping of the telephone. He pulled the sheets over his head then, because the bedroom light was hurting his eyes.

A man came shortly after that; he had a kind, creased face, and he carried a large black bag, and he sat on Leo's bed and looked in his eyes and took his temperature, then asked Leo to try to sit up and to bend over to touch his knees with his forehead. When Leo could not do this, he said, dear, oh, dear, this was worrying, and Leo must be taken to Deadlight Hall. There was an outbreak of something – a word Leo did not know – which was affecting a number of children in the area. The man used the word brain several times, which was terrifying, and said all the children who had this illness were being kept together and nursed. He would take Leo to the Hall himself, right away, he said. Perhaps Miss Hurst would kindly pack a few night things.

Farmer Hurst demurred at first, saying it was a lot of fuss about what was nothing more than a bilious attack; children in his day had not had illnesses with fancy names like meningitis, and it was a bad journey to Deadlight Hall in this snow, what with the lanes being iced up and more snow to come. But the man who Leo supposed was a doctor insisted it must be done, and then Leo was sick again, which seemed to decide matters.

The journey to Deadlight Hall was horrid. It was growing dark, and the car jolted and slithered on the icy roads, and twice ended up in the hedges, and the doctor had to drive and reverse over and over again to get back on the road. Leo, wrapped in a blanket, huddled miserably on the back seat clutching a pudding bowl in case he was sick again, thought they would go on and on driving through the darkening world with the sky bulging with snow waiting to fall, and that they would never get anywhere. But in the end they did get somewhere; they got to Deadlight Hall, and that was when, as well as feeling dreadfully ill, Leo had started to feel frightened.

Deadlight Hall was not a real hospital. It was a horrid dark house with old trees all round it, so that it seemed to crouch behind them as if not wanting to be seen. There were round, staring windows and creeping shadows, and oil lamps glowing in corners like yellow watching eyes. The doctor carried Leo up stone steps and inside.

'You'll be all right, my boy,' he said. 'It'll be all right.'

As they went inside, Leo could hear cross voices; somebody was saying something about it being ridiculous to expect them to turn a dingy old place into a hospital overnight, absolutely crazy it was, and no proper supplies and goodness knew how many more children to come.

The doctor carried him into a long room with high, narrow beds, and a squat iron stove glowing in one corner. There was a smell of hot metal and shadows flickered from the stove's light. Leo began to think he might have died and gone to hell. He knew about hell by this time – the real place, not the swear-word some of the older children used at school – because the Hursts talked about it. Mr Hurst said it was where sinners went: the devil carried them down into hell and watched them burn for ever and ever. So Leo must be very watchful that he did not become a sinner. Miss Hurst had said, glumly, that even if you did not commit sins of your own, you might be held accountable for the sins of your ancestors. The devil had you all ways.

Leo had thought he had been watchful as Mr Hurst said, and he had not thought he had been bad enough to be counted as an actual sinner, but clearly either he – or somebody in his family – must have been, because this place looked as if it was the hell that Mr Hurst had talked about.

There were children in the room with him – he had not known that there was a part of hell kept specially for children, but that was what it looked like, because there were about ten of them, some quite small, one or two around Leo's age, and they were all lying on narrow beds, crying with pain, or struggling to get away. But the people in charge would not let them get away, even though they were fighting and even though some of them were shouting, and others were beating the air with their fists. Leo, bundled on to a chair while a bed was made up for him, stared at everything, and through the red shimmery haze that kept coming and going in front of his eyes, he saw that the people in charge were really devils. They wore ordinary clothes, and they said ordinary things like, 'Drink up your medicine' and, 'You mustn't try to get out of bed,' but Leo thought they were devils, as sure as sure. When they moved to and fro across the squat iron stove, their eyes shone red and glinted from the glow.

It was not until later that night that he discovered that Sophie and Susannah were there as well. He was not sure what he felt about this. He liked having them with him, but not if it meant that they too were bad, black sinners, and going to burn in hell for ever and ever.

They managed to wave to one another, and when no one was in the room, they both tiptoed across to his bed and sat on it, one on each side.

'Are you ill?' Leo said in their own language. They were not supposed to use it at school, but it was friendly and reassuring to use it now.

Sophie glanced towards the door, then said, very softly, 'No. We pretended because we wanted to get away from the house. We've been so frightened.'

'What of? Why did you pretend?'

'We saw that man again,' said Sophie. 'The one who talked to us in the street that time.'

'In our own language.'

'It's what our parents and Schönbrunn told us to be careful about,' said Sophie. 'We're worried that somebody came after us when we left our village. All the way to England.'

'We've seen other people watching us,' said Susannah. 'Standing outside the house for ages. In the rain and everything.'

'Hiding behind trees and things.'

Leo said, 'But why would anyone do that?'

'We thought it might be something to do with – you know – the Ovens.'

Leo stared at her in horror. The Ovens: the nightmare from home.

'And then some children near us got ill with this menin-thing, and they were brought here,' said Sophie. 'Susannah thought if we pretended to be ill as well, we might be safer in here. We didn't think anyone could get at us. But . . .' Sophie broke off and glanced nervously around again. 'But now we aren't sure.'

'And,' said Susannah, 'the really bad thing is that now we're here, we think . . .'

'What?'

'We think this is where the Ovens are.'

'But they're at home,' said Leo, after a moment. 'That's why we had to come here.'

'We think they're here,' said Sophie. 'We can smell hot iron, like a huge stove burning.'

'Isn't it the stove over there you can smell?' said Leo. The stove was in the corner, and it was hissing quietly to itself. It was not a friendly kind of stove, like the one at home; it was fat and swollen and ugly, and it had short iron legs.

'No, it's a bigger heat. Massive. And old. Ancient. We can sort of hear it.'

Sophie did not try to explain what she meant by hearing the massive old heat, and Leo did not bother to ask, because this was the kind of thing the twins often said. He asked what they would do.

'We don't know. We might try to run away. Properly, I mean. Miles and miles away.'

'But it's snowing,' said Leo, horrified. 'And where would you go?'

'We don't know yet.'

'People in stories run away and they're usually all right,' said Susannah. 'Somebody always finds them and takes them to wherever they want to go. Sometimes it's in a forest, and there's a cottage. But it's always all right in the end.'

They all knew this was true.

'But the really frightening thing,' said Sophie, whispering even more softly, 'is that our mother used to talk about the *Todesengel* coming for us.'

The *Todesengel*. Leo was able to think partly in English now, and he said, half to himself, 'The Angel of Death.'

'Yes. We aren't sure what she meant, but she was really frightened about it. We think it had something to do with the Ovens.'

'We think,' said Susannah, 'that it might be here now, that Angel.'

'But angels are good, aren't they?' Leo knew this from Sunday school.

'We don't think this one is. We heard Mother tell our father she would do anything to stop the Angel of Death getting us. So we think it'd be better to run away, even in the snow.'

Leo could not decide if this was sensible or not. He felt too ill to think about it clearly; his head hurt too much, and he thought his bones were burning. But he said, 'If you run away, I'll help. I'd come with you if I could.' He would not care if he was dying, he would still help his beloved twins, and he would run away with them if they asked him to.

'Will you? We'd like that. We've brought the silver golem with us. My father said it would protect us, and Schönbrunn said so as well, so it must be true.'

'It's your golem, really, of course, so we think it'll be extra good,' said Susannah.

'Although we might need to sell it to get some money.'

Leo started to ask how they would go about this, but the door opened, and the twins gasped, and scurried back to their own beds. A thin lady with narrow, bony shoulders, scraped-back hair, and fingers like dry sticks, came in and walked round the beds. There was to be no talking, she said. Her name was Sister Dulce, and she was here to make them better. They must all do what she told them. It seemed to Leo that she stared at the twins when she said this.

Shortly after this, two men came in and did something to Susannah as she lay in the bed. Leo could not see what it was, but there was a large needle and a metal tray, and whatever was done made Susannah cry and squirm with pain. He clenched his fists and wished he dared go over to the bed to stop them, but he was not brave enough. He heard some of what was said, but he did not really understand it. One of the men used words that sounded like lumbar puncture, which was puzzling because Leo thought punctures were what cars had, and then another talked about spine fluid, which sounded terrible. One of them said, 'Look here, can't we put the child out to do this?' and Sister Dulce said, 'We can't. You know that. She'll have to endure it.'

'What about her sister?'

'Leave it until tomorrow morning. I'm still not sure about her.'

'How about that one?' said the man, looking across to Leo's bed. 'He's only just been brought in, hasn't he?'

'Yes, but leave him as well for the moment.'

Leo burrowed back under the sheets, and shut his eyes, and through the haze of pain and fear he heard Sister Dulce say they must all go to sleep, because it was eleven o'clock at night, which was no time for children to be awake. She went out, closing the door, and the room became silent, apart from the occasional sob from Susannah's bed. Sophie was next to her; Leo could see her hair spilling over the pillow. Most people could only tell them apart because Sophie's hair was redder than Susannah's. If Susannah was hurt, Sophie would be hurting as well. Leo knew this, and he hated it for them.

He lay on his side, watching the stove. If he half-closed his eyes, he could make it seem to move. Or was it moving by itself anyway?

Yes, it was. It was waddling forward towards the nearest bed. Leo half sat up, alarmed, and he was just wondering whether to call out to the others, when he heard another sound. This time it was not anyone crying or the stove, it was someone walking around outside this room.

It ought not to have been frightening to hear those footsteps, because people had been walking around ever since Leo got here. But these footsteps were different. They were slow, sort of dragging. Across the room, Sophie sat up and looked towards Leo's bed.

'Can you hear that?' said Leo, as loudly as he dared.

'Yes.'

'Who is it?' Leo did not dare ask if it might be the Angel of Death, the *Todesengel* so feared by the twins' mother, but Sophie heard the thought, of course.

He said, 'Is Susannah all right? What did they do with that needle?'

'It hurt a lot,' said Sophie, her voice wobbling. Leo knew she was trying not to cry. 'They dug it into Susannah's back, into her bones. They're going to do it to me tomorrow.'

'And to me,' said Leo, remembering this with a shiver.

'And after they've done that,' said Sophie, her voice trembling even more, 'they'll take us to the Ovens. That woman – Sister Dulce – she's the one.'

'But where—?' began Leo, then broke off. 'Someone's coming,' he said. 'Lie down. Pretend to be asleep.'

Sophie flopped down at once, and Leo turned on his side, watching the door. After a moment, it began to open, not quickly and firmly in the way Sister Dulce and the others had opened it, but slowly and stealthily, as if whoever was there did not want to be seen or heard. Leo's heart started to race. Very gradually, the door opened wider, and a shadow fell across the floor – it was a black shadow, but the red from the stove ran in and out of it. Leo lay absolutely still, waiting for it to go away, but it did not. It stood in the doorway as if looking round.

Then a low blurred voice said, very quietly, 'Children, are you here . . .?'

Leo was shaking uncontrollably, and his head was hurting so much he thought it might explode.

'Children, are you here . . .?' There was a pause. 'I'll find you . . . Wherever you are.'

It's come for the twins, thought Leo, sick with the horror of it all. This is what they saw – it's what followed them to England, and watched their house. It's followed them in here.

The shadowy figure stepped back into the passage, and Leo sank gratefully back into the pillows. It was all right. Whatever had been there had gone away. The twins were safe and everything was all right.

Except that everything was not all right. There was a movement across the room, and to his horror he saw two small figures walking hand in hand to the door. Sophie and Susannah.

They went very quietly across the room, almost like shadows themselves, not looking towards Leo. Sophie's arm was round Susannah – Leo thought Susannah must be still hurting from the needle pushed into her bones earlier. They went through the door and it closed with a soft little click.

Were they running away as Sophie had said? Surely they would not go out into the snow by themselves? And Leo could not believe they would run away without telling him, either. Sophie had said they would like it if he went with him. Or did they think he would follow them? We'll always be linked, they had said that night. We'll always know if one of us is in trouble.

Leo did not know what to do, but what he did know was that the shadow was still out there – he could feel that it was. Which meant the twins would walk straight into it.

His whole body was still burning up and his bones felt as if they were melting with the heat, but he would put up with worse than this to help his beloved twins. He got out of bed and went across to the door.

SIX

At first he thought he was not going to manage it, because he felt so ill that it was difficult to walk. Mr Hurst had talked about people cast into hell being made to wear iron cloaks, and Leo wondered if this had happened to him now. It seemed perfectly possible.

But somehow he got out to the big hall. It was in shadow, but it was not completely dark, and he could smell hot metal. Was that the old heat that Sophie had talked about? She and Susannah had thought the scent was from the Ovens. Leo was just thinking that rather than risk the Ovens he would go back to his bed, when there was a movement ahead of him. His heart bumped and the hot confusing mist swirled around him. He stood very still, then two figures walked in and out of the shadows, and Leo, fighting not to fall over, saw the unmistakable tumble of Sophie's hair.

They half turned to look back at him, and one of them put up a hand to beckon him. They're running away, thought Leo. They're running away from the *Todesengel*. But they had beckoned to him to follow them, and he would have to try, so he took a deep breath and went across the hall and through the door after them.

The door opened easily, and on the other side were stone steps going down. There was a bad smell of damp and decay, but Leo, by now feeling dreadfully ill, managed to ignore it, and made his shaky way to the foot of the steps. Now there was a narrow stone passage. It was not absolutely dark because there were oil lamps fixed to the walls near the ceiling, which someone had lit. They were like huge swollen eyes staring down and Leo hated them. He began to walk along the passage, forcing himself not to look up at the bulgy eyes, willing the twins to appear. Once he thought he heard the whispery voice calling the children again, but then it faded and he thought he had been mistaken. He would probably reach the twins at any minute, although if they were running away, he was not sure if he would manage to go with them. And where would they go anyway?

The oil lamps flickered, blurring his vision and making him

feel sick all over again, but he stood very still and eventually the sickness went away and the red mist melted a bit. Several doors opened off the passage – moving very cautiously, Leo opened them, because this would be exactly the kind of place the twins might be hiding. The rooms were all quite small and narrow, and they smelled dreadful. Leo thought it was not just damp and dirt – it was as if something very bad had happened in these rooms, and as if the badness was still here. But there was no sign of the twins.

The hot iron scent was stronger, and he could hear sounds as well now – hoarse gratings and clankings, as if some huge rusting machine was struggling into life. But nothing bad had happened to him yet and he had to find Sophie and Susannah, so he went a little further along. The shadows were thicker, but now they had crimson ragged edges, as if they had been dabbled in blood. Leo was careful not to tread in these shadows.

The oil flares flickered, and Leo saw the twins again – they were a little way ahead of him, moving away from him. He went towards them, but his head seemed to be opening and closing, and the passage was becoming endless, stretching out and distorting, like the dark passages in nightmares did. Each time he thought he was catching the twins up, they seemed to whisk away.

Then, quite suddenly, Leo was directly in front of a black door, with thick bands of iron across it. He stood still, staring at it. It was a dreadful door, an old, *old* door, and the iron pieces might be to shut people out. Or – and this was a really dreadful thought – they might be to shut people in.

The top half of the door had a round window. The glass was smeary and cobwebby, but beyond it the red-dabbled light glowed, and the machinery sounds were clanking. The Ovens, thought Leo, fighting down panic. That's what is in there. That's why there are those iron pieces across the door. Sophie and Susannah were right.

He still could not see the twins – did that mean they had they gone through that terrible door? Or perhaps there was a way outside. If he stood on tiptoe he could look through the window and see into the room. Only I don't want to, he thought, with a fresh wave of panic. I want to run away, a long way away, and not know what's in there.

But there was nowhere else the twins could be, and he would have to find out what had happened. With his heart pounding and his head aching worse than ever, he went up to the black iron door, and stood on tiptoe to look through the glass.

At first he could not see very much at all, because the thick glass blurred everything. But gradually he made out a huge furnace, a bit like the one in the schoolhouse at home, although that one had been much smaller. But it had growled in the same wheezing, coughing way, and the older children had sometimes tried to frighten the younger ones by saying there was a monster hiding inside it.

This furnace crouched blackly against a wall, and Leo thought it really must be one of the terrible Ovens. Huge thick pipes hung down from both sides, like a giant's arms, and they were juddering and clanking. There was a round door at the front with a massive bolt across it, and all around the rim were spikes and trickles of flames.

Sophie and Susannah were in there. Leo could see them, not clearly, but enough to know they were there – he could see the way Sophie's hair always tumbled forward when she had not tied it back properly. They were standing almost in front of the furnace, and with them was something wrapped around with a sheet. He tried hard to see what it was, then, with a fresh wave of horror, realized it was a person. Someone was a prisoner in there – someone who was tied up in a sheet. He rubbed the glass to make it a bit clearer, then with sick fear he realized the tied-up person was Sister Dulce. He could see the narrow, bony shoulders, and when a bit of the sheet fell back, he saw the scraped-back hair. The twins must have got her into this room somehow, and they were keeping her prisoner. Because she had hurt Susannah and was going to hurt Sophie in the same way tomorrow? Or was it because she had been going to feed them to the Ovens, as Sophie had seemed to think?

He would have to go in there to tell the twins to let Sister Dulce go. But there was no handle or latch on the door – there was only a big square lock with a keyhole. Leo pushed against this, but the door did not move. It's locked, he realized in horror. They're locked in there. I'll have to tell someone what's happening.

But this was the twins, his dear Sophie and Susannah, and Leo could not begin to think what kind of punishment they might get. And it seemed as if anything he did would be too late, because they had got the door of the furnace open – Leo did not know how, but Susannah was holding a long hooked rod, and one of them must have used it to unbolt the furnace cover and pull it open. Heat, fierce and almost blinding, was blazing out, smearing the glass window so that Leo could only make out shapes moving back and forth. But after a moment or two a small piece of the window cleared, and as Leo stared in, the whole scene, blackly dreamlike already, spun itself into the worst nightmare ever. The two girls were holding the helpless woman, and they were thrusting her head-first into the open furnace. Utter terror gripped Leo, and he shouted and banged on the glass, but either the twins did not hear or they did not care.

He pushed uselessly against the door again, then began to have wild thoughts of running to the main part of the house to call for help. But his legs were so weak and the floor kept tilting, and he was not sure if he could even stand up for much longer, never mind run for help.

He thought for a moment there was someone else in the room with the twins, but it was only a smeary kind of shadow, and Leo thought it was simply a drift of smoke.

And now it was too late. The furnace roared up greedily, and there was a massive clanging sound as the iron door of the furnace was slammed back in place. And that woman – Sister Dulce – was inside. Burning. Sick dizziness closed over Leo in a huge engulfing wave, and he fell against the cold stone wall of the passage, his mind spinning. She was in there, that woman who had hurt Susannah and threatened to hurt Sophie, and who might have been going to feed them to the Ovens. But she had been fed to the Ovens instead, and she was burning alive. Leo knew that burning alive was the worst thing in the whole world. He crouched shivering in the darkness, wanting to wrap the shadows around him so no one could see him, wanting them to smother the pictures in his mind.

But the pictures were there in his head – he thought they would always be there – and the pain in his head exploded. A shuddering, uncontrollable sickness swept over him, and he bent over, retching helplessly, his eyes streaming, unable to see or hear or think.

When at last he managed to straighten up and wipe his face with his handkerchief, the room was in darkness and the iron door was still locked. All he wanted to do was lie down and go to sleep, but he could not leave the twins. Were they still in there? Hiding until it was safe to creep out? Leo did not think they had crept out while he was being sick. You could not be sick and look around you at the same time, but he was sure he would have known if they had come out.

He looked through the window again, but the furnace was cool and dark, and nothing moved. He leaned against the door, listening. And then – he had no idea how he knew this – but someone inside the room did the same. Leo could not hear it and he could not see it, but he knew someone had come to stand on the other side of the door, and that someone was pressing its face against the hard cold surface of the iron. Whoever it was, they were inches from him.

He forced himself not to flinch, and he laid his hands flat against the door. In their own language, he said, 'Sophie – Susannah. It's all right. I shan't ever tell anyone what you did. I promise I'll never tell anyone.'

The words came out very softly, but the twins would have heard. They would know they could trust him. They would know he would keep his promise and never tell anyone what they had done tonight.

There had never been any sign of Sophie and Susannah again, not that night or the next, and not throughout the confused, pain-filled days that followed, with the agonizing lumbar puncture Leo had to endure. He had to stay in Deadlight Hall for what felt like a long time, together with the other children – it was not until a long time afterwards that he understood they had all suffered from an illness called meningitis.

It was a strange time. Leo thought some of the children died, but no one actually said this, and the freezing, blizzard-torn winter made it difficult for people to visit. Two of the younger nurses devised games and simple puzzles for the children, and one found a store of children's books somewhere in the house. They had been very old books and Leo had not understood them all, but he had liked listening when the young nurse read them aloud. He would have liked to take some of the books back to Willow Bank Farm, but it seemed they must go back to wherever they had come from.

He heard afterwards that there had been a search for Sophie and Susannah, although the frozen ground and incessant blizzards made it difficult. But the police combed the area, using dogs, and the children were all questioned, although none of them knew anything. Leo said he had seen the twins, but that was all. He had not said anything about the Angel of Death, or about the twins' plan to run away.

Miss Hurst told Leo later that the search had gone on for a long time, but nothing had been found. Mark her words, said Miss Hurst, they would never hear of Sophie and Susannah Reiss again.

Nor did they. In the end people stopped searching, although it was a long time before they stopped talking about it.

Leo believed the twins had run away as Sophie had said, and he tried to think they had reached somewhere safe. Perhaps they had been found in the storm by a kindly person, like in stories. There was sometimes a woodcutter. To reassure himself he read all the books that were stored at Willow Bank Farm – the books that had been Farmer Hurst's and Miss Hurst's when they were children. There were people in forests in those books who were often disguised, but always good, and children did not get lost because they marked the way by scattering pebbles or bits of bread. Reading about all this, Leo thought the twins would surely be all right.

For a long time he kept hoping that one day they would write to him, but they did not.

*

The School House, Nr Warsaw
December 1943
My dear M.B.

Your letter reached me yesterday, and came as a blow to the heart. We had taken so much care to ensure the children would be safe, and to hear that the Reiss girls have disappeared is devastating.

I know you will spare no effort to trace the twins. I know, as well, that Schönbrunn will be tireless in his search. As to their eventual fate, I know you are right to say their pronounced gift of telepathy will make them an attractive proposition for Mengele and to warn me that they would always have been in extra danger because of it. I always knew it, but still I cannot bear to think his people could have found them. If you should track down the informant or the agent, I beg you will let me know. There is an old maxim that to know one's enemy is to be strong.

Your friend, as always,
J.W.

Prague
January 1944
Dear J.W.

As part of our search for the twins, Schönbrunn is going to put out discreet enquiries among jewellers and dealers in England, to see if the Reiss golem is offered for sale anywhere. I shall be helping him with that – I have a few contacts in England in that field.

The figure was not found among the possessions the twins left, and Schönbrunn believes this to be hopeful – indicating they were able to take it with them when they vanished, which does not suggest force. If we can trace the golem, that may provide the start of a trail that could lead us to them. Both those figures are distinctive and the hallmarks recognizable.

It is possible the family with whom the girls lodged have lied to our agents, and are keeping the Reiss golem in secrecy, intending to sell it for themselves. Schönbrunn thinks that unlikely, though. Our information is that the girls were with an English couple who had lived in the same small market town all their lives, and were known and respected. It seems unlikely that they would realize the worth of such an item or, indeed, know how to go about selling it.

We have never heard of Mengele's agents casting their net as far as England, but our information was very clear that the doctor wanted Sophie and Susannah Reiss for his evil work. That intelligence came from Schönbrunn and I have never known him to be wrong. This may sound harsh, but truly I would rather think of those two girls begging in the streets of England – of any country – than to think of them in Mengele's laboratories.

I will not believe that Mengele's people found Sophie and Susannah Reiss, and took them to Auschwitz, though. I will *not*.

Good wishes to you, as always,

M.B.

The School House, Nr Warsaw
January 1944
My dear M.B.

We trust Schönbrunn to be careful, and to do nothing to draw attention to himself or, of course, to the twins.

I was glad, though, to have your more recent letter, with the news that Leo Rosendale is safe, although I fear the disappearance of the twins is likely to distress him. Those three were extremely close, and at times Leo seemed almost to share the twins' disconcerting gift for sensing the thoughts and emotions of others.

I have made the decision not to tell the Reiss family yet that their daughters have vanished. Letters are almost impossible between this country and England now, and I believe the Reisses will not be overly concerned if they do not hear from their daughters for a little time. This is a decision I may regret, but at the moment the deceit seems justified. It will be a heavy secret for me to bear, but I will spare them the pain and the fear as long as I can.

Kindest regards, as always,
J.W.

SEVEN

Nell thought the trouble with becoming extremely close to another person was that you started to sense that person's thoughts and emotions. She was finding she was doing so with Michael, more and more. On the whole, this pleased her. She had had something similar with her husband – almost a subliminal sensing of emotions. On the day he died in the motorway pile-up, Nell, alone in their house, had felt a sudden overwhelming sensation of panic and immense confusion before the phone rang. In the crashing pain and anger that followed Brad's death, she had thought she would never experience that shared understanding with anyone again. She had not, in fact, wanted to experience it, because it had been something between her and Brad exclusively. And then Michael had walked into her antiques shop. Nell smiled, remembering. 'Whoever loved, that loved not at first sight,' he had once said, hiding behind a quotation, as he often did when he was feeling deeply emotional. But the meeting had been a happy one, and it had led to delighted intimacy. She thought Brad would not have minded her closeness with Michael, not after four years, and she liked to think he would have approved of Michael.

But that mental closeness meant you sensed the other person's thoughts and sometimes that could make for a difficult situation. Particularly if there was something you wanted to keep to yourself.

'I'll be devastated to leave Quire Court,' Godfrey Purbles, from the antiquarian bookshop adjoining Nell's shop, had said, two days earlier. 'But I've always wanted to have a shop in Stratford – well, who hasn't? It's going to cost me an utter fortune and I dare say I'll end up in a debtors' gaol – do they still have debtors' gaols nowadays? – but the premises are quite near the Rose Tavern, which couldn't be much better, on account of the tourists flocking and cavorting everywhere. And as a hunting ground for rare books and theatrical memorabilia it'll be tremendous.'

'You'll probably end up discovering the famous unknown play,' Nell said, smiling.

'Yes, and I'd probably pay several fortunes for it, only to find afterwards that it's a Victorian fake.'

'I'm glad for you, but I'll miss you.' Nell liked Godfrey and found him companionable.

'Oh, you'll visit me, of course. And I'll come back to Oxford. But here's the thing, Nell. The shop.' He looked at her hopefully, clearly wanting her to voice an unspoken thought.

Nell said, 'The shop? Your shop, d'you mean?'

'Yes. It'll have to be sold, because I can't afford both places. At least, the lease will have to be sold. Assigned, they call it, I think. How would you feel about taking it over? I mean in addition to yours, not instead of.'

Nell was very aware that life often presented you with odd twists, and quite often you had long since seen or suspected what those twists might be. But this was not a twist that had ever occurred to her.

'The lease is probably the same as your place as far as ground rent and repairing obligations and whatnot,' said Godfrey. 'But there's about thirty years left to run on mine. And the two shops adjoin – I'll bet you could knock them into one.'

'The freeholders would have to approve that,' said Nell, looking round Godfrey's shop with the rows of bookshelves, and the lovely old tables for customers to consider the wares and discuss them in leisurely fashion.

'It would double your present floor area,' said Godfrey. 'It might even more than double it – I think this shop is a bit bigger than yours.'

'Godfrey, I don't know if I could afford . . .' But Nell was already remembering the insurance payout from Brad's death, some of which the bank had invested in various funds and bonds, most of them incomprehensible, but all of them paying reasonable dividends, even in the current depressed and depressing market. If she called them in, would there be enough to take over Godfrey's shop? And even if there was, would she want to use all of that money, which she had meant to keep for Beth? But then she looked round Godfrey's shop again – yes, it was larger than hers – and she found herself thinking that she could turn the annexe behind her own shop, where she and Beth currently lived, into a big workshop which would allow her to return to renovating furniture, which she loved doing.

'Come and see the rest of the place anyway.' Godfrey was already leading the way. There were two more book-lined rooms, and a large alcove for prints. The living part at the rear had a beautiful large sitting-room looking on to a paved courtyard, with a small dining area leading off. There was a big square kitchen. Everywhere was immaculate – Godfrey was inclined to be fussy in a slightly old-maidish way – and the place would not need so much as a lick of paint.

'Two huge bedrooms and bathroom up here,' said Godfrey, starting up a spiral staircase. 'From the main bedroom you can see across to All Saints Church.'

For a wild moment Nell saw herself waking in this room – Michael would be there on some mornings – and seeing the misty silhouette of All Saints against the dawn with him next to her. This was such an alluring prospect that she thought she had better slow down before she got carried away.

'And a couple of storerooms at the top of these steps,' said Godfrey, going across a small landing and up four more stairs. 'I've never really used them – except for storing old stock. This one's directly under the roof, as you can see. But I should think you could make two more bedrooms up here, or a study, if you wanted.'

'Yes,' said Nell, looking about her. 'Yes, you could.'

But as they went downstairs, she said, 'Godfrey, we have to be very straight with each other about this. I'm attracted to this, but I've only got a certain amount of money, and it really is all there is. I'm not going to start borrowing from banks or building societies.'

Godfrey beamed, and pattered into the little office to put the kettle on. When he came back, he was wearing the rimless spectacles which he always donned for serious work, and which made him look like a pleased owl.

'Let's work out some figures over a cup of coffee,' he said.

The figures worked out surprisingly well.

'We're making a few assumptions,' said Godfrey. 'And we don't know how much it would cost to knock the two shops into one. But I don't think we're very far out.'

Nell hoped they were not, because it was looking as if this really would be affordable. It would be a bit of a risk, because it would take most of the squirrelled-away investments, but it would not take all of them. The money earmarked for Beth would not need to be touched. She promised Godfrey that she would give

him her decision within the next two days after she had talked to
the bank and perhaps to a builder as well, then she went back to her
own shop. Awaiting her was a message from some Japanese customers
who wanted to buy a pair of Regency sofas which Nell had been
trying to sell for six months. This was so encouraging, and would
replenish the coffers so well, that Godfrey's project looked even
more promising.

After supper, when Beth embarked on her music practice, Nell
caught herself thinking that if she took on Godfrey's shop, Beth
could have a bedroom in one of those unused upper rooms, and one
of the present bedrooms could be turned into a music room. She
was immensely proud of Beth's progress and pleased with Beth's
continuing interest in the lessons, but it had to be acknowledged that
the annexe was a bit small when it came to the practising of scales.

'Would you like a proper music room, Beth?'

Beth's small face, so heartbreakingly like her father's at times, lit
up. 'I'd utterly love it. Where could I have it? Here somewhere?'

'No, not here. But if we were to move to a bigger shop you
might. It's only an idea at the moment.'

'We wouldn't move away from Oxford, though? We couldn't
move away from Oxford, and leave Michael.'

Beth sounded anxious, and Nell said, 'No, not away from Oxford.'
Certainly not away from Michael, she thought. 'But perhaps to a
bigger shop here in the Court.'

'That'd be lavishly good,' said Beth, and by way of expressing
her approval, started in on a lively Mozart piece which her teacher
had transposed and simplified for her.

'It hasn't happened yet and it might not happen at all. So don't
say anything to anyone,' said Nell. 'Understood?'

'Um, yes, OK. Not even to Michael?'

'No, I'll tell Michael myself. And isn't it your bedtime? In fact,
isn't it past it?'

'One more Mozart. You *like* Mozart,' said Beth, hopefully.

'Yes, but if you play any more tonight you'll never sleep – your
mind will be too active.'

'I bet Mozart wasn't made to go to bed when he didn't want to.'

'Mozart didn't have double geography and an arithmetic test in
the morning. Yes, you do have,' said Nell, as Beth opened her mouth
to protest.

'I hate geography.'

'Well, how about if we just do a few capitals of countries. And afterwards you can play one short Mozart.'

'Um, OK.'

Beth diligently chanted a few capitals, identified one or two outlines of countries in Google Earth, then enthusiastically banged out a truncated version of a rondo. She finally went happily to bed, and burrowed down into sleep straight away. Nell, following some time later, found her own mind was too active for sleep. The prospect of taking over Godfrey's shop was becoming very enticing. She was already thinking how she would retain part of the book section for Godfrey's Oxford customers, and how she would have the space to hold small antique events and weekend courses for eager amateurs, as she had in Shropshire.

Punching the pillow for the tenth time, and trying not to look at the beside clock ticking through the small hours, she thought she would phone Michael early tomorrow, and ask him to supper so she could tell him about the project. She considered this to see if it fell into the category of not being able to make her own decision without his approval, and concluded it did not. Then she spent a further half hour wondering how much she ought to take into account Michael's presence in her life in reaching a decision about the shop. But this opened up such a complicated tangle of emotions that Nell put the problem away, sat up in bed, switched on the bedside light, and reached determinedly for her book. She fell asleep before she had read two pages of it.

The next morning brought a large envelope from Ashby's Auctioneers in London. Inside was a sheaf of photocopied letters, with a covering note from her contact in the sale rooms. He wrote, cheerfully, that they were looking forward to dealing with the silver golem for her client, and that he had been doing a little research of his own.

'I'm fairly sure that it's one of the pair I mentioned to you. They both disappeared around 1942 or 1943, but interestingly and rather intriguingly Ashby's archives have some correspondence relating to one of them. (We have archives going back to the company's inception in 1853, would you believe?)

'I thought it might interest you, and your client as well, to see these letters, so I'm enclosing photocopies. And if the figure you've been offered really is one of that vanished pair, what we'd like to know, of course, is where the other one is!'

Nell did not dare immerse herself in the photocopied letters yet. She oversaw Beth's breakfast, then bundled her into the car and whiled away the short journey by chanting through the capitals of the world once more. Beth went happily into school, prophesying she would be top in the geography test, and Nell drove back to Quire Court, forcing herself to keep to the speed limit.

It was ten minutes to nine, and she did not usually open the shop until ten, so she had a clear hour to read the material from Ashby's. She poured a cup of coffee, carried the envelope into the small office behind her shop, and slid the contents out. There were only four sheets, and with a pleasurable sense of anticipation, she began to read the first.

It was not quite what she had expected. The phrasing – even allowing for the stilted formality of correspondence in the 1940s – was awkward, and Nell thought the letter struck an odd discord.

> *Department for Criminality and Theft*
> *Post Box No B7921*
> *London*
> *February 1944*
> Sir
>
> I act for a private firm of investigators who try to trace two silver figures, of Jewish workmanship, in the form of the Jewish emblem, the *golem*. Both figures were taken illicitly from a synagogue just outside Warsaw several months since, and enquiries inform us that they were smuggled to England by the thieves.
>
> Please could you tell us if you have been offered such a figure, and if so, the present owner's identity. I remind you that it is a duty of all citizens to assist in cases where crimes may have been committed.
>
> Yours respectfully.

The signature was indecipherable, and across the foot of the letter, someone who was clearly an Ashby's employee had written, 'No such department exists. Treat this one with caution – recommend advising Inspector George Fennel at New Scotland Yard. He will know how and if this should be investigated.'

New Scotland Yard,
London
February 1944
Dear Sirs

I am most grateful to you for notifying us of the contents of the somewhat curious letter regarding the apparent theft of two silver golem figures. As you surmised, there is no 'Department of Criminality and Theft' here.

Enquiries with our Warsaw people reveal that two silver figures of this description did indeed vanish from a small synagogue in a village just outside Warsaw. However, no formal report seems to have been made of any theft, although you will appreciate that it is difficult to obtain information from that part of Europe at present.

At first look, there seemed no reason to suspect any espionage activity. However, the post box address has proved to be an accommodation address in London's East End – a small general shop, which we have had under what we term 'light' surveillance for some months.

It seems unlikely that enemy agents would go to such trouble to trace the whereabouts of two Jewish objects, however valuable. It is more probable that it is the 'singer not the song' that interests them – that it is the present owner or owners of the silver golems they wish to find. We cannot hazard a guess as to why they might be going to all this trouble to find the whereabouts of one or two people, but that is our conclusion.

I advise you to send a polite acknowledgement, saying you have no record of these figures. If you receive any reply, I would be very glad if you would notify me at once.

If, of course, you do hear of such figures being sold, either by your auction house or by any other similar establishment, I would be glad if you would send word to me without delay.
Yours faithfully,
Inspector Geo. Fennel.'

Carbon copy of letter sent by Ashby's of London to Post Box B7921.

February 1944
Dear Sir

We have to hand your enquiry regarding two silver *golem*

figures, but have not, at this present, been commissioned to deal with anything matching your description. However, should we be requested to handle such a sale, we will be very happy to advise you.

Yours faithfully,

for and on behalf of Ashby's of London.

Department for Criminality and Theft
Post Box No B7921
London
February 1944
Sirs

We thank you for your prompt reply.

The golem figures are ones we are anxious to trace. If you hear of their whereabouts, or of any persons trying to dispose of them, we will be most grateful to know.

They are both stamped with an extra mark, alongside the main hallmark, but separate from it. One of those marks is of three vertical lines jutting up from a horizontal line. I sketch it at the foot of this letter for you so you may identify that figure if offered to you.

Yours respectfully.

This letter bore the same scrawled, illegible signature. The sketched symbol was the one Nell had found on Professor Rosendale's figure. The symbol Michael had also found inside Deadlight Hall. She looked at it for a long time, then turned to the next two letters.

Carbon copy of hand-delivered letter to Inspector Fennel
Ashby's Auction Rooms
London
March 1944
Dear Inspector Fennel

We have received a further enquiry about the Warsaw golem figures. This, however, comes from someone with whom we have dealt several times over the years, and who we believe to be a genuine dealer in jewellery and *objets d'art*. He is a Jewish gentleman of Polish extraction, modestly known in his particular field, and as far as we know, entirely trustworthy.

It is, however, a curious coincidence, and in view of the contents of your last letter, we are hesitant about trusting this to the normal postal service, hence the special delivery.

Yours sincerely,

for and on behalf of Ashby's Auction House.

City Postbox 2991
Prague
March 1944
Dear Sirs

I write to enquire whether you ever have for sale silver objects with a particularly Hebrew connotation. A well-established client who collects such things is interested in acquiring a *golem* figure, and has commissioned me to make tentative enquiries. I am addressing the same question to other auction houses and appropriate jewellery establishments, but having dealt with your excellent company a number of times in the past, am hoping you may be able to help.

If you were to find yourselves offering such an item, I should be most obliged if you would let me know. Postal services to my country are, of course, erratic and unreliable in these times, and my work necessitates a degree of travel, so I have provided a *poste restante* address. As an alternative, Drummonds Bank, Charing Cross, can be used.

Sincerely yours,

Maurice Bensimon

Ashby's Auction Rooms
London
March 1944
Dear Mr Bensimon

We have to hand your enquiry re. a silver golem figure, but have to advise you that we have no such object at present in our catalogues.

This is something of a specialist area, as you will appreciate, although we do occasionally receive commissions to sell such objects. If we should be asked to deal with such a piece, we will inform you at once.

If you wish us to undertake a search for the figure, under the arrangement we have agreed with you in the past, we would

be happy to do so. To this end, we enclose a note of our charges
and commission fees.

Assuring you of our best intentions at all times, and with
our very best wishes,

Yours sincerely,

for and on behalf of Ashby's Auction House.

Hand delivered note to Ashby's Auction Rooms
New Scotland Yard,
London
March 1944
Dear Sir

Thank you for letting me have sight of the letter from Mr
Bensimon. I return it herewith for your records.

It now seems as if two sets of people are trying to trace
either these silver figures or (more likely) the present owners
of them. My department will continue to look into this.

Our initial investigation accords with your information, and
suggests that Mr Bensimon's enquiry is indeed genuine. Indeed,
our intelligence hints that he is part of a certain discreet network
in that part of Europe – a network which we have no wish to
disrupt or endanger.

With kind regards,

Yours sincerely

Inspector Geo. Fennel.

The soft chimes of one of Oxford's many churches broke into Nell's
absorption. Ten o'clock. She slid the letters back into their envelope,
forced her mind into the present, and went through to the front of
the shop to unlock the doors. She stood for a moment, looking out
into the court.

She liked Quire Court at this relatively quiet time of the morning.
Michael, when he was caught up in one of his romantical flights,
sometimes said this was the hour when any lingering ghosts were
whisking themselves back to their shadowy half-worlds, shamefaced
and rather apologetic, like guests who suddenly realized they had
stayed too long at a party. If you had opened your door a few
seconds earlier you would have seen them, he said, spinning one
of his stories for Beth, who loved them. And they were not ghosts
you would ever have to be afraid of, he explained; they were all

the people who had once lived in Quire Court, and who liked to occasionally pop back to see how it was getting on.

Beth, round-eyed, had wanted to know more about this. 'Do dead people sometimes come back like that? Might my dad?'

Nell had paused in the act of serving out food, trying to think how best to answer this, but Michael had been ahead of her. He said, 'Yes, certainly he might, Beth. Don't expect to ever see him though, will you? But he could be around now and again. Just briefly, just to know how you're getting on. And I'll tell you something else. If he does, he'll be so pleased to see you doing well at school and being happy. He'll be really proud of you.'

'Um, well, good,' said Beth, with the awkward shrug she accorded to most emotional topics and particularly to anything to do with her father.

Without missing a beat, Michael had merely said, 'Yes, it is good. Nell, is that casserole ready, because if so I'll open some wine to go with it, if you want. Beth, shall we chunk up some of that French bread, as well?'

Nell, looking out at Quire Court, remembering that conversation, suddenly wished, deeply and painfully, that she could have talked to Brad about extending the shop into Godfrey Purbles' premises. But whatever I do, I can make the decision myself, Brad, she said, in her mind. And if you do ever nip back, like the ghosts in Michael's story, you'll be able to see I'm doing all right. I really am.

Across the court, Henry Jessel, the silversmith, was unlocking his door. He waved to Nell, and pointed skywards, turning up his coat collar and miming a shiver. Nell grinned, and went back inside to hunt out soft cloths and beeswax to give the curled and carved walnut frames of the Regency sofas an extra buffing before the Japanese customers arrived. There was a small inlaid table of around the same date: she would set that alongside the sofas with something tempting on it. There was a really beautiful Feuillet workbox with enamelled painted panels, which might be sufficiently unusual to attract them.

She might bring one or two things in from the small workshop at the back of the shop as well, in preparation for the weekend. Saturdays were often busy in Quire Court.

But her mind was still filled with the 1940s, and that strange, sinister enquiry about the owner of the silver golem.

There was no point in wondering, all these years later, if the anonymous person had been successful.

EIGHT

There were three emails in Michael's in-box on Monday morning. The first was from Owen Bracegirdle in the History Faculty, responding to Michael's request for help in tracing Deadlight Hall's past.

'A good source would be Land Registration documents and Searches or Transfers of Title, at the Rural Council Offices,' wrote Owen. 'They're publicly accessible documents, and it's a legitimate request to look at them – particularly if the place is being chopped into flats and sold off piecemeal. Tell me you aren't chasing spooks again – no, on second thoughts, don't tell me that at all, because I love a good mystery, and you and Nell do seem to get into such intriguing situations.'

Michael replied suitably to Owen, then consulted his diary, and found that apart from the weekly meeting with his faculty head, he was free until late afternoon. This meant he could spend most of the morning tracing Deadlight Hall's past. Professor Rosendale would certainly not be expecting him to spend so much time delving into the subject for him, but Michael was curious. There was something strange about the place, and he wanted to find out more. If he could uncover anything that would help or reassure the professor, all to the good.

The next email was from the photographer, who had called the previous day to take the publicity photographs of Wilberforce for the new book.

Hi Michael

Great to meet you yesterday – just love the shots we got of your fantastic rooms.

I'm sure we can get the camera stand and the light meter repaired – again, please forget about paying for that, I've got oodles of insurance, and if I haven't your publishers will probably stump up the dosh, although don't tell them I said that.

I hope Wilberforce's tail hasn't suffered too badly. My word, he can yowl when he's annoyed, can't he? And I hope you can get the curtains mended and the cushion re-stuffed.

I'll come back early next week to photograph him properly. It would be good if you can actually get him to sit down this time. Have you thought about trank pills – most vets do them. I'm sure they'd help.

Best,

Rafe

The third email was from Michael's editor, who was hoping to hear that the photographer had got some fabulous shots of Wilberforce.

Michael would be pleased to hear they were going to set up a separate fan page for Wilberforce on their website, inviting the cat's many young fans to write in. Perhaps Michael might dash off a few words telling the eager young readers a little about Wilberforce's background? A sort of potted biog, only not too potted. Around 750 words would be good. There was no real rush, but it would be nice if they could have it by midweek.

Michael sent a polite note to the photographer, and then, ignoring the claims of several essays on the metaphysical poets which were waiting for his critical attention, sat down to write a background for the fictional Wilberforce. In the event, he rather enjoyed creating several colourful ancestors, which included various piratical gentlemen, a fruity Thespian personage whom family legend credited with having written most of Shakespeare's plays, and a Tower of London cat who had unintentionally foiled a Gunpowder Plot shortly before Guy Fawkes' famous conspiracy. ('And Master Wilberforce forgot to bring the matches, so the City of London and the King were saved.')

He reread this, frowning. Were Guy Fawkes and Shakespeare too advanced for the seven- and eight-year-olds who devoured Wilberforce's adventures? No, surely they would have heard of both gentlemen, and it would probably please a number of parents to think their offspring were picking up odd snippets of history. It would also allow the illustrators to have a field day. Michael emailed the biography to his editor before he could change his mind, and went off to his faculty meeting.

His return was greeted by the vet's bill for de-turpentining Wilberforce, which had been brought up to his rooms by the porter on the grounds that it was marked 'Urgent'. The porter pointed out that it was not part of his duties to hand-deliver missives, but you could not ignore an 'Urgent' letter, could you, so here it was, Dr Flint, and begging pardon for being so out of breath, but climbing those bloody stairs played havoc with the tubes of a morning.

'It's very good of you,' said Michael, reaching for his wallet. 'Have a drink on me to help the tubes out.'

By the time the porter had departed, his tubes considerably appeased by the tip, and Michael had recovered from astonishment at the amount requested by the vet, his editor, who had the uncanny ability of reading most things at the speed of light, had emailed again. She liked the Wilberforce biog so much she wanted him to expand the Gunpowder Plot idea, with the aim of starting a spin-off for a set of children's historical tales. Michael could doubtless dash off one or two books on this theme, could he? Not too teachy, but underpinned by accurate historical information.

Michael wrote a cheque for the vet, smacked a stamp onto the envelope, then sent a deliberately non-committal email to his editor, saying he thought the Gunpowder Plot book was a very good idea.

These annoying interludes and interruptions dealt with, he set off for the Rural Council offices, encountering the Bursar as he crossed the quad, and spending ten minutes listening to the Bursar's discourse on the unreliable nature of modern workmen. The decorators, it appeared, could not finish the painting that day as arranged, because they'd had to order an extra twenty litres of paint which would not arrive until Thursday. College would therefore have to continue in its present dust-sheet and stepladder disarray for at least another week. The Bursar found it all very annoying and did not know what things were coming to if a firm of decorators could not calculate how much paint was needed for a few perfectly ordinary stairways.

Michael's request at the Rural Council offices for a sight of the Deadlight Hall records was received as an everyday occurrence. Certainly he could be given sight of Searches and Land Registrations and Transfers, said the helpful assistant. They had had quite a few people asking to see them recently, what with the place being renovated. The records might not be as complete as they would like – there had been some bomb damage to the old Council offices during WWII – and she believed there were a number of 'lost years', which sounded rather romantic, didn't it. There was, however, still a fair amount of stuff, and everything was scanned on to hard disk, all the way back to 1800. The viewing room was just through there, there was a coffee machine in the corridor, and if he needed any assistance of any kind, please to let her know.

Michael always found it vaguely wrong to use a computer screen for this kind of research. If you were going to make an expedition into the cobwebby purlieus of history, it ought to be by means of curling parchments with crabbed writing penned by long-dead monks and scribes, or through faded diaries chronicling forgotten loves and hates and wars and friendships. It had to be acknowledged, though, that computers were more efficient and a great deal faster than the parchment/diary method. Michael collected a cup of coffee from the machine, sat down at the screen, and waited for the past to open up.

At first he thought there was not going to be anything of any interest about Deadlight Hall. There was the original land purchase which showed the Hall had been built in the early 1800s, but it then seemed to vanish into what the assistant had called its 'lost years'.

There was an apology on the home page for the incomplete state of some of the documents, and the total absence of others, but explaining that the ravages of time, not to mention mice, damp, and the attentions of the Luftwaffe, had all wrought substantial damage. The main archives department in Oxford might, however, be able to fill in any gaps.

Michael scrolled forward patiently, and was relieved to see that Deadlight Hall sprang back into being in 1877, when a worthy-sounding organization called the Breadspear Trust had acquired it. He made a note of this, and moved to the next entry, which dealt with the Trust's obligations and administration. It seemed to have been partly governed by a philanthropically minded Mr Breadspear, and partly by the Parish and the Poor Relief Committee. He was rather intrigued to discover that the present Welfare State descended from the original Vagabond Act of the 1400s, a fearsome-sounding law that had required the arrest of vagabonds and persons suspected of living suspiciously. The legislation had apparently been repealed a great many times, and it was probably as well that an original clause requiring these hapless (or perhaps they had been merely feckless) souls to be set in the stocks, pierced through the ear, or handed the materials to build a house of correction, was no longer in force.

The next page opened up a series of letters, which had apparently been attached to the transfer of title to the Trust, and which had been scanned in as being of possible interest to students of local history. At first sight they were so indistinct as to be almost illegible, but letters were always promising, so Michael zoomed up the viewing, which helped, and began to read.

The letters commenced with the appointment of one Mrs Maria Porringer (widow of this parish), to a slightly ambiguous-sounding role at Deadlight Hall. It appeared to be a combination of house-keeper, superintendent and general factotum, and required her to be responsible for:

> The well-being and moral behaviour of all children placed in Deadlight Hall . . . To ensure such children are brought up to be honest, sober, God-fearing and grateful . . . To ensure that, as soon as the said children are of sufficient age, they are sent to places of work where they must be obedient, punctual, diligent, and honest.
>
> Remuneration to the said Mrs Maria Porringer to be as agreed and set down in correspondence with her dated the 10th day of August in the year 1878.
>
> Signed, for and on behalf of, the Parish Council.
>
> Augustus Breadspear, Salamander House.

Salamander House, thought Michael. Dragons and elemental fire-creatures, and a Victorian gentleman with a name that might have come from the pages of Charles Dickens.

At first sight, the documents struck a benevolent note, as if the young persons in question were being housed and schooled by kindly mentors or teachers. 'Brought up to be honest, sober and God-fearing' was fair enough, particularly given the era, but Michael did not like the sound of 'grateful'. The places of work might mean apprenticeships in the old and good sense of the word – the indenturing of boys and girls to skilled masters to learn a useful trade. But the nineteenth century had had a grim habit of employing young children from poor backgrounds, and forcing them to work impossibly long hours in mills and manu-factories. The literature of the time was filled with brutal places that had housed children, from Dotheboys Hall to the baby farms of *Oliver*

Twist, and it was peppered with Mr Creakles and Daniel Quilps. All fictional places and people, but based on grim reality.

Michael scrolled on to the next set of letters.

Deadlight Hall
September 1878
My dear Mr Breadspear

Please accept my sincere thanks for confirming the appointment agreed by the Trust last month. I am most grateful for this opportunity, particularly since, as you know, Mr Porringer passed on recently. He was an apothecary, in a good way of business, but after his death the shop had to pass to a distant cousin. However, I helped with running the shop for many years, and I dealt solely with the accounts. I permitted no nonsense of any kind from staff we employed, and did not tolerate impudence or familiarity from customers. You can therefore be sure that I shall wield a firm hand within Deadlight Hall.

I suppose if Mr John Hurst from Willow Bank Farm wants to provide some lessons for the children, that will be acceptable, although it should be made clear that we have no funds for such things.

On a separate note, the other, private arrangement you propose is acceptable. Carpenters and workmen have already been engaged and given specific instructions.

Very truly yours,
Maria Porringer (Mrs)

Michael frowned at the handwriting, because he had the strong impression that he had seen it before. But each century had its own style and fashion in writing, and probably most letters from the late 1800s would have been written in the same kind of hand. He would simply be recognizing the style of that era.

He reread the last paragraph, intrigued by the mention of a 'private arrangement', then read on.

Deadlight Hall
September 1879
My dear Mr Breadspear

You will be glad to know that the incident last week (I wrote to you about it) has been satisfactorily resolved, and I have taken steps to ensure it cannot be repeated. You will note the lock-smith's accounts in this month's figures. There will also be a further carpenter's bill, for it was necessary to strengthen the door at the same time.

Mr John Hurst calls every Saturday afternoon, although I am not happy about this. Last week I asked him not to teach the children poetry and suchlike, never mind if it is Shakespeare or Lord Byron, and yet only yesterday I caught him reading some high-flown verses to them, actually describing the behaviour of devils, such ungodliness. When I challenged Mr Hurst, he had the impudence to say he was reading John Milton's *Paradise Lost* to the children, and it was one of the world's great classics.

'Well,' I said, 'the classics may be all very fine, but filling up children's heads with rubbish about the drunken Sons of Belial seems most unsuitable.'

'But,' said the infuriating man, 'we should always be wary of demons and devils, Mrs Porringer. Indeed, the Testament of the Twelve Patriarchs warns us against Belial in particular – it tells us that fornication separates man from God and brings him near to Belial.'

Well, Mr Breadspear, I did not know where to look for the shame of such language, and the worst of it was I believe the man was laughing at me. I have yet to meet a more impious and disrespectful person than John Hurst.

I am respectfully yours,

Maria Porringer (Mrs)

Deadlight Hall

March 1880

Dear Mr Breadspear

I am a plain-speaking woman, and I am not best pleased by our sparse financial arrangements since the start of the year. I hope I am not one to be what the Bible calls greedy of filthy lucre, but the labourer is worthy of his hire. I am quite run off my feet, what with feeding and clothing the small ones, which is something to be considered, even with the charitable donations from ladies of the parish, including Lady Buckle's cast-offs, which usually smell of boiled cabbage and Sir George's pipe tobacco.

In addition to all that, I now have the two Mabbley girls, who came here in January as you know. (I was not at all surprised to be asked to take those two, for we all know what kind of come-day, go-day creature Polly Mabbley is). This means a total of fourteen children in all, and a deal of hard work.

As well as that there is, of course, the other duty I am performing, which takes up a considerable amount of my time.

In the past fortnight I have had approaches from two gentlemen looking for workers for their manufactories. If better arrangements cannot be made between us, these gentlemen's terms might suit better, and I shall have to think whether it would be advantageous to send some of the children to them (once of working age, of course) rather than to Salamander House.

I would be glad if you would oblige with an early reply.

Yours respectfully

Maria Porringer (Mrs)

Infuriatingly, this was the final letter from Maria Porringer, and the only document following it was a note of some land attached to the Hall being transferred in 1948. Michael glanced at this rather perfunctorily, and saw that the land had in fact been transferred to an S. Hurst. Might that be the same family as Jack Hurst who was renovating Deadlight Hall? And was the irreverent John Hurst referred to by Maria Porringer a forbear?

There were just two more documents relating to Deadlight Hall and, as with some of the earlier documents, they were incomplete – in fact the first was very nearly fragmentary. It seemed to relate to an inquest, but the edges were so jagged it was difficult to make out the heading. The whole thing had the appearance of having been Sellotaped together and scanned onto the computer by somebody who had probably said, 'It isn't much, but it's a corner of local history, so let's include it.' The section bearing the name of the deceased had been torn away altogether, but the place of death was clearly stated as having been Deadlight Hall.

The verdict on the unfortunate unknown was Death by Misadventure, and a handwritten note in the 'Cause of Death' section simply said, 'Unable to determine cause due to extreme and severe damage and incomplete condition of remains.'

Near the bottom was a rider from the jury, to the effect that Deadlight Hall be fenced off and secured against further mishap.

The second document was a tender for work at the Hall and although the date was blurred by time or damp, it seemed to follow from the recommendation of the Coroner's jury. It gave an estimate of £75.12s.6d for the work required and trusted this would be acceptable.

'Work to include disconnecting, so far as possible, all plumbing and heating outlets and all furnace vents as per our detailed list, to include labour, materials, and making good. Duration of work would be one week.'

A note had been added, explaining that it would be 'nigh on impossible to disconnect the entire contraption on account of the plumbing being integral to the water supply as well as the hot water heating system.'

The writer had never come across such an arrangement, not in all his years as a master plumber, but it was his opinion that if you took out the whole contraption, you would very likely end up causing the collapse of the entire ground floor. He did not, therefore, recommend complete removal under any circumstances, and would not do it if fifty Coroners' juries were to tell him to.

The Deadlight Hall documents ended with this, and there did not seem to be anything more.

Michael managed to fathom the printing procedure, and printed two copies of the inquest notes and scrappy tender, together with Maria Porringer's letters. He would let Professor Rosendale have copies as soon as possible.

Returning to College, he was greeted by the news that Wilberforce had caught a sparrow during his morning perambulation, which he appeared to have partly eaten, before losing interest and leaving the remains in a pink suede boot belonging to a second year. The second year, who hailed from Kensington and seldom let people forget this, complained vociferously to Michael. The boots, it seemed, were Philip Plein, they had cost an absolute fortune, and Mummy and Daddy were going to be seriously furious over the entire thing.

Michael, who had never heard of Philip Plein, made a mental note to check his provenance with Nell and rather fruitlessly explained to the second year that cats only left these offerings to people they liked. The second year was having none of this. She said it was a disgrace the way flesh-eating predators preyed on poor defenceless little birds and ripped them to shreds, in fact Mummy was president of half-a-dozen wildlife societies and it so happened that the second year was currently canvassing for contributions on Mummy's behalf.

Michael promised to invoke various insurances for the replacement of the boots, after which he signed up for a twelve-month donation to one of the wildlife societies. The second year was somewhat mollified at this, thought she would replace the pink suede, which was rather last-year, with grey, and helped Michael dispose of the corpse in one of the flower beds.

Honour being satisfied all round, Michael escaped to his rooms to immerse himself in the relative sanity of the essays on the metaphysical poets.

He put what he was already calling the Porringer letters into a drawer, ready to show to Professor Rosendale, and started to read the first of the essays which was by a particularly promising first-year student who was already showing signs of heading for a Double First, providing he could stay on track.

NINE

London
Spring 1944
Dear J.W.

I think I may have been slightly mad or possibly even a little inebriated when I agreed to travel to London to meet Schönbrunn. But Schönbrunn has that effect on people, so, as you see, here I am and we shall start the search for the Reiss twins at once. I will try to leave *poste restante* addresses for you, so that if the twins do send a message to their parents (and I pray they will), you can let me know. For the moment, any correspondence sent in care of Drummonds Bank in Charing Cross will reach me.

London is war-torn – not quite as badly as our own Warsaw and Prague, but certainly battered. I have always liked this city, just as I have always liked this country. The British are a resilient race, with a truly remarkable way of seeing humour in misfortune and tragedy. They have made up raucous and very derogatory songs about Hitler, which they sing in their theatres and public houses. Even during an air raid, people in the shelters will make rude gestures to the Luftwaffe, making light of the fact that German bombs might be exploding their homes to splinters as they do so.

I am hoping I pass as sufficiently English not to arouse any suspicion. My knowledge of the language is fairly good, I think, although I am careful not to speak unless necessary, because my accent could so easily be taken to be German. Schönbrunn, on the other hand, could pass in almost any country in the world as a native, and he has the most extraordinary gift for blending into any company. I have now been with him into several public houses, and incredibly in each one there is someone who puts up a hand in a gesture of greeting and recognition. Or, of course, it may be that he is simply choosing places where he knows there will be contacts.

You are right not to tell the twins' parents yet that they

have vanished. We should not worry them until we know the truth.

Tomorrow Schönbrunn is taking me to a small village in Oxfordshire. This is where the twins and also Leo Rosendale were originally placed – Leo is still there, we believe – so Schönbrunn feels that is where we must begin.

I wondered if we should seek out Leo, who might remember something useful about the twins – those three were such friends – but Schönbrunn thinks it better not. It could distress Leo unnecessarily, he says, and there is also the point that we do not want to draw attention to ourselves. Two strangers in a small country place, talking to a child, may attract notice.

I have no idea if this letter will reach you safely or if it will do so in its entirety, but as usual Schönbrunn has friends within some kind of secret network, and assures me he can get letters to you. For that reason I feel able to write in more detail than I should otherwise dare.

As always, I send my kind regards and very best wishes. Stay safe, my good friend,

M.B.

Oxford
Spring 1944
Dear J.W.

As you see, we have reached Oxford. Travelling is difficult, although not impossible, but the trains seem to take the longest route between two places, and there are all kinds of papers and proofs of identity to be shown along the journey. Schönbrunn, as you will guess, has provided us with all the necessary documents. I have not asked how or where he acquired them – I have not dared! I am just grateful that they are accepted.

Oxford is a beautiful city, even in the midst of this war, and we have managed to find rooms in a small boarding house which is modest, but clean and comfortable. Somehow Schönbrunn has acquired a motor car – a shocking old rattletrap it is – and also petrol (again, I dare not ask). However, a car will make things much easier, although he is a terrible driver. I clutch the dashboard as we bounce along, while Schönbrunn wrestles with gears and steering, and swears at the other motorists in various languages.

Sophie and Susannah Reiss were placed with a family in a village just outside a place called Wolvercote. Schönbrunn was involved in the arrangements and knows the way, so we shall drive there tomorrow and call at the house, presenting ourselves as Ministry Officials. Apparently the British are accustomed to people knocking on their doors and asking the most intimate questions. I dare say this is the fault of various War Departments.

Our questions will be based on food consumption which Schönbrunn thinks will not seem offensive.

Best regards,
M.B.

Oxford
Spring 1944
Dear J.W.

The food consumption ploy has worked perfectly. We did, though, have to knock on the doors of at least half a dozen other houses so as to appear credible, and I am now in possession of a great deal of information regarding potatoes (half the crop suffered something called blight), carrots (a quarter of these were lost to black rot) and Brussels sprouts, which, according to most people, are not liked by anyone, except at Christmas, when you have to eat them on account of it being a tradition. There are, however, hopes for the spring yield of tomatoes and lettuces – providing, that is, the Government doesn't snaffle the best of the crop. (I am unsure of the precise meaning of this word *snaffle*, but Schönbrunn says it simply means steal.)

Sophie and Susannah Reiss lived with a couple called Battersby on the village outskirts. Mrs Battersby, a generously proportioned and garrulous lady, insisted on our coming inside, the better to complete our questionnaire.

And now I am setting down, to the best of my recollection, an account of the conversation. It began with a well-judged question from Schönbrunn about how many people lived in the house, and this caused Mrs Battersby to open up about the two small girls taken in the previous year.

'Dear girls, they were,' said Mrs Battersby, dispensing tea (very strong), and slices of seed cake (delicious). 'And Mr Battersby and I were more than happy to give them homes, not having been blessed with children of our own. But those poor lambs were so bewildered and vulnerable at first it broke my heart.' Then, to me, 'I can assure you we were careful about their attendance at school each day – a very good village school we have here.'

I nodded and made a diligent note.

'Church every Sunday, and Sunday School in the afternoon. Mr Battersby was a bit concerned about that, them being Jewish, but I said they'd find God just as well in a good English church as in a synagogue. You'll forgive me, Mr— I'm sorry, I didn't catch your name, but I realize you aren't English, and so if that remark is offensive to you, I apologize. I was brought up a good Anglican, you see, and it's difficult to change.'

Schönbrunn smiled at her (he is shameless at times), and she blinked, then went on.

'They seemed to settle down so well, although missing their homes dreadfully, of course, but they were such good, well-behaved little mites, we thought they were adjusting. So bright and clever they were, and we noticed a remarkable thing – to teach one of them something was to teach both the same thing.'

Neither Schönbrunn nor I made any response to this, but we both knew it was this extraordinary vein of telepathy that Mengele's people had been so greedy for.

'Then,' said Mrs Battersby, 'what do they do but up and run away.'

'Run away?' I said in surprise, for I had not been expecting this, but before I could say more, Schönbrunn was commenting on what a sad thing that was to hear.

'Well, it's the only conclusion we could reach,' said Mrs Battersby. 'They became ill, you see, that was how it started. Not from any lack of care on my part, I'd like it known.'

'I'm sure not.'

'Meningitis, it was. A dreadful cruel illness, and a real epidemic. Half the children hereabouts caught it. The authorities set up a temporary isolation hospital, and to my mind they didn't do so badly, given the difficulties.' Again, this was directed to me, and I nodded.

'We weren't allowed to visit them,' said Mrs Battersby, 'but we were glad to hear that at least they had a friend with them – Leo Rosendale, who came to England with them. He's living with the Hursts over at Willow Bank Farm – very strict, they are, but I have to say they made everyone very welcome last Christmas – a Boxing Day supper it was, although a pity that Mr Porringer was there. Mr Battersby has no time for Mr Paul Porringer and neither do I, nothing but a jumped-up counter-pusher, he is, for all he likes to boast how his grandfather had his own shop in the days of the old Queen.'

('Old Queen' clearly refers to Queen Victoria, who is still remembered by elderly people here.)

'But the little girls vanished?' I managed to say. 'From the hospital itself?'

'Clean disappeared late one night. The doctors reported it at once, and the police came to tell us, and Mr Battersby went straight along to the police station to help organize a search. Most of the village turned out. Searched all night and all the next day. The police went on for several days – notices at railway stations, photographs in the newspapers, even a piece on the wireless. And they talked to the other children, those who had been in the hospital that night. Leo Rosendale, and one or two of the others. But none of them seemed to know anything, and of course they'd all been so poorly. I don't mind admitting I was chilled to the marrow to think of those little mites out there, such a bitter cold night it was, straight after Christmas, and them still poorly from that menin-gitis, even though the doctors said they hadn't got it very severely.'

Schönbrunn said quickly, 'But they were found in the end?' I could feel him willing her to say the twins had turned up – that news had been received of them since he and I had arrived in England.

'No, they weren't found,' said Mrs Battersby. 'Not hide nor hair nor whisker. There were all kinds of suspicions and rumours that some nasty-minded person might have taken them. Some folk said they had seen a stranger hanging around, offering children sweets. But the police thought it unlikely anyone took the girls. They were in the hospital, you see, with other children, and nurses and doctors all around – very strict isolation it had to be, and they kept all the doors locked and didn't allow anyone in apart from the doctors and nurses. They wouldn't even let the parents in.'

'An isolation hospital,' said Schönbrunn, thoughtfully. 'Yes, it would certainly have been difficult for anyone to get in there.'

'It's my belief the girls weren't as poorly as we thought, and they ran away to get back to their homes. I can only trust to the good Lord that they found their way there, and that some Christian soul helped them, for the thought of them out there in the snow and ice . . . I keep hoping we'll hear something. I wake up many a night, thinking I can hear them chattering away to one another in their bedroom – although Mr Battersby believed they didn't always need to speak to understand one another, if you take my meaning. And then I think, well, perhaps tomorrow there'll be a letter or a telephone call to say they're all right.'

'I do hope there will,' I said, and I meant it more than she could have known.

'Mr Battersby took it very badly. There's nights he goes out and walks the lanes – even though walking any distance is a sore trial to him, having taken a bullet in the last war – but he can't get rid of the idea that he might come across some clue that's been missed. "Girls," he'll call, just softly like, not wanting to alarm them if they're in earshot, which of course they aren't. He knows it's illogical to call for them, but he says he can't seem to help it. "Girls," he calls. "Where are you?"'

I wanted to tell her who we were and how we, too, were trying to find the twins, for the thought of that poor man wandering the lanes calling for the lost girls was almost more than I could bear. Schönbrunn sent me a warning glance.

'Folks said it was the infirmary's fault they went,' said Mrs Battersby, 'but I never believed that, for those doctors and nurses were good as gold to those children, and you'd maybe like to put that in your forms as well, Mr . . . er . . . I did hear the Sister in charge left the place almost immediately afterwards, though. I don't know what happened to her – there was some story that she couldn't face having lost two of her charges, and that she simply walked out that same night or it might have been the next day.'

Schönbrunn frowned, and I could see he was wondering if this might be a useful line of enquiry. But he did not say anything, and I managed to ask about the infirmary itself. Had it been near here?

'Oh, yes. Ugly old place it is, just a few miles away. If you're going back to Oxford you'll likely see it across the fields. The nurses scrubbed out a few of the rooms and disinfected them to use as wards, and the men carried in beds and suchlike.' She shivered. 'I dare say the children'd be too ill to notice much, but I wouldn't want to be in that house. A gloomy place it is, built more than a hundred years ago, and an odd history it's got, if you can believe all you hear. At one time it was made into some kind of orphanage – Victorian days, that was – and they say all manner of cruelties went on there. But you can't believe all you hear.'

I was about to ask outright for the name of the place, but Schönbrunn forestalled me, saying, 'It sounds something of a landmark.'

'Oh, it is. You ask anyone hereabouts about it and they'll tell you that Deadlight Hall is a real local landmark.'

On that note, we made good our escape, thanking Mrs Battersby for her hospitality. Schönbrunn shook her hand and assured her the details she had provided would be used in a responsible and discreet fashion. I said they would be of immense help to the government.

'I'm a black liar,' I said, glumly, as we careered back to the high road. 'And so are you.'

'But in a good cause.'

'We deceived that good, trusting woman.'

'Are you sure she was all she appeared?'

'For pity's sake, you aren't telling me she might have been a German agent? Or working for Mengele?'

'I'll admit it's unlikely,' he said. 'But we trust no one. You'll have to square the deceit with your conscience as well as you can.'

'I shall have my just deserts one day,' I said, resignedly. 'And when I die, I shall very likely be cast into Gehenna.'

'What—?'

'The place of fiery torment.'

'I *know* what Gehenna is,' said Schönbrunn. 'I was going to say what did we do with the road map, because if we're going to find Deadlight Hall before it gets dark, we should start looking out for it.'

It was then that we rounded a bend in the road, and saw it

across the fields. The house with the bad history. Deadlight Hall. I stared at it with a feeling of cold dread gathering at the pit of my stomach. If ever the Jewish Gehenna existed – if ever there really is a place of torment for sinners and non-believers, a place where the worshippers of Moloch burned their sons and daughters in fires – then it would look exactly like this grim dereliction.

And now, of course, as you read this, you'll be saying, 'Oh, dear me, here's old Maurice Bensimon being dramatic again,' but I promise you, my friend, this place was as menacing and as forbidding as anything that ever came out of the Torah's darker pages, or, indeed, out of a Gothic tale of horror. (No, I do not read such books, but I have eyes, also ears, and I know about such things.)

Schönbrunn stopped the car and we both sat looking at the Hall for several moments. Then he said, 'I think we had better go inside.'

I had never felt less inclined to enter any building, but he said, 'This is where the twins vanished from, remember. There could be all kinds of clues.'

'That ward sister.'

'Yes, certainly.'

'At least the place is empty,' I said, but Schönbrunn pointed to a long window on the side of the main doors.

'It isn't empty,' he said.

The window, like all the windows, was almost glassless, but jagged shards still clung to the stone lintels. Framed in the opening, its outline distorted by the broken glass and blurred by the dying afternoon light, was the shape of a figure. Its head was tilted away from us, as if it was looking for something within the house. Then, as we stared, it turned and looked outwards, as if watching our approach.

Schönbrunn restarted the car and drove it on to a small patch of grass near the front of the house.

'Are we still going in?' I said, and saw the gleam in Schönbrunn's eyes I had once seen in the shadow of Buchenwald, when he faced a dozen Nazi guards and shot most of them.

'Oh, yes,' he said, softly. 'We're going in.'

TEN

The lock was broken on Deadlight Hall's massive doors – not just rusted away, but clearly torn from the frame, splintering the wood in the process. There could have been a perfectly innocent explanation for this – a tramp wanting to break in for a night's shelter – but there could also be several less innocent explanations.

There was no particular need for stealth – if challenged, we had only to say we were strangers to the area and curious about a local landmark – but we both moved quietly and cautiously. Schönbrunn and I have been in some strange places and menacing situations during the last two or three years, but I don't think either of us had ever encountered anywhere as eerie as Deadlight Hall.

As we paused in the doorway, I said, very softly, 'There's no sign of the figure we saw. It was at that window by the door, wasn't it?'

'Yes.' Schönbrunn produced a torch and shone it warily. 'There's thick dust on the floor,' he said. 'But it's undisturbed, as if no one has walked in this hall for a very long time.'

'No footprints,' I said, and as I spoke, I felt as if something cold and unpleasant twisted at my stomach. 'And yet to get to that window a person would have to cross the floor.'

'Undoubtedly.'

'Perhaps we didn't see anyone after all. Perhaps it was a trick of the light.'

'I think there was someone there,' said Schönbrunn. 'He – it could even have been a she – was standing in that window recess, looking out.' He frowned, then said, with decision, 'We mustn't become distracted. We're here to search the house, nothing more. Because if we're believing that woman's story, it's from here that the twins vanished that night. So we need to find out if there are any clues.'

'The police searched the house,' I said, uneasily. 'Mrs Battersby said so.'

'Yes, but the police wouldn't have been looking for the kind of clue we're looking for.'

'What kind of clue are we looking for?'

'I don't know until we find it,' he said, which was exasperating, but Schönbrunn can be very exasperating sometimes.

'But it was the depths of winter when they vanished. If they wanted to run away, wouldn't they have waited for better weather?'

'It would depend on why they ran,' he said, then, with a note of near-violence, 'I hope they did run away,' he said. 'Because if they didn't, it means they were taken.' *Taken by Mengele's people . . . Taken because he wanted Sophie and Susannah Reiss inside Auschwitz, and his agents had specific orders . . .* The thought was in both our minds.

'So,' said Schönbrunn briskly, 'it's imperative that we pick up their trail. You marked what the Battersby woman said about people thinking there'd been a stranger hanging around – offering the schoolchildren sweets?'

'Oh yes.'

Neither of us needed to say more. Both of us were aware of Dr Mengele's behaviour inside Auschwitz; of how he played the part of a kindly uncle, securing the children's trust by giving them sweets and sugar lumps, all the time luring them closer to the door of his laboratories.

Forcing the images away, I said, 'Where shall we start?'

We surveyed the hall. I suppose we had expected to encounter a scene of dereliction, but although the plasterwork was peeling and the floorboards were dull and scarred, it was not as bad as we had expected. There was a stench of damp and mildew, but there was none of the miscellaneous, often squalid rubbish so frequently seen in abandoned buildings. You and I, my friend, have seen too many of those since our country was ravaged. I sometimes think I shall never wash away the clinging stench of bomb-damaged, smoke-blackened ruins.

Schönbrunn said, 'They'd keep the children together, I think, so it's likely they'd use the biggest rooms.'

'Here on the ground floor.'

'Yes. Let's start here, at any rate.'

I don't know what we expected to find, but what we did find, in an inner room, at least confirmed Mrs Battersby's story. Carved on a wall, low down, at child height, was the Jewish symbol for *S*. I do not need to describe it to you, my friend, but to both of us, that mark was as clear as a curse. Sophie and Susannah Reiss had indeed been here – they had left their initial.

'It's reassuring on one level and terrifying on another,' I said, straightening up from examining the mark. 'And why would they leave their initial here?'

'It needn't be sinister,' he said. 'Did you never carve your initials on a schoolroom desk?'

'I don't think so.'

'You must have been an inordinately well-behaved child. We'd better explore the upper floors.'

'Still no footprints,' I said, as we reached the first floor.

'No. So the figure we saw didn't come up here. But why hasn't he – or she – come out to challenge us? We haven't been particularly noisy, but we haven't tiptoed around.'

'He might be hiding,' I said. 'There could be all kinds of perfectly innocent reasons for that, though.'

We looked into all the first-floor rooms, then we went up to the second floor ones, which were smaller. All the rooms were empty – some had a few pieces of furniture, and some of them were draped in dust sheets, making strange ghostly outlines in the dimness. Schönbrunn pulled the dust sheets away, but nothing lurked or crouched beneath any of them.

'There's nothing,' I said. 'In fact—' I broke off as Schönbrunn grabbed my arm. 'What's wrong?' I said, instinctively lowering my voice.

'Listen,' he said.

At first I could not hear anything, then, between one heartbeat and the next, came a soft voice.

'Children, are you here?'

There was silence, and I dug my fingernails into the palms of my hands. I was aware of Schönbrunn listening intently. The voice came again.

'Children, where are you?'

It's difficult to convey in a letter how extremely disturbing that soft voice and those words were. There was almost a fairy-tale quality – a grim echo of all those wicked stepmothers and witches in gingerbread cottages – all the hungering ogres who hunted little children, and carried them off to dark castles. I remembered again Josef Mengele, the Angel of Death, who stalked children and carried them off to his own dark castle: the fortress called Auschwitz, where he performed his experiments. Experiments that included amputations, chemicals injected into eyes to change their colour, the attempts to create conjoined twins by sewing sections of their bodies together . . . Twins.

'It's coming from above,' said Schönbrunn.

'Attics?'

'There's nowhere else it could be.' He was already going towards a small, narrow flight of stairs. I followed slowly. I will not use the word reluctant.

The attic stairs were steep, and I was slightly out of breath when we reached the top, but Schönbrunn was already exploring. Those attics were dark and dingy, oppressive from the closeness of the roof directly above, and thick with a dreadful despairing loneliness. I must have flinched, because Schönbrunn said softly, 'Whatever happened here, happened a long time ago.'

'I hope it did. I can't make out very much anywhere, can you? Unless – is that a door in that corner?'

'Yes,' he said. 'Take the torch, while I try to open it.'

The door resisted at first, but it eventually yielded, and swung inwards.

I cannot quite say that something was in that room, for we did not actually see anything, but there was the strong sense that it was not empty. I moved the torchlight slowly over the cobwebbed walls, seeing an old bed frame and a marble washstand. But for a moment my heart bumped with fear, because surely there was someone standing at the far end, immediately where the wall met the roof slope – someone wearing pale draperies, the head turned to watch us . . .

'Children, are you here? If you're here I'll find you . . .'

The whisper came again, as faint and insubstantial as the drifting cobwebs, and we both spun round. But there was no one there, and when we turned back to the room the outline had gone, and there was only a fall of tattered curtain, moving slightly in the ingress of air from our opening of the door.

'There's nothing here,' said Schönbrunn after a moment, but for the first time ever I heard a note of concern and puzzlement in his voice. 'Nothing,' he repeated, more loudly, and closed the door, turning the handle so firmly I think it probably jammed. 'Let's go back downstairs and see where else to look.'

'There was a door under the stairs,' I offered. 'Probably it leads to a scullery and store rooms. Places where a child – two children – might have hidden and left more clues.'

'Indeed so.' He sent me an approving glance.

The door, which was set well back in the hall, opened with a scratch of sound – it was not a particularly loud noise, but it was enough in that old house to make me look nervously over my shoulder. But nothing moved – or did it? For a moment I thought I saw the figure in the window recess again, but when I shone the torch it was only the silhouette of an old tree immediately outside, dipping its branches towards the window.

'There's a flight of steps,' said Schönbrunn, peering through the door. 'I can't see much else. There's a disgusting smell, though. Where's the torch?'

The torch's beam cut a triangle of cold light through the darkness, and Schönbrunn began to descend the steps without hesitation. There was no indication that this would lead to sculleries, or that it would lead anywhere at all, but we had to make sure.

At the foot of the steps was a narrow passageway, and Schönbrunn pointed to the ground again.

'Still no footprints,' he said, then stopped and turned to look back along the dark passage.

'Something there?' I said, but even as I spoke I could hear it.

Footsteps. And the sound of someone breathing – doing so with difficulty, like a sufferer from asthma might.

'Whoever it is,' said Schönbrunn, very softly, 'is in this passage with us. Between us and the door leading to the hall.'

Fear clutched at me all over again, but Schönbrunn called out, and his voice was perfectly steady.

'Hallo? Who's there? We're down here. Two of us. We're exploring the house.'

That 'two of us' was clever. It indicated that we could put up a fight if necessary. Not that I was ever much use in a fight. Masterly inactivity has always been my strength.

We waited, shining the torch back towards the door.

'There's no one there,' I said, after a moment, but still speaking softly.

'I can't see anyone. No – *look there!*'

But I had already seen it. A shadow cast on the wall at the end of the passage, as if someone was standing there, just out of sight, but had not realized its shadow was visible. It was not particularly tall and there was a deformed look to it. The shoulders were hunched, and the head was bent to one side.

Schönbrunn called out again, and the figure seemed to listen intently. And then it vanished. One minute it was there, the next it had gone. It was as if it had been made of a cluster of spiders' webs, and as if something had blown chill breath on it, causing the webs to shrivel. The reality, of course, would simply be that whoever was there had darted silently away.

I said, in a determinedly practical voice, 'Whoever that was has gone.'

'It was calling for the children. And,' said Schönbrunn, 'who were we told does that? Still calls for them, weeks after they vanished? Who is it who constantly walks the lanes around here, trying to find them?'

'Battersby,' I said, eagerly. 'Of course. Except . . .' I looked back uneasily, remembering the broken lock on the main doors. 'That figure was misshapen,' I said.

'Yes, but Mrs Battersby told us that walking any distance was a trial to her husband, because he had been shot in the last war. There's no one else it could be.'

'Of course there isn't.' I felt a surge of gratitude. 'You,' I said to Schönbrunn, 'are probably the sanest, most logical person I've ever known.'

'Logical? I hope so. Sane? I sometimes wonder.' But the edge of the torchlight caught his face, and he was smiling. 'We'll leave Mr Battersby to his sad search, and we'll see what else Deadlight Hall can tell us.'

The passage was dark and dank, but opening off it was a series of small, separate rooms. I went into the first of them, and that was when I knew we were not in Gehenna at all – that we had never been in Gehenna, for Gehenna, if it ever did, or ever will, exist, will be blisteringly, soul-shrivellingly hot. Those rooms were cold: a deadly coldness that would seep into your bones if you were in them too long and destroy you. I went into each one, and in every one I felt the misery and the loneliness soak down into my bones. I thought: people lived here, slept here, *despaired* here.

So strong were the feelings that in the last room, I swayed, and had to put out a hand to the wall for support. It was with real gratitude that I felt Schönbrunn's hand close around my arm.

'It's all right, you know,' he said, very quietly. 'There's no one here.'

I wanted to say, Oh, but there is. There are fragments of people still here – tiny splinters of lost, forgotten people, and although I have no idea who they were, I know they experienced terrible things – unhappiness, fear, deep aching loneliness – and I know it because those emotions still live.

I did not say any of it. Indeed, I surprise myself to see I am writing it now, even to you, my oldest friend. I shall leave it as I have written it, though, and no doubt when you read it, you will think once again, 'Ah yes, poor old Maurice Bensimon, he is certainly growing fanciful as he gets older.'

'One more room,' said Schönbrunn, leading the way to the very end of the corridor. I wanted to say we should not bother, that we should go back to our lodgings, but of course I followed him.

At the end of the short passage, facing us square on, was a black door, bound with thick iron strips. Set into the upper half was a round window, like a single unblinking eye. I had the feeling it was trying to stare at us, that lidless eye, but that it could not quite see us because its surface was smeared and filmed with grime, as a man's eye can become smeared and filmed with a cataract. I stared at this dead, blind eye, and thought, *So this is the 'dead light' of this house.* But Schönbrunn had taken the torch and he was shining it on to the door, and I forced myself to stand next to him.

'It's a furnace room,' he said. 'If you stand close to the glass you can make out the furnace itself.'

He lifted up the torch and I wanted to tell him not to wipe the eye clear of its cobwebby film, to leave it in its semi-blind state so that nothing could look through at us, but instead I peered through the glass. The furnace was there – black and crouching and ugly. Thick pipes snaked away from it and the surface around its door was scarred and pitted with heat. I hated it instantly, but I said, 'Yes, I see. It doesn't tell us anything about the twins though, does it?' I thought: so now, let's go back upstairs, and get away from this place as fast as possible.

But Schönbrunn was already reaching for the heavy handle

and if the door was unlocked we should have to go inside. But before he had turned the mechanism his expression changed, and he spun round, directing the torch on to the incomplete stone wall behind us. This time there was no need for him to tell me to listen, for I could hear the sounds clearly.

Footsteps – not the slow, difficult steps we had heard earlier, but firm, heavy footsteps ringing out on the cold stones.

There was no time to think who the footsteps might belong to, or how we would deal with this new situation, because he was already there, stepping through the narrow opening in the wall. And this was no elusive, amorphous shadow spun from spider webs, or forlorn figure calling for two lost girls; this was a solidly built man in his forties, with a jowly face and small mean eyes. And in his hand was a gun which he was pointing at us.

He said, 'Schönbrunn. They told me you were coming.'

At his smoothest and most urbane, Schönbrunn said, 'My companion and I are merely exploring this unusual building.'

'We'll forget the rubbish about you being travellers or men from some nameless ministry,' said the man. 'I know perfectly well who you are.' He studied Schönbrunn for a moment. Me he seemed to hardly notice. He said, 'It's a remarkable moment to meet such a well-known figure. You aren't in the least what I was expecting.'

Schönbrunn said, politely, 'You, on the other hand, conform exactly to the pattern of Nazi spies. Even to the stench. Corrupt and rotten.'

His voice was polite and not emphatic, but his eyes were glowing with that reckless courage.

The other man's eyes snapped. He said, 'I do know why you're here, of course. You're here to find out what happened to the Reiss twins. I'm here to prevent you drawing attention to the fact that they disappeared – which in turn might draw attention to my own activities.'

'May we know your name?' said Schönbrunn.

'My name is Porringer. Paul Porringer.'

The courtesy dropped from Schönbrunn as if it was water running off oiled feathers. In a voice like iced steel, he said, 'Porringer, where are the Reiss girls?'

'No longer here.'

'I know that. Mr Porringer, we do not bandy words. You

are a German sympathizer and a Nazi spy. You are also British, which makes you a traitor to your country.' This last was said with such contempt I almost expected the man, Porringer, to shrivel. He did not, of course. 'I suppose,' said Schönbrunn, 'that you pass here as an ordinary Englishman.'

'I am an ordinary Englishman,' said Porringer, at once. 'I've lived here all my life. I run my family's pharmacy business. I'm a pillar of the local church, friendly with my neighbours, and accepted by them all. None of them has the least idea of what I am. And once you're dead, they'll never know the truth.'

'Ah, but "What is truth?" as jesting Pilate once asked. What, for instance, is the truth about the Reiss twins?'

'They were wanted for research. To help with important work.'

'We knew that already. We think you took them away, although we don't know how.'

Schönbrunn waited, and Porringer, as if he could not resist boasting about his own cleverness, said, 'Several of the children developed meningitis – they were brought here. It became a temporary isolation hospital. No one was allowed in, except for medical staff. And,' he said, 'a helpful chemist who had a well-stocked shop and could bring various drugs.'

'You?'

'Yes.'

'So you got into Deadlight Hall?'

'Yes.'

'And you took the twins? Where are they now?'

I thought there was an unmistakable hesitation, and I thought Schönbrunn marked it as well, because he made as if to move. Then Porringer said, 'Their whereabouts need not concern you.' He gestured with the gun towards the furnace room. 'And now put down the torch, let its light shine into the furnace room, then open that door and get inside.'

'And then?'

'And then I shall shoot you and leave your bodies down here.'

'You'll be found out,' I said. 'Our bodies will be found – it will be traced back to you.'

'Believe me, gentlemen, I will not be found out. You won't be found, either,' he said. 'No one ever comes to Deadlight Hall. After I've shot you, your bodies will lie down here for years, and they'll quietly and slowly rot.'

ELEVEN

With those words, Deadlight Hall's shadows crept nearer, and the blind dead eye seemed to peer more intently through its smeary film.

Then Schönbrunn said, 'Execution in a furnace room? Not worthy of you, Porringer, or your Nazi masters. Almost squalid, in fact. Or is it sufficiently bizarre to hold some distinction, I wonder?'

He turned to me as if for confirmation of this and, realizing he was playing for time, I said, 'Squalid rather than bizarre, I'd have thought.'

Schönbrunn nodded, then set the torch on the floor as Porringer had ordered, angling it to shine on to the iron door. When he grasped the thick old handle it turned, and he pulled the door open. There was a faint sound as if ancient breath had been released, and a stench of old soot gusted out. For a moment I thought there was a movement in the corner near the furnace, almost as if our entrance had disturbed something, but it was only black beetles scurrying away from the light. Schönbrunn seemed hardly to notice. His eyes were already scanning the room, and I knew he was searching for a means of escape.

Porringer nudged the torch with his foot, so that the light fell more fully into the room, and gestured to us to move back to the wall. The furnace was on our left, and as the light fell across it, I saw that it had a round door, held in place by a long steel rod, placed diagonally and thrust into grooves. The rod would make a good weapon, but I could not see any means of snatching it from the door without Porringer seeing.

He seemed in no hurry to shoot us. Clearly he was relishing having the legendary Schönbrunn at his mercy, and would no doubt brag about it to his paymasters in Berlin.

Schönbrunn said, 'What exactly is this place? Come now, Porringer, if this is to be our tomb, you can at least tell us where we are.' He took an unobtrusive step towards the furnace, and my heart skipped a beat, because I knew he, too, had marked the steel rod.

'We're in the bowels of Deadlight Hall,' said Porringer.

'What is – or was – Deadlight Hall?'

Porringer gave a small shrug, and said, 'A hundred years ago this house was a cross between an orphanage for the bastards of the rich and respectable, and what used to be called an Apprentice House. A sort of hostel for the orphans who were brought up here and sent to work in the local industries. As a matter of fact an ancestress of mine ran the place. Maria Porringer was her name.'

'I shouldn't have thought this part of the country would have much industry,' I said, strongly aware of Schönbrunn taking another step nearer to the furnace, and wanting to keep Porringer's attention on me.

'There was more than you'd think,' he said. 'In particular there was a glass-making manufactory. Salamander House it was called. Most of the children who lived here worked there. It's long since gone, of course.'

'This house has a bad feeling. As if violent things have happened here.'

'Oh, the locals will spin you any number of stories about Deadlight Hall,' said Porringer. 'No one will live here. It's been empty for years, and—'

The sentence was never finished. Schönbrunn dived for the furnace door, seizing the steel rod and dragging it free, so that the door creaked slightly then began to swing open.

Faced with two victims in separate parts of the room, Porringer fired at me, but I had already dropped flat to the floor. (I may not be as resourceful as Schönbrunn, but I do have some instincts.) The bullet went harmlessly over my head and into the wall behind me. Tiny chips of stone and plaster flew out.

Schönbrunn did not waste time; he simply threw the steel bolt directly at Porringer. It caught the man a glancing blow and although it did not actually disable him, he instinctively threw up one hand in defence. In doing so the gun fell from his hands, clattering to the floor, and Schönbrunn snatched it up at once. Porringer bounded towards him, but then – I could not quite see how it happened – his body jerked abruptly backwards as if a string had been looped around his neck and tugged hard. He fell back, against the furnace, banging his head on its side. The round cover, already released by the removal of the steel rod, flew open, revealing the black yawning interior. Porringer scrabbled to get back to his feet, but he was slightly stunned by the blow to his head, and he could not get up.

Schönbrunn levelled the gun at his head. 'Tell us where the Reiss twins are,' he said, but Porringer seemed not to hear or understand. He was still half lying against the furnace, but he had grasped the rim of the opening and was using it as a lever to push himself back to his feet.

'Listen to me, Porringer,' said Schönbrunn very coldly. 'If you don't tell me where the Reiss twins are, I will shoot you in each ankle.'

Porringer shook his head, although whether in refusal or because he was trying to clear his head, I have no idea. I was in fact bracing myself for the sound of gunshot when the open furnace cover suddenly swung back, as if someone had pushed it to shut it. It was a massive, thick slab of iron and it crunched against Porringer's head and on to his hands, which were still grasping the edges, knocking him halfway into the furnace's mouth, and trapping him. He gave a dreadful grunting cry, and I sprang forward, grasping the edge of the door to pull it back.

'Help me,' I said to Schönbrunn, desperately. 'It won't move – it's stuck – or the hinge has broken, or something. But it's so heavy – it's smashed the back of his skull half open—'

Schönbrunn thrust the gun in his belt and knelt next to me, at the side of the furnace. 'Porringer,' he said, 'can you hear us? Listen then, if you tell me where the Reiss twins are, I'll free you, I swear. I'll get the door up somehow and we'll get you out, and get you to an infirmary. But first tell me where they are.'

Porringer was struggling, and blood was dripping from his hands, which were trapped between the edges of the door, and he was shouting for help, his cries echoing hollowly from within the furnace.

But when Schönbrunn rapped out that question, Porringer said, 'Damn you, no!'

'For pity's sake, man—'

'You'll only – shoot me – as a spy . . .' The words were slurred and distorted and blood was running from his neck. Schönbrunn and I exchanged glances.

'You won't necessarily be shot,' said Schönbrunn. 'You could change sides. Become a double agent. I'd help you.' I knew he would have promised Porringer almost anything to find out what had happened to the twins. 'Where's the torch?' he said to me, urgently. 'Shine it on to the door's hinges. Between us we can lever it open, surely.'

Porringer's lower body was twitching spasmodically, and he was groaning. Schönbrunn and I grasped the edges of the door, and threw all our weight into pulling it open. In the cold torchlight we could both see that blood had spattered the iron – blood, with tiny splinters of bone in it. I began to feel sick. As you know I am apt to be annoyingly squeamish.

But I said, with as much force as I could, 'Porringer, tell us. We're trying to get you free, but tell us about the twins, and we'll do our best to help you.'

But either Porringer would not or could not speak by now, and I said, 'We must get him out. There's blood and brain matter spilling out. We can't leave him like this—'

'If there was something we could use as a series of wedges to force the lid open,' said Schönbrunn, looking round the room, 'we could get him out and to an infirmary.'

'Should one of us try to find a doctor? There'd be one in the village – Mrs Battersby would know, I could ask her. Or if her husband's still prowling around upstairs . . .'

'I think Battersby must have gone,' said Schönbrunn. 'If he was still here he'd have heard us and come down to investigate. As for going in search of a doctor – by the time we managed to get one here . . .' He looked at the trapped man and gave an expressive shrug.

'Also,' I said, very softly, 'to do any of that would blow our cover.'

'Quite. Dammit, there must be something we can do.'

That was when we heard the other sounds. A kind of rhythmic ticking, like the heartbeat of some invisible creature. We both looked towards the door leading out to the dark passage, but nothing moved. Then came a dull roar. At first I had no idea what it was, then Schönbrunn said in a voice of extreme horror, 'Dear God, it's the furnace.'

'What—?'

'It's firing,' he said.

'It can't be.'

'But it is. Can't you smell the hot iron? The door mechanism must have released something – set something working. If we don't get him out in the next few minutes he'll burn alive. His face—'

The thick pipes feeding the furnace were already scorchingly hot, and the smell of hot iron was increasing.

The torch spluttered and the battery died. We were in the pitch dark.

Porringer's screams will, I believe, echo through my nightmares until I die. It is a terrible thing to hear the screams of a man whose brain has been partly crushed, and whose face is about to be burned off by the roaring heat of an ancient furnace.

After the first few nightmare minutes the darkness was not quite so absolute, because a flickering light began to glow from the furnace. That meant we could at least see what we were doing, but it would not have mattered if a hundred suns had shone down on us, or if a thousand bright lights had poured into the room, because there was nothing we could do to save Porringer.

If we had known how to disable the furnace that might have saved him, but we did not know, and we did not dare waste time trying to find out. Instead, we tore our hands to shreds trying to get the door open. To no avail. The door resisted our efforts as firmly as if something was leaning heavily against it, or as if – and this really will convince you I went temporarily mad in that hellish place – as if something on the inside was pulling hard on it to prevent it being opened. In the end, the heat became so unbearable that eventually we were forced to stop. Even so, we both had badly blistered hands for some days.

I cannot tell you how long it took Porringer to die, because time ceased to exist in that hellish place. The glow from the furnace turned the room into something from one of the ancient visions of hell. Our shadows, distorted and grotesque, moved across the old stone walls, and more than once I thought other shadows moved with them. Smaller, more fragile silhouettes, their arms outstretched. The old deadlight set into the room's iron door was bathed in the sullen light; it watched us unblinkingly.

Porringer was screaming, and there was a stench of burning flesh – I cannot find words to describe that, nor is it something that should be described. But at one stage the nausea over-whelmed me, and I was sick, helplessly and messily, spattering on the floor. I think Porringer was dead by that time, for the sounds from the furnace had ceased.

One of the most bizarre, most sinister aspects of the entire incident was that once Porringer was dead, the furnace began to cool. The angry glow faded and the sound of the pipes clanking and growling ceased. There was a ticking as the metal cooled.

We left him – what remained of him – in that room, closing the iron-bound door, and groping our way back through the dark passages. I could not stop thinking about that smeared, blinded deadlight, and how it had seemed to watch everything that happened. That is something else that is in my nightmares.

I suppose Porringer's body will be found sometime, but I am not sure if it will be possible for it to be identified. I don't know if there will be enough of it left.

Schönbrunn and I walked rather shakily from the furnace room. Neither of us spoke. Both of us wanted, I believe, to simply reach the good fresh air and the normal world, and to get away from Deadlight Hall as fast as we could.

Neither of us can explain what happened to Porringer. There was no one else with us in the furnace room. It can only be that when Porringer fell against the furnace, the cover was dislodged by his fall and the hinges broke, so that when it swung closed, it somehow locked into place. That, we have agreed, is the likeliest explanation.

But we cannot explain how the furnace itself fired.

As we went up the stone steps to the main hall, Schönbrunn said, 'There was no trace of the twins here, was there?' and I heard a note of appeal in his voice.

'No trace whatsoever. We've done all we can here to find them.'

'Did he really know anything, do you suppose?' I said, as we crossed the big hall. 'Because there was that hesitation when we asked him.'

'I marked that, as well. But . . .' He stopped. 'Listen.'

'I can't hear anything,' I began, then broke off, because I was hearing it now. Through the dim dereliction of Deadlight Hall came the strange and vaguely sinister call we had heard earlier.

'Children, where are you?'

'It's Mr Battersby,' I said, but even I could hear the uncertain note in my voice.

'I don't think it is,' said Schönbrunn, speaking quietly as if fearful of being overheard.

'Then who?'

'I have no idea.'

We went out of the old house without waiting to find out who was calling for the children – I don't think either of us really wanted to know who it was. We stood for a moment, thankfully breathing in the fresh air, then we drove back to Oxford and our lodgings.

As to Sophie and Susannah Reiss, we still have no information. Porringer wanted us to believe Mengele had them, of that we are sure. And yet there was that hesitation. But we shall not stop trying to find out what happened to them.

Tomorrow I am going to London, and I will follow the twins' trail from another source – that of the Prague golem that they took when they were smuggled out of Warsaw. It is just faintly possible that whoever took the girls will have tried to sell it – it's so obviously valuable that it would be a considerable temptation. It's also sufficiently unusual to be remembered. I have a few contacts in the jewellery quarter of London and I shall approach them – using extreme discretion, of course. I am not very optimistic about finding anything, but it is an avenue that must be explored.

As always, my best regards to you,

M.B.

London 1944

Dear J.W.

Forgive the rather long silence between letters, but since reaching London I have been very much involved in the search for the golem. Sadly, my cautious forays into the jewellery quarters of London have provided no information at all. My approaches met with courtesy and efficiency, but no one could help. One fine old auction house here – Ashby's by name – has promised to correspond with me if they do hear of such an item being offered, and I have given the name and address of my bank for any possible letters. I am not, though, very hopeful.

I had to put off writing this letter for a while – the Luftwaffe had mounted one of their raids on London, and it was necessary to make for the nearest air-raid shelter. It was full of all kinds of people, and they passed round beer and sandwiches, after which they sang an extraordinary song which referred in the most derogatory of fashions to the physical, and very personal, limitations of the Führer and Herr Himmler. Schönbrunn sang as enthusiastically as anyone (I have no idea how he knew the words) and after the second verse I too found myself joining in. Then the All Clear sirens sounded and everyone went back into the streets and on their separate ways. These are remarkable experiences, even for people such as Schönbrunn and myself, who have seen cities laid waste and devastating tragedy across half of Europe.

Three days ago Schönbrunn heard, through one of his networks of informers and spies, that Dr Mengele currently has three sets of twins in his laboratories – and that two of the sets are girls around the age of the Reiss twins and closely match their descriptions. I do not need to tell you what a bitter blow this is. It may not be Sophie and Susannah, of course, but we dare not take any chances. Schönbrunn is making plans to leave England. His eyes shine with that reckless light, and there is the sense that the air around him crackles with an electrical force.

He has not asked if I will accompany him when he leaves England. I have no idea what I shall say if he does.

My good wishes to you,

M.B

London
1944
My dear J.W.

This morning a letter was delivered to my lodgings from Schönbrunn.

It seems that he left England four days ago and is now on his way to Oswiecim. My heart sinks even to write the name. For you and I, my good friend, know that the name of Oswiecim has been changed by the Nazis. And that it is now known as Auschwitz.

Auschwitz. The name strikes such terror into the soul.

Schönbrunn, cautious as a cat, puts no details of his plans in the letter, and clearly he arranged for it to be delivered after he had left, so that I could not try to dissuade him. Would I have done so? I have no idea.

He says nothing of how he intends to get into the camp, but of course that is what he means to do. You and I know he has got into other concentration camps, and has managed to bring out several of our people. But this is Auschwitz.

He has said he does not wish me to accompany him. 'You would never pass unnoticed, my friend,' he says, and I know this to be true. I cannot blend into a crowd; I cannot appear or sound anonymous. He also writes, 'If you do not hear from me, do not assume I have failed.'

I think I do not need to say he will rescue the children whether they are Sophie and Susannah Reiss or not – assuming any rescue to be possible, you understand. But, as with everyone who has ever known Schönbrunn, I have utter faith in him. I cannot imagine he will go unchallenged on his journey, but you and I both know his capacity for creating an illusion – both of appearance and of nationality.

I intend to remain here for a little longer, following my own search for the golem.

My good wishes, as always, and a hope that I shall be with you again before too long – as well as a hope that the families we all know will one day be reunited.

M.B.

TWELVE

Over the years, Leo had come to accept that his family had been lost to him. He had never known what had become of his parents or any of the people in the small village just outside Warsaw. There had been times when he had thought he would go back and try to find out, but when it came to it, he had not wanted to do so. He had been afraid of finding that those beloved people had been incarcerated in the concentration camps, and that some had died in the gas chambers. The Ovens, thought Leo. That was our childhood fear. We didn't really understand, but we were all afraid.

And yet the years with the Hursts had not been as unhappy as they might have been. Simeon Hurst and his sister had been severe and strict; they had not understood about Leo being Jewish, and they had force-fed him with Christianity. But he had come to understand that this had not done him so ill a turn; it had given him his ability to view religion with a wider lens than he might otherwise have done, and had probably led him to studying philosophy and theology – a study that had proved so rewarding and that had led him to his beloved Oriel College. He sometimes thought that because of the Hursts he had worked hard, and because of that he had managed to get to Oxford. More, he had managed to remain at Oxford, and it became his life and his family.

The years at Willow Bank Farm had settled into a degree of stability. There was school and singing in the choir, and there were school activities and friends. The sad memories of his home began to fade a bit. The other memory of that pain-filled, macabre night at Deadlight Hall did not fade, though; Leo did not think it ever would. He did not think the memory of the twins would ever completely fade, either.

But he liked school and he had liked most of his lessons. The Hursts made sure he did his work diligently and thoroughly, and occasionally handed out a few sparse words of praise. Surprisingly, they never missed attending a school concert or a prize-giving, Simeon wearing his Sunday suit and polished boots, Miss Hurst in a knitted hat and black lace-up shoes. They always sat in the front row, and afterwards talked earnestly to the teachers about Leo's progress. One year, when rationing was starting to ease, the school offered a cold buffet after its Christmas carol service, with a fruit cup rather daringly flavoured with sherry. It was unfortunate that the headmaster, wanting to be hospitable, and pleased to talk to the guardians of his promising young pupil, poured Miss Hurst several glasses of this, after which, inspired by the carol singers, she began her own rendition of 'Once in Royal David's City', slightly off-key, and had to be helped out to the battered truck which Farmer Hurst drove. She sang 'We Three Kings' all the way back to the farm, then collapsed in a bundled heap in a fireside chair and smiled foolishly at the plate of stew which had been simmering on the stove while they were out.

After that night, Leo had usually managed to steer her away from any alcoholic beverage that was on offer, although it was sometimes difficult, because Miss Hurst made her own elderflower and parsnip wines, which she liked to bring out for visitors. Sometimes, if the vicar called, she became quite bright-eyed and giggly, and said, 'Oh, Vicar, the things you say.' Leo thought Farmer Hurst did not like to see his sister being giggly and prodding the vicar with a pretend-stern finger. If the vicar's sister was there, she always folded her lips tightly like a drawstring purse.

Simeon and Mildred Hurst both said Leo must continue to study hard. Simeon said if God had given Leo the gift of intelligence Leo must be sure to make use of it.

Occasionally they talked about their disgraceful ancestor.

'A wastrel,' said Simeon. 'And he lost us a lot of money.'

'And land,' chimed in Miss Hurst. 'Don't forget the land.'

'I don't forget the land, Mildred, I've never forgotten the land. We don't covet our neighbour's goods, of course, Leo, and a man cannot serve God and Mammon both—'

'But that land was once Hurst land and rightfully this family's,' put in Miss Hurst, firmly. 'Our ancestor sold a large piece of land all those years ago,' she told Leo, by way of explanation. 'To pay his debts, so we've always understood. Women, mostly.'

'And drink.'

'Yes, that, too, and woe unto them that rise up early in the morning that they may follow strong drink,' said Miss Hurst, putting a half-empty bottle of parsnip wine back in its cupboard.

'He squandered his substance and sold his birthright for a mess of pottage,' said Simeon. 'So think on, young man, think on, and avoid suchlike temptations.'

Leo said he would think on, although he did not really know what Simeon meant. But shortly after his twelfth birthday, it appeared that the Hursts now had a chance of regaining the land so wantonly sold by their forbear.

'A reasonable price they're asking,' said Simeon. 'I don't know but what we mightn't manage it, Mildred.'

'They'll expect you to haggle.'

'D'you think so? Yes, I dare say they will. I dare say it's usual.' For the first time Leo saw Simeon Hurst uncertain of himself, and he guessed it was because the farmer was not familiar with the buying and selling of anything, and particularly not land.

He said, a bit timidly, that he remembered people at home always haggling a bit; it was part of almost any purchase you made.

'I told you that, Simeon. They'll expect you to haggle, I said.'

With slightly more confidence, Leo said that what you had to do was to start at a much lower price than you were prepared to pay. Then you increased the figure a little at a time.

'Is that how it's done? I tell you what, Simeon, you take Leo with you. It'll be good for him to know about the land and the running of the farm.'

'That's a good suggestion. Leo, you'll come along with me, and while we're there, you'll mind your manners and not speak unless you're spoken to, remember. Get your coat, and we'll be off to see if we can buy back our field.'

Leo, interested in this unexpected departure from routine, sped up to his room to get his coat.

'We'll take the old carriage path,' said Simeon Hurst, lacing up his boots. 'You've never been along there, have you, and it's a nice walk of a fine morning. You'll see how the two fields march along-side Willow Bank land, and you'll understand why it'd be good for this farm to have the fields back. We'll be back for dinner.'

Miss Hurst said there would be rabbit pie, which Simeon and Leo thought would do very nicely after their long walk.

But if Leo had realized the land adjoined Deadlight Hall, he would have found a reason to remain at the farm. He had never managed to completely push down the memory of the night when Sophie and

Susannah vanished. Even though he had clamped a lid over it, the lid sometimes became dislodged, so that the seething memories escaped in little scalding dribbles, like Miss Hurst's stews sometimes hissed and spilled out on the stove.

As they walked along the carriage path, Simeon pointing out wildlife and flora as they went and explaining about the different crops and how crop rotation worked, a slow horror was stealing over Leo. They were going towards Deadlight Hall. Deadlight Hall, with its iron-bound room and the furnace that roared greedily away. The place where his beloved twins had burned someone to death and then disappeared. But I promised I'd never tell anyone what they did, thought Leo. I promised, and I've kept the promise.

As the Hall came into view, a man walked along the path to meet them, hailing Farmer Hurst cordially. This was the present owner of the land, who might be prepared to sell it back to the Hurst family. Leo was secretly pleased when Mr Hurst introduced him as if he had been a grown-up. He shook hands politely as he had been taught, and stood quietly while the two men talked. Most of it was incomprehensible – there was a good deal about boundaries and rights of way, and Leo tried not to be bored. Then the man said, 'Perhaps your boy would like to look around, would he?' And, to Leo, 'There's a badgers' sett nearby. And someone saw a heron near the canal last month.'

Leo understood that the man would prefer not to talk about the land in front of him, so he said thank you, yes, he would do that, and went off. No, he would not get lost, and yes, he would come back here.

He had not meant to go into the Hall, but it seemed to call to him. All the time he was looking for the heron he could almost feel the house pulling him. Perhaps he should let it. People said you could get rid of a nightmare by looking it in the face, and at home there had been a very old man, a rabbi and a scholar, who had told the children that you could drive out evil spirits by confronting them. You simply had to hold fast to your courage and your faith.

Leo did not think he had very much courage, but in this bright, clean, sunshiney morning, he thought he might have just about enough to look his nightmare in the face. He walked across the overgrown grass, and up the steps to the double doors. As he grasped the handle he was whispering a plea that the doors would be locked, but they were not, and they swung inwards with only a small protest.

The scent of damp and age and despair came out, and the bad memories swirled up, like a cloud of rancid flies. He flinched and almost turned back, but having got this far he must at least step inside. And once inside, it was not so bad. He did not remember much about the main part of the Hall – he supposed he had been too ill that night – and he looked around with curiosity. The schoolhouse at home had had an entrance a little like this – not as large, but there had been the same kind of floor, and the same wide shallow stairs leading to the upper floors. There was the door that led down to the furnace room. Someone had propped it open, and he could see the stone steps.

As he hesitated, trying to make up his mind to go through the door, something glimmered in the darkness beyond it. Something that was small and pale, and something that had long chestnut hair . . . As Leo stared, caught between fear and fascination, the outline half-turned, and he saw that a second figure, almost identical, stood there as well. Hands, small, soft, fragile, came up and beckoned to him.

There are moments in life when what you most want in all the world suddenly seems within your grasp, and logic deserts you. In that moment, Leo was aware only of a surge of delight. Sophie and Susannah! he thought, and went eagerly into the dark corridor and down the flight of stairs.

At first he could see them clearly, but as he plunged through the dimness, they seemed to recede and several times their outlines blurred. Then they were there again, moving away from him. Sophie turned and beckoned once more, and Leo went forward eagerly. This was where he had come that night, struggling against the pain in his head, fighting the fever and nausea.

Expecting at any minute to see the twins, he went on, towards the row of doors he remembered. He was level with the third door, when he realized that footsteps were coming into the corridor behind him, from the main hall. He stopped and looked back. Had someone followed him in? Perhaps it was almost twelve o'clock and Mr Hurst had come to look for him.

And then cold horror washed over him, because a soft voice came out of the dimness.

'Children, where are you?'

It was the thick, breathy whisper Leo had heard all those years ago. It was with him, here in this narrow passageway. As he tried frantically to think what to do, a figure appeared in the corridor. It was indistinct in the uncertain light, but Leo could see that it was small and hunched over, as if the person was deformed. To walk towards it was unthinkable, so Leo turned and plunged towards the furnace room. Towards Sophie and Susannah, said his mind. They would be waiting for him. 'We'll always be linked,' they had said on the night they had left Warsaw. 'We'll always know if you're not all right, or if you're in trouble.'

But that was six years ago, said Leo's mind. They vanished six years ago; they can't still be here, looking exactly the same, they *can't*.

The words reached him again.

'Children, are you here? I'll find you wherever you are . . .'

And underlying the words, as if tapping out a rhythm, was a clicking. Machinery, thought Leo, and his mind looped back over the years. Old machinery starting up.

The furnace room was only a few yards away now. If he could get in there, he could slam the door against that horrid whispering figure. The iron door was closed, but a faint glimmer of light showed through the thick round window.

'Children, where are you?'

The words trickled through the shadows, and Leo gasped, and went towards the iron door. Light, crimson and baleful, poured out, lying across the worn old stones, and he could smell the burning iron. An ancient heat, Sophie had called it.

Sophie and Susannah were not really here. It had only been his mind that had pretended to him that he could see them. He would not see them again.

But he did.

Framed by the iron staves of the old door, as if to make a macabre painting, was the same scene that had printed itself so deeply on his mind all those years ago. The black lump of the furnace, its innards glowing with the fierce, ancient heat, and the figures of the two girls moving through the red light. There was the struggling, squirming figure again, exactly as Leo remembered it.

The heat of the furnace was scorching his eyes, making them water and blurring the scene before him. But even though he could not see it clearly, he knew what was happening, and he knew who was in there. Sophie and Susannah, and the sharp nursing sister

– Sister Dulce – whom they had believed was going to feed them to the terrible ovens – the ovens their parents had dreaded. The twins had killed her all those years ago, rather than face the ovens, and they were killing her again today. She would burn alive, all over again.

Leo began to pray that he was asleep and having a nightmare, and that he would wake up at any minute, because none of this could possibly be happening. Then he thought: but what if I'm being given a second chance? A chance to stop it happening? He took a fearful step closer, and behind him the iron door made a slow grating sound. Leo spun round, and managed to grab the door's handle, dragging it back before it could close. It was much heavier than he had expected, and he had the sudden terrifying impression that someone was standing on the other side, just out of sight, pulling the door back into its frame. In another minute it would clang shut, and he would be trapped.

He did not dare look back to where the twins were. He only wanted to run away and find somewhere safe to hide. He had hold of the door handle and if he could manage to pull it a bit wider, he could dart out into the passageway before it closed altogether. The hunched-over figure might still be out there, but Leo would rather face that than be shut in here with the blazing furnace and the twins, who had suddenly become sinister and menacing. He knew they were still here; even though he had not looked back into the room, their shadows were moving on the walls.

He had not realized he had been shouting for help, but he heard his voice reverberating along the narrow corridor. There would not be anyone to hear, but he went on shouting anyway. Once, something seemed to move in the dark corridor, and Leo yelled to this something to help him, no longer caring that it might be the hunched figure.

He was nerving himself to let go of the handle and trust to luck that he could run out before the door swung shut, when other footsteps rang out in the corridor – real footsteps. A moment later came Simeon Hurst's voice, calling his name. Leo drew in a shuddering breath of relief, and shouted for help.

'I'm in here! I'm trapped – I can't get the door open.'

The farmer was coming towards him. Leo could hear Mr Hurst's firm heavy footsteps. He was aware of relief, because no one – not horrid whispering voices or shadowy figures – would dare to oppose Mr Hurst.

He shouted again. 'I'm in the furnace room! The door's trying to close – I can't get out! And the furnace is burning—'

Simeon had reached the door – his thick, comforting bulk filled the doorway, and Leo had never been so glad to see anyone in his life. Simeon did not waste time in asking questions; he dragged at the door. It seemed to resist, then Hurst's extra strength and weight prevailed, and he pulled it wide, banging it back against the stone wall. Leo tumbled through, and half fell against the passage wall.

The furnace was still roaring up, and Simeon, clearly puzzled, went towards it. Leo, huddled in the stone passage, saw two shapes creep out of the shadows. Their outlines were densely black against the red glow, but they were small and fine-boned, and they had long hair.

'No!' cried Leo, in panic. 'Come out! Come out now, oh, please.' He scrambled to his feet and started towards the iron door, but Simeon did not seem to hear him. Instead, he went up to the furnace, and picked up a long iron rod with a black hook at one end that was lying nearby.

Simeon Hurst's outline was silhouetted blackly against the roaring crimson furnace, like a cut-out figure. He was intent on shutting the furnace door, and he was slotting the rod in place, so he could push the cover back. Leo started forward, then paused, fearful that the door might start to close again and trap them both inside.

Simeon almost had the furnace door closed, when a sheet of flame seemed to spit outwards, and a tiny crackle of flame caught the edge of his coat. He cried out and the rod slipped from his hands and clanged noisily on the stone floor as he beat at the tiny licking fire. Leo darted across to him, but Simeon had already fought himself free of his coat and had flung it down, stamping out the flames to douse them. Without looking round, he said, 'Leo – stay clear – it's not safe.'

'But—'

'Stay clear, I tell you.'

There was such a commanding note in his voice that Leo did as he was told. Mr Hurst's jacket was no longer burning, and he would know what to do about the furnace. It would be all right.

Hurst reached for the hooked rod again, but in doing so he seemed to miss his footing or perhaps he tripped on the uneven floor. He stumbled forwards, flinging up his arms. Leo cried out and bounded across the floor, but it was too late. Simeon Hurst fell head first into the scarlet roaring depths.

The furnace blazed up and there was the nightmare, never-to-be-forgotten sound of Hurst screaming through the fire, and of the triumphant roaring crackle of the fire itself. Leo grabbed the iron rod, hardly noticing that its heat blistered his fingers, and tried to thrust it into the furnace. He was panic-stricken and terrified, but through the panic he had a confused idea that Mr Hurst might somehow be able to grasp the rod and be pulled out.

He could not, of course. There was a moment when Leo could see his silhouette within the flames – writhing, the hands clawing as if for freedom, his hair blazing and flames shooting out of his eye sockets. Then he simply folded in on himself. The fire died down, licking greedily over what was left.

The worst part was the smell. It was exactly the same smell as the kitchen at Willow Bank Farm when Miss Hurst roasted their Sunday dinner. Hot and greasy. A scent that would normally make you think of gravy and potatoes. Leo's mouth filled with water, then he bent over retching.

He had no idea how long he remained like that, cold and sick, but when finally he was able to go back up the stairs the hunched-over figure had vanished. Leo was shivering so violently he felt as if his bones might break apart, and despite the blazing heat of the furnace a short while ago he was so cold he thought he would probably never be able to get warm again. But he took a deep breath, squared his shoulders, and went to find someone who would tell him what should be done.

What had been done became a nightmare of confusion and grief, but men had come in response to Miss Hurst's telephone call, and had taken charge.

Later, ashes had been scraped out of the now-cold, now-quiescent furnace so that a funeral service could be held and decent burial be given. There was some kind of official enquiry, and Leo had to explain to a policeman what had happened. He tried to do this as clearly as he could. Mr Hurst had stumbled, he said, and fallen into the furnace. No, he did not know how the furnace came to be alight. No, he had not touched anything – of course he had not. Asked why he had been there in the first place, he said he had been exploring; he remembered being there when he had meningitis as a small child, and he was curious to see the place again. He did not say anything about seeing Sophie and Susannah, because he was no longer sure if he had seen them, and he did not say anything about the figure who had called for the children.

The policeman said he had done very well, and he was not to worry. He would not have to attend the enquiry or the inquest.

People in the small farming community were shocked and horrified at Simeon Hurst's terrible death, although several hardier souls asked if it was true that it had not been possible to distinguish the contents of the furnace from his remains, so that the funeral might be read over nothing more than, well, over bits of clinker?

The verger said that this was unfortunately true, but the vicar was going to hold the service anyway, and they must just trust in God that they would be chanting the Twenty-Third Psalm and praying for the resurrection of life over some remaining bits of Simeon Hurst at the very least, and not over pieces of anthracite. As for those attending the wake at Willow Bank Farm afterwards, the vicar had said they were please to remember not to refer to funeral bak'd meats under any circumstances whatsoever.

Several ladies from the neighbourhood came to the farmhouse on the morning of the funeral to cut sandwiches and make tea and coffee, because Miss Hurst, poor soul, could not be expected to cope. Leo could perhaps help with handing round the sandwiches, could he? When Leo said he could, the ladies were pleased and told one another what a very nicely behaved boy he was, and how well repaid Simeon and poor Mildred had been for taking him into their home.

Mildred Hurst lay on her bed and sobbed for two days, after which she got up, put on a black frock of ancient cloth and forgotten style, netted her hair, and presided ferociously over the sandwich-cutting party. The sandwiches were egg and cress, cheese and chutney, and shrimp and anchovy paste. Leo heard one of the ladies say that ham was the usual offering, but that nobody had had the heart – or the stomach – to bake a ham.

During the sandwich-cutting Miss Hurst was given several glasses of elderflower wine by one well-meaning lady, and several glasses of brandy by another, neither of whom realized what the other had done, both of whom thought it would help the poor soul to pluck up a bit. After the second round of brandy, Miss Hurst said that she was perfectly all right, and Simeon would not have wanted a lot of wailing and beating of breasts. Everything must be devout and respectful, and please would people cut that bread thinner for the sandwiches otherwise it would not go round and she was not made of money.

Leo sat next to her during the service, and hoped nobody noticed that she took frequent and furtive sips from a small silver flask. Before the congregation went out to the graveside, she sprayed the front of her fur tippet with a scent bottle labelled *Attar of Roses*. It smelled peculiar, but it helped cover up the brandy fumes.

During the wake at the farmhouse, Leo heard the vicar's sister say that Deadlight Hall had been shut up and a fence put round it. 'Downright dangerous,' she said, disapprovingly, and the lady to whom she was speaking said, in a low voice, that it was not the first time there had been a dreadful tragedy there.

'I suppose they'll try to sell it,' said her listener.

'Oh, they'll try,' said the vicar's sister. 'But I shouldn't think they'll succeed. Nobody will want it.'

THIRTEEN

L ife changed after Simeon's death. The farm began to fail, not all in one tumble, but little by little. Things that wore out were not replaced. Livestock dwindled. Crops did not have just one bad year, which most farmers expected, but several in a row.

Miss Hurst employed a manager, but the place became less and less prosperous. She herself did not change very much with the years; she continued to have her elderflower wine – 'Just a little nip for comfort,' she said – and the vicar continued to call regularly. Miss Hurst was always pleased to see him – a very kind gentleman, she said, entirely trustworthy, and most helpful over financial affairs. She did not understand these things, and Simeon had always handled such matters. If she had to go to the bank or the solicitor's offices, the vicar always accompanied her, and his sister went along as well, because dear Cuthbert was an unworldly soul, and must be guarded against hussies such as Mildred Hurst. So they had gone all together in the vicar's little rattletrap car, Miss Hurst in the back, her feet primly together, the vicar's sister seated in the front so that Miss Hurst could not throw out any lures.

After Mildred's death, there was a note for Leo which the solicitor handed to him.

'I can't leave Willow Bank Farm to you, Leo,' she had written. 'I should like to, but there are cousins who have a legal claim and there's nothing I can do about it.' Reading that, Leo had supposed there was some kind of entail. He had never expected to be left the farm, anyway. But Mildred Hurst had left him a fair sum of money. 'The life savings of my brother and myself,' the note said. 'Dear Leo, you were the son I never had.'

Leo had cried over that, quietly and genuinely. He wished he had known what she meant to do, because he could have told her how very grateful he was, not specifically for the money, but for the home she and her brother had given him.

The vicar's sister had been right in saying nobody would want Deadlight Hall. It had crouched on its patch of scrubby land, quietly decaying, its windows falling in, its stonework gradually covered by creeping moss and lichen. Sometimes Leo had frightening dreams about the misshapen shadow who had walked the dark corridors, and the voice calling for the children. After a while the dreams became less frequent, but they never quite went away.

He never forgot Deadlight Hall. Of course he did not – it was not the kind of place anyone could forget. It was reassuring, though, to remember that it was still standing empty. No one will ever live there, he had thought. It will fall down of its own accord in the end, and the shadow and whatever was in that furnace room will go.

But if he was able to push Deadlight Hall into the corners of his mind, he was never able to do the same thing with Sophie and Susannah. Just as Deadlight Hall was not the kind of place to forget, Sophie and Susannah were not the kind of people to forget, either.

As the years slid past he gradually accepted it was unlikely he would ever find out what had happened to them.

London
1944
Dear J.W.

Later today I shall try to get on a train for the journey home, although it is not easy to do so, and I may have to make several attempts. All the trains are constantly crowded with service men and women, some wounded, others who are joining or rejoining their regiments. So although I hope to be home in the next few days, it could be longer.

Yesterday I heard from Schönbrunn – a letter sent from the very lip of Auschwitz itself. I cannot begin to imagine how he was able to get a letter out from there, but it should not surprise me that his remarkable network stretches even to the town of Oswiecim. He has never talked much about that network, but from time to time I have had glimpses of it – of people with whom a letter or a message can be left . . . A small shop in an unobtrusive side street where the shopkeeper can be trusted . . . Stone bridges spanning narrow rivers where there are cavities within the stones, allowing messages to be left for collection . . .

At times I almost wonder if Schönbrunn is real, for he seems to inhabit the pages of an adventure story or some strange and vivid fantasy. There have been occasions in his company when I have remembered the old legends, and in particular that of the Golem of Prague – the real one, that is, not the two that Leo and the Reiss twins had. You know the old tale, of course – indeed, it is part of our heritage. How that Golem was constructed of clay, and brought to life to defend the Prague ghetto How, later, it was entombed in a hiding place in the Old New Synagogue, and how, when the tomb-like hiding place was broken open at the end of the nineteenth century, no trace of it was found. And how it is prophesied that the golem will be restored to life again if it is ever needed to protect our people.

I have reread those last two sentences, and I wonder, as I have often wondered, how people can say there are no links between the great religions of the world.

I dare say you are smiling as you read all this, and saying, 'Oy, that Maurice Bensimon, he is such a dream-spinner.' If ever I were to write my memoirs, the dreams I would spin of these years would be dark ones. So on consideration, I shall never do so. I will only say, instead, that whatever Schönbrunn is, or is not, he has the most extraordinary strength of mind and will of any man I have ever met, and his courage is humbling.

It seems too much of a risk to entrust his actual letter to the post, so instead I am copying down the main information here for you. Performing such a mundane task will help to calm my mind and will fill up the hours until I can be on my way to Waterloo Station.

Schönbrunn writes:

'One of the curious things about this place is that when the word *Auschwitz* is uttered, one simply thinks of the camp itself – the grim grey barracks inside the barbed-wire, as if it is a desolate and solitary entity set amidst a wilderness. But although wilderness there is, the old town of Oswiecim is quite nearby, and people still live in it. I will not say they live in normality, but they pursue their lives as well as they can.

'The Germans have drained the swamps that once lay everywhere, but traces of the dank, misty bogland still linger, and it is as if a dark miasma hangs over the old town – as if the misery and the fear has seeped outwards from the camp itself.

'Since the occupation, the population has dwindled to a sad fragment. A great many people have been driven from their homes, and numerous small villages have been wiped from the map entirely. It saddens and angers me to think of those lost villages – their histories vanished, their stories and their people wiped from the landscape for ever.

'In happier circumstances I would have wanted to delve into Oswiecim's history, but I shall not do so. I want no memories of this place to lodge in my mind.

'Part of me is praying Sophie and Susannah Reiss will not be here – that this will prove to be a false lead. But there is another part that hopes they are here, because that will mean I can take action to rescue them. But if Mengele does have them I cannot bear to contemplate what may be happening to them.

'I beg you, do not let the Reiss family know any of this.'

Schönbrunn then went on to write that he had found lodgings in the town.

'They are not good, but I have stayed in worse. My landlady is a lugubrious but kindly soul, and this morning she told me how everyone in the area knows what goes on inside the camp.

'"They think they keep the secrets of what they do in there," she said, "but we all know that exterminations go on all the time. And there are the experiments, also – performed by the one they call the Angel of Death."

'My mind sprang to attention at this, but as if I had never heard the name – as if it is not burned into my brain – I only said, "Who is the Angel of Death?"

'"He works on the children," she said. "Terrible things, they say he does. He is not always there – he has other places he visits and where he works. But I have seen him walk around occasionally. He looks for the children – it's said he always has sweets in his pockets for them. He talks to them and listens to their tales." A pause. "And then he carries them off to his laboratories," she said.

'"What happens to them there?"

'"No one knows. But few of those children are ever seen again."

'"You know that for certain?"

'"No. I know the other deaths are for certain, though. When

the wind is in the right direction the stench comes into the town. It cannot be mistaken – it is from the continuous burning of the bodies," she said. "Thick, sweet, mixed with the acrid stench of the heat. You taste it in your nose for days. You would like coffee now?"

'The coffee is terrible, gritty and sour, but today I drank it thankfully, hoping it might wash away her words. It did not, of course.

'Oh, M.B., one day this may all be part of the past and they may build monuments and memorials to the people slaughtered here, but nothing anyone can ever do will succeed in wiping from my mind the things I am seeing – the hopelessness and the fear in the faces of the people being herded along the railway tracks towards the camp. Those images have seared into my mind like acid, and they will always be black and grey and drenched in despair, threaded with spider webs of railway lines that all lead to one place. There will be no colour in my memories of Auschwitz.

'Please remember that if you do not hear from me again, you should not assume I have failed.'

The letter ended on this half-optimistic, half-warning note. But despite the optimism I fear we shall not hear from him again – not ever. This morning came a visit from one of the miscellany of people who make up that secret network. How the man had tracked me down in this modest boarding house on London's outskirts – how he even knew of my existence – I have no idea. But he did find me somehow.

'I believe we have lost him this time,' he said, facing me in the dingy guests' lounge, sipping tea (we cannot get coffee at the moment).

My heart did not sink at his words; it seemed to constrict as if iron bands had clamped around it.

I said, 'He's indestructible.'

'Not this time.' He looked at me very levelly. He has that direct look Schönbrunn's people almost always have. 'I saw him for myself. I saw him go towards those gates—'

'Auschwitz?'

'Yes. I was waiting for him in hiding – there is not much hiding, but Schönbrunn found a place. But I was close enough to even read the legend above the gates. *Arbeit Macht Frei*.'

'Work will free you,' I said, half to myself.

'Yes. Was ever there a crueller irony than those words? Beyond those gates are the barracks with their rows of grim cell-like rooms – and the places about which those dread rumours have circulated. We do not need to name them. We both know what they are. Schönbrunn waited until he heard army trucks coming along the road. Then he walked out and waved them down.'

'Why?'

'I don't know.' A shrug. 'He never tells anyone all of his plans. I could not see what the trucks carried – not prisoners, I don't think. Supplies of some kind, perhaps. There was some interchange between Schönbrunn and the driver – I could not hear it, and it was in rapid German anyway. Then three of the soldiers sprang out of the truck and almost threw him into the vehicle.'

'And?' I said, as he broke off.

'They drove through the gates into the camp,' he said. 'My belief is that he had some story ready to tell them – he has used several, as you know.'

'But this time they did not believe him.'

'Or,' said my companion, 'this time someone was one step ahead and had warned the Nazis that he was coming.'

'A traitor among his own people?'

'I'm afraid so. In which case, Schönbrunn will now be dead.'

If Schönbrunn is dead I cannot see how we will ever find out what happened to Sophie and Susannah. But I shall stay hopeful that being taken into Auschwitz was part of his plan – that he intended to get in there all along, and that he spun those Germans a deliberately thin cover story. But it is a vain hope.

And so the whereabouts of the Reiss twins is as unknown as it ever was. I fear we may never find out the truth.

M.B.

FOURTEEN

Nell was having a good Monday morning, following an excellent weekend. On Saturday the Japanese customers had not only bought the Regency sofas, they had also bought the inlaid table. There had been much courtesy and compliments, and Mr Hironaka had extended an invitation to Nell to visit his family if ever she were in his country.

She had spent most of Sunday morning applying Danish oil to a late-Elizabethan dower chest, which would replace the sofas in the shop window, and at midday Michael had taken her and Beth to lunch at one of Oxford's many riverside inns, after which Beth had gone to spend the rest of the afternoon with a school friend. Nell and Michael had ended up at Quire Court and had made slow, deeply satisfactory love, with the light fading gently on the Court's old stones outside and sun slanting across the bed. Afterwards Michael had said something about the serenity of ancient, undisturbed ghosts, and Nell had thought it might be better not to tell him yet that she was considering bashing down walls and demolishing ceilings, and risking plunging the serene ghosts into distracted madness and probable mass exodus.

Monday had dawned full of sunshine and promise, and over breakfast Beth had talked with exuberance about Michael's latest project for the Wilberforce history books.

'Elizabeth the First and Guy Fawkes and stuff. He's going to write about Wilberforce's ancestors and I'm going to help.'

'He'll enjoy doing that. And it'll help your history lessons as well.'

'I thought,' said Beth, giving her mother a cautious look, 'that he could have a musician Wilberforce somewhere. Um, like when they had minstrels. They travelled around and wrote their own music and stuff. A bit like pop stars today,' said Beth, with unexpected perception.

'That sounds quite a good idea.'

Beth beamed, then said, 'D'you think I could suggest it to Michael? Only I don't want him to think I'm trying to kind of push in on things.'

'I think it would be fine to suggest it,' said Nell. 'But I'm pleased you asked before you actually said anything to him.'

'If you and Michael got married,' said Beth, hanging over her breakfast so that Nell could not see her face, 'I 'spect he'd wouldn't live in College any more, would he?'

'I expect not, but we're fine as we are, and you're—'

'Entering into the realms of fantasy,' finished Beth.

'Yes. Are you having any more toast? And have you got your gym things ready?'

'Yes and yes. Don't *fuss*,' said Beth.

After Beth had been delivered to school, Nell spent an hour with Godfrey Purbles, inspecting the rooms in the bookshop, and discussing with him how practical it would be to knock through from her own premises to make one large shop.

'If you could make it double-fronted,' said Godfrey, 'that'd make really lovely premises. The thing to do is to get a good builder to take a look. You don't want to go smashing sledge hammers into supporting walls and bring the upper floors and the roof crashing in.'

Nell remembered Michael's serene ghosts, and said, no, certainly she did not want to do that.

'I tell you who'd be good to ask about the work,' said Godfrey. 'Jack Hurst. His firm have been builders in Oxford for ages – he did that archway for me last year. Wait a bit, I've got his phone number somewhere.'

Nell took the phone number gratefully, and went back to her own shop to phone the bank, pleased to be told that someone could see her later that day. After the meeting she would tell Michael what she was considering. Would she find she could open up to him about the finances of it all? Money was one of the few things they never really discussed. When, two years earlier, it had been decided that she would move to Oxford and she had found the Quire Court premises, he had made a cautious enquiry as to how she would be financing the move – doing so with a diffidence that suggested he found the subject a difficult, unfamiliar one. Nell, who had still been finding her way through a number of minefields after her husband's death, but who had been determined to be independent, had said, rather abruptly, that she was fine, thank you, there was enough dosh in the kitty.

Michael had said, 'Well, if not . . .' and left it at that.

Remembering this, Nell wondered if he would make a similar semi-offer when she told him about Godfrey's shop, and if so what she would do about it. To have a business partnership of any kind would cement their relationship in a rather odd way. Not matrimonially but fiscally. Always, of course, assuming he had money to invest and that she had not misunderstood that previous conversation. She had no idea what a don's salary was, or what he earned from the Wilberforce books.

How likely was it that he had been subconsciously or subliminally thinking the two of them might eventually get together under one roof? Nell had a sudden tantalizing image of a tall old house somewhere on the city's outskirts, not too far from Oriel or Quire Court, filled with books and music, often invaded by Michael's colleagues or even his students. It was a good image, but Nell was not sure if it was a workable one. Michael's place seemed to be his rooms at Oriel. Her place seemed to be here, in Quire Court.

She locked up and went out to the little house behind the shop to put on a business-looking suit for the meeting with the bank. Assuming it was all favourable, when she got back she would telephone Godfrey's builder, Jack Hurst, and ask him to give her a quote for the work.

She was perfectly prepared for the bank to try to dissuade her from cashing in the bonds, and to counsel extreme caution over the proposed plan. What she was not prepared for – what she angrily realized she ought to have foreseen – was that the bonds, if cashed before their expiry date which was two years away, would not yield anywhere near as much as she had calculated. There were penalties for early redemption and, to compound the problem, the bonds themselves had suffered from the disastrous economic situation of the last couple of years.

'They'd recover if you left them,' said the Small Business Adviser, whom Nell was trying not to think looked as if she had just left school. 'The interest would roll over and mount up in the last twelve months, like endowment mortgages used to. See now, going on the figures you've given me, you're several thousand short of the amount you want. It's not a huge sum, though, and it's not necessarily unreachable. We could see if a short-term business loan might be accepted. To cover that shortfall.'

'I'm a bit hesitant about that. If I'm going to draw on these bonds and have a loan on top . . .'

'Yes, you wouldn't have much of a safety net, would you?' She nodded, obviously understanding this, and flipped to another screen on her laptop. 'You've got that separate fund for your daughter with us as well, haven't you?'

'Yes, but that's cast-iron untouchable. I used one of my husband's insurance payouts for that.'

'It's looking fairly good,' said the adviser, turning the laptop so Nell could see. 'Enough to put her through university comfortably, or provide a deposit for a house.'

'Or backpack round the world,' said Nell, smiling.

'And why not? I'll do a printout for you so you've got up-to-date figures for that.' She set the printer whirring, then said, 'I like your concept for these two shops, though. I think it could be profitable, and I hope we can work something out for you. That idea you've got about using the annexe behind your own shop for weekend courses – I love that.'

'I've organized those courses before,' said Nell, grateful for this approval. 'When I lived in Shropshire. It works well – you book people into nearby pubs and hotels, depending on what they want to pay, and hold simple workshops and even have a visiting speaker over the two days of the course. Bookbinding or the history of glassware or something like that. And perhaps throw in a conducted tour around a suitable historic house in the vicinity.'

'I'd sign up for all that,' said the adviser. 'I think though, at this stage you need to get some more exact figures. The cost of assigning the lease to you and a builder's estimate – maybe even an architect's as well – for knocking the shops into one unit. Once we've got that, we can make a more precise forecast and go from there.'

'That would be sensible,' said Nell. 'Godfrey – Mr Purbles – has already asked the landlords for a figure on the lease. And I'll get quotes for the work – he's recommended a builder, as well. As soon as I've got those I'll contact you again. Thank you very much.'

'I haven't helped much so far,' said the business adviser.

'No, but you've clarified things. And you've been encouraging about the whole idea. That means a lot.'

She went back to Quire Court, still undecided, and spent the next hour unpacking some pieces of glassware she had acquired at a house sale the previous weekend. Beth had come with her to the sale and had loved the tension and the excitement of the auction. They had chosen the pieces they wanted beforehand and Beth had been entranced by the bidding procedure. It was pretty cool, she said afterwards, to have a mum who did things like that.

The glass was going to look very good indeed, and Nell washed it all carefully. But as she did so, one level of her mind was replaying the meeting at the bank. The thought of using up almost all of her careful stash of funds was suddenly alarming, and the prospect of a loan on top of that was outright terrifying. Supposing the venture failed? Supposing there was an even worse plunge in the economy? Supposing she became ill and could not run the shop? There would be absolutely no funds to fall back on, because Beth's fund was indeed untouchable. As she placed the glassware in the smaller of her two windows and set out some Victorian jewellery with it, she thought it would be a bitter blow if she had to back out.

But when Godfrey came into the shop just before she was closing, clutching a letter and looking anxious, the prospect of backing out loomed even closer.

'The freeholder's figure for the assignment?' said Nell, glad for once that there were no customers in the shop and they could talk freely.

'Yes. Oh, Nell, it's much higher than I thought it would be.'

'How much higher?'

'They're saying that because the lease was created more than ten years ago, they're now allowed to ask whatever figure they want for assigning it. There are stages in the life of the lease, apparently, and this is one of them. I thought the figure would be pretty much the same as I paid, but it isn't . . .'

'Godfrey, how much higher?'

'Fifteen thousand pounds higher,' said Godfrey, miserably.

Nell sat down abruptly. 'Oh, lord, that really is higher.'

'We can negotiate a bit,' he said, hopefully. 'I dare say they aren't expecting to get the exact amount they're asking, but they've said this is a prime spot. Nell, I do hope I haven't got you all fired up about this, only to find it's impossible.'

'It isn't like that at all,' said Nell at once. 'But that extra fifteen thousand pounds might stretch it too far.'

Michael had intended to spend most of Monday morning drafting notes for a lecture on eighteenth-century novels. There was the usual faculty meeting at nine, and he had a tutorial at eleven, but apart from that he was free. He thought he might try to track down Salamander House later. He would also see if Professor Rosendale had a spare half hour somewhere, to let him have the Porringer letters.

When he got back to his rooms after the meeting, Wilberforce was nowhere to be seen, but he made his presence felt in the form of an email from the photographer doing the publicity shots for the new book. They had rescheduled the shoot, and the photographer would like to come along to Oriel on Thursday morning. They would bring their own props this time, to save any further damage to Michael's rooms, but it would be really helpful if Wilberforce could be persuaded to cooperate – although remembering the first shoot, Rafe could not think how this might be achieved.

Hard on the heels of this was an email from Michael's editor, who expressed herself as thrilled (it came over as 'thrrrilled') to report that the editorial meeting absolutely loved the idea for a set of historical books set in Wilberforce's world, using his ancestors as characters. They would like to make this a joint venture with their educational books department (who were very keen on the project) and they would, of course, be sending a formal offer, commissioning the series. But in the meantime, it would be great if Michael could let her have a treatment for the first couple. They ought to be sequential, of course. Perhaps Michael could start with King John and Magna Carta – the Wilberforce of the day might be a scribe, constantly losing writing materials or falling into ink pots. After that, maybe Elizabeth the First, in which a Tudor Wilberforce could be a swashbuckling court cat embarking on a life of piracy, bringing home treasure chests of doubloons. Although they must be careful not to plant the idea in the children's minds that robbing and pillaging was good. And it was only an idea, of course. But could they say next March for delivery of Book One?

And while writing, here was a link to the website the marketing people were building for Wilberforce. Michael should remember it was a work in progress, and everyone was sure it would be possible to change the colour of Wilberforce's fur in the illustrations, although so far nobody had admitted to making it that peculiar tangerine shade when it was well known by them all that Wilberforce – the fictional one at any rate – was black and white.

Michael regarded the orange splodge intended to represent Wilberforce with dismay, then typed an email to Beth, asking what her year and the year below her were currently learning in history at school. He added a line about her now being editorial consultant, which he thought would amuse and please her, and sent it off.

By this time his student had arrived for the tutorial, and an absorbing hour followed, in which the student, who was Michael's particularly promising first year, displayed some satisfyingly original thinking, and argued his points with polite insistence.

After the student had left, Michael put in a couple of hours on his lecture, covering his desk with books, and enjoying himself wandering along paths in the company of such people as Jane Austen, Oliver Goldsmith, and Fanny Burney. He added Tobias Smollet and Henry Fielding to the mix to spice things up a bit.

It was mid-afternoon before he was able to tell the professor about the Porringer letters.

'I should like to see them very much,' said Leo. 'Are you free at the moment?'

'I am,' said Michael. 'I'll drop them in now, shall I?'

'Yes, do. I'll get someone to bring coffee.'

Michael, seeing the rooms for the first time – seeing the charm of their clutter and feeling the gentle atmosphere of books and scholarship – understood why they were a small legend of their own within Oriel. Seeing the professor bestow his smile on the bearer of the coffee, he also understood why the tray had been carried up three flights of stairs without demur.

Rosendale read the letters with deep interest.

'I don't know if they'll provide any answers for you,' said Michael, when Leo laid them down, 'but it's all useful material. It might be worth delving into Salamander House, as well – oh, and you note the suggestion that there was some kind of private arrangement between Breadspear and Porringer – something off the record, as it were.'

'Oh, yes.' Leo thought for a moment, then said, 'Dr Flint . . .'

'Michael.'

'Michael, I think I told you I lived near to Deadlight Hall as a child. I was one of a group of children who were smuggled out of Poland in 1942, and I was sent to live with a brother and sister. Simeon and Mildred Hurst, at Willow Bank Farm.'

'Maria Porringer mentions that place,' said Michael eagerly, reaching for the printouts. 'And the name Hurst, as well. Yes, here it is. John Hurst, of Willow Bank Farm.'

'Yes. And I rather think,' said Leo, 'that John Hurst might be the man Simeon and Mildred referred to as their shameful ancestor. "Wild and godless" they called him, usually with the Biblical line about the sins of the fathers, as well.'

This was the most Michael had ever heard the professor say about his background – he thought it was probably the most anyone at Oriel

College had ever heard him say. Not wanting to intrude, but interested, he said, 'Were they good to you, that farmer and his sister?'

Leo smiled. 'They were strict and rather severe, but they were kind in their own way. But when Mildred Hurst died, she left the contents of the farmhouse to me. Furniture and china and so on. I sold most of the furniture – it was nearly all Victorian and rather florid, but one of the things I did keep was that old blanket box.' He indicated an oak box beneath a latticed window. 'It stood outside my bedroom at Willow Bank, so it felt like a bit of my childhood. The Hursts used it to store odd papers and photographs. None of them were relevant to me, but it seemed wrong to destroy them.'

'Are they still there?' said Michael, hardly daring to hope.

'Oh, yes. I've never really looked at them, but I always felt they were a fragment of a particular era of history, so I kept them.'

'Professor, when you say papers . . .?'

'Mostly old letters and photos and the odd newspaper cutting, I think. It's a bit of a jumble.' He was already crossing the room to the carved box. Sunlight filtered through the window, laying chequered patterns on its surface.

'It's been under this window . . . well, ever since I've been here,' said the professor. 'I've used it as an extra shelf.'

'So I see.' The grain of the lid showed dark oblongs where books had lain for years, and where the sun had gradually faded the rest of the surface around them. Michael knelt down and lifted the lid. It tipped back smoothly and with only the faintest creak of old hinges. He waited for the scents of age to engulf him – old paper and forgotten memories – but there was nothing. Was that because there was nothing of the past in here? No, he thought. It's because the darkness is too dense. This is dead light in every sense.

He became aware of the professor explaining that the papers might go quite far back.

'Even as far back as Maria Porringer and John Hurst,' he said. 'So take as long as you like to look through them. But if you wouldn't mind, I'll leave you to do it on your own.' He stared into the trunk for a moment. 'I don't know what there might be in there,' he said. 'And I'm not sure if I want to find it. I don't mean there'll be anything criminal or damning or scandalous – at least, I shouldn't think so – but whatever is there is a link to some very mixed memories for me. I think, you know, that's why I decided to sell the silver golem.'

'I understand,' said Michael.

'So I'll walk along to the Radcliffe for a couple of hours. That coffee's still hot, so help yourself to a refill.'

Left to himself, Michael carefully lifted out the top layer of the contents. And now, finally, the stored-away aura of the past did reach out to him. These were not letters and documents efficiently and neatly stored on computer hard drives or microfiche screens; this was the faded fabric of the long-ago – the curl-edged photographs, the ink-splodged missives, the cobwebbed, candlelit writings that were dim with age and that might even be illegible . . .

And there's something here, thought Michael. I know there is. By the pricking of my thumbs . . . With the thought came another image – a half-memory of something he had seen very recently, something to do with cobwebs and a dim old place where there had been a shelf holding old books or documents . . . He waited, but the memory remained annoyingly elusive, and he left it alone and focused on what lay in front of him.

There were two or three shoe boxes filled with black and white photographs – even some that were sepia. Michael glanced at these briefly, seeing self-consciously posed gentlemen wearing wing collars and Sunday-best suits, and ladies with flowered frocks and shady hats. Nell would seize on these with delight, of course; he would ask the professor if she could see them. But for the moment he put them to one side, and reached for two large packages, virtually parcels, both wrapped in the old-fashioned way, with brown paper and string.

The knots in the string parted easily after so many years and, his heart starting to beat faster, Michael unfolded the contents.

At first look there did not seem to be anything of particular interest, and nothing looked likely to relate to Deadlight Hall. On the top was a handwritten note, addressed to 'Dearest Mildred'. That's Miss Hurst, thought Michael, remembering what Professor Rosendale had told him. Mildred and Simeon Hurst. He smoothed out the letter, trying not to split the paper where it had been folded for so long.

It was undated, and there was no address. Michael had the impression of a quickly written note, either delivered by hand, or thrust into a parcel.

Dearest Mildred,

It is very kind of you and Simeon to agree to store my things at Willow Bank Farm until I can send for them. I dare say the bits of furniture can go in your attic, and in these packages are a few old family papers – nothing valuable or even particularly important, but mostly old photographs and a few letters from my great-uncle's time, which my mother always kept. I expect you'll be surprised to find me being so careful – and even sentimental – but I'd like to think they were in safe-keeping. With the future so uncertain and everything being blown to smithereens around us, it seems somehow important to preserve the past – even though parts of this particular past are not very creditable!

I will write soon.

Fondest love to you and Simeon,

Rosa.

Rosa. By her own admission, there was nothing especially interesting in the papers she had left for her good friends Mildred and Simeon Hurst to store. It was slightly odd that if the papers had meant so much to her, she had never reclaimed them, but there could be any number of reasons for that. There was no date on the letter, but it sounded as if it had been written at the height of WWII, when there were all kinds of upheavals and tragedy in people's lives. Curious to know what Rosa had wanted to keep for posterity, Michael turned over the next layer.

Two names leapt out at him at once. The first was that of Augustus Breadspear, the vaguely Dickensian-sounding name familiar from the documents found at the Archives Office a couple of days ago.

The second was Deadlight Hall.

Moving with extreme care, almost expecting the thin brittle pages to crumble into dust beneath his hands, Michael lifted out the little stack of papers, and carried them to the deep wing chair in the corner of the room.

He placed them carefully on the small side desk where the gentle sunlight filtered through the window, sat down in the deep wing chair nearby, and began to read.

FIFTEEN

Deadlight Hall
October 1882
My dear Mr Breadspear

Tomorrow I am sending you Douglas Wilger, who should be sufficiently strong for the work, being twelve years old, but could pass for fourteen. He may need discipline, for he has turned out to be a wilful and ungrateful child, one as needs a firm hand. Already he has had the impudence to say that to work at Salamander House is what he calls 'beneath him'. He also makes objection to the hours, which he says are very long, and adds that it is a dangerous place.

I do not know what the world is coming to when a child born in shame is so ungrateful, although I will allow that his father – whoever that may be – pays our accounts very prompt.

To my mind the work at Salamander House is easy and the hours reasonable. My goodness, I should like to see how these young people would fare if they had to stand behind a counter in a busy apothecary's establishment all day, as I did in Mr Porringer's establishment.

The Wilger boy will come to Salamander House tomorrow morning at 7.00 sharp.

Respectfully yours,
Maria Porringer (Mrs)

Following this letter was what appeared to be an official report from the same year.

DEADLIGHT HALL TRUST
ENQUIRY HELD INTO INJURY AT SALAMANDER HOUSE.

Governing Chairman of Enquiry Board and author of report: Sir George Buckle.

Statement made by Mr Augustus Breadspear, owner, managing director, and Chairman, of Salamander House Glass Manufactory.

I attest that the boy, Douglas Wilger, was employed by me

for work in the furnace room of my manufactory at Salamander House commencing on the 10th day of October, in the year 1882. His hours were from seven o'clock in the morning to seven o'clock each evening. (Saturdays are seven o'clock until four o'clock, and Sundays, of course, are a day of rest, although I make sure all my apprentices attend Church service.)

My workers are looked after properly and considerately. They are allowed half an hour for breakfast at half-past eight, and another half an hour for dinner at midday. I provide breakfasts and dinners for them all – which is more than I can say for a great many other factory owners – and good substantial food it is at Salamander House, none of your rubbishy bread and dripping or onion broth. There is a delivery each day from Hurst's Farm, of fresh eggs and milk, as can be seen from my account books, which are all kept in proper order and can be inspected by anyone who wants to see them.

Douglas Wilger's duties were to carry the blown glass objects from the manufactory benches to the furnaces for firing and finishing, to lever open the furnaces and to ensure the doors remained open while the products were placed inside. He had also to assist the glass blowers to arrange such products on the inner shelves of the furnaces.

So Salamander House was a glass manufactory, thought Michael, coming up out of the nineteenth century for a moment. Of course it was. The clue's in the name.

He returned to Augustus Breadspear's statement.

I am unable to give precise details of the tragedy, since I was not in the kiln room at the time it happened. I can say, though, that the Wilger boy was unsatisfactory. He was resentful of the tasks assigned to him, and during his first week was reprimanded for carelessness three times.

I am very sorry about what happened to him, but no blame or responsibility can be assigned to Salamander House or to my overseers. Douglas should have looked where he was going. An entire tray of expensive work was ruined by his clumsiness – work that had taken considerable time and skill to produce, and my customers will now be kept waiting.

I believe Douglas may have to come on to the Parish for his

upkeep, which is a further burden on funds that are already sparse, although I should like it known that I subscribe generously and regularly to the Parish funds. For the moment the boy is still living at Deadlight Hall, in the good care of Mrs Maria Porringer.

It should be borne strongly in mind that any statement made by Mr John Hurst about this incident is likely to be biased and even spiteful, Hurst being a troublemaker. Since I discovered *certain disreputable facts* about his private life he is keen to discredit me in any way he can. A mannerly reticence as well as a gentlemanly respect for the lady in question (perhaps that should be 'ladies') forbids me to disclose those facts, even if this were the place to do so, which it is not.

The next statement was considerably longer, and Michael saw that it was indeed made by John Hurst of Willow Bank Farm.

Statement made by Mr John Hurst of Willow Bank Farm, in this County.

I attest that on the morning of 22nd day of October, in the year of 1882, I was making a delivery of provisions to Salamander House. As a result, I saw exactly what happened in the firing rooms, and you can take this statement as completely true, never mind the moonshine flummery that Augustus Breadspear will have spun you.

A regular order for eggs, milk and butter is placed with my farm by Mr Augustus Breadspear, who would like everyone to believe the food is for his workers. This is not true. The delivery is taken to Breadspear's private house, which is next to the glass manufactory, although separated from it by a high wall, as you know – and if you do not know it, George Buckle, then you should, and you a Justice of the Peace.

Not a morsel of the food delivered to that house reaches the workers in the manufactory, not so much as an egg yolk or a scrape of butter. A more mean-spirited individual than Mr Breadspear I hope never to meet—

The next line had been vigorously scored through, so that it was almost impossible to read it, but Michael, tilting the paper closer to the window's light, made out the word *skinflint*. He read on.

It is normally the business of my herdsman to make milk and egg deliveries to customers, but on that morning I took the Salamander House order myself. You may well ask why I should do such a thing, being so busy with the farm, but I am compiling evidence against Breadspear. It's my firm belief that he half-starves his apprentices, works them every hour God sends, and gives not a jot of care to their safety. They labour for hours on end in the firing rooms, and constantly suffer burns and blisters. Their eyes are often affected by the constant heat of the kilns, and their lungs become dry and scorched. In extreme cases I believe there can be permanent impairment to their sight, and that damage to the lungs is often permanent, as well. If any of those wretched creatures survive much beyond thirty years of age I should regard it as a miracle.

I make no secret of my suspicions regarding Augustus Breadspear, so you may write all this down fair and true, George Buckle, and I shall look at it very sharply before I put my name to it, to be sure it is exactly as I have said. Nor I shan't listen to any nonsense about knowing my place and respecting my betters, for I farm my own land and Willow Bank came to me fair and square by inheritance and an entail. In short, I am as good as you – in fact I am as good as any man and a sight better than most. I pay my dues and I owe no man a brass farthing, which is more than can be said for a great many folk hereabouts. As well as that, I know my rights, because I have read Magna Carta, which I'll wager is a sight more than you have.

On the morning of 22nd October I had resolved to see the firing rooms for myself while they were in full working operation. I wanted to catch Breadspear and his overseers at their cruel ways, which would give me evidence for a formal charge. The laws are disgracefully weak when it comes to the treatment of young people in manufactories (Magna Carta did not provide for every eventuality), but I am resolved to fight for what is right and kind. If it means a change in the law, then that is what I will fight to achieve. No, I am not an anarchist. If I am anything, I am a reformer.

I took the dray along the lanes and across Watery Toft, and delivered the eggs, milk and butter to the kitchen door of Breadspear's private house. I dislike that house. I do know what happened there a couple of years ago – even as a relative newcomer

to the area I have heard about it – but I take no notice of the tales
spun by the credulous and the spiteful. It is simply an ugly, mean-
looking house, in which a bad and tragic thing once happened.

It is nonsense for Breadspear to say I slunk into the manufactory and crept through the corridors like a homing tomcat.
I unlatched the gate in that wall and walked openly across the
courtyard, entering the manufactory through the main doors.

It was a little before eight o'clock, but even at that early
hour there was a thrum of machinery and a clatter of steel and
metal. I followed these sounds, opening several doors, but
finding only store rooms or packing bays. Trays of glass ornaments were set out, ready for packing, and in Breadspear's
favour I will say he has a thriving manufactory and the trinkets
and goblets and decanters he makes are of a beautiful quality.
That, however, does not excuse his treatment of his workers.

In the end it was easy to identify the firing rooms; the heat
from the kilns belches out into the corridors, and as you
approach that part of the building the very stones glow with
uncomfortable heat. In the height of summer it must be an
unbearable place in which to work.

The instant I opened the door of those firing rooms I felt as
if a burning fist had dealt me a massive blow. My eyes prickled
and heat scoured my skin. I put up a hand instinctively to shield
my eyes, and when I felt able to remove it, for a wild moment
I believed I had stumbled into a living depiction of hell's deepest
caverns – that a painting by one of the dark masters had sprung
into life around me. Bruegel perhaps, or Hieronymus Bosch, or
Botticelli who mapped the diagram of Dante's Nine Circles of
Hell – Yes, I will spell those names for you, although you should
think shame, George Buckle, that you do not know them.

At the centre of the firing room was a large six-sided structure, almost like a summer house or the kind of folly that rich
men sometimes build. Thick stone pillars stretched from floor
to ceiling, but between those pillars – inside the structure – the
kiln itself blazed. It was fiercely, intensely hot, and impossible
to look at directly, but from where I stood I could make out
rudimentary shelves within the fire, with trays of objects I took
to be the glass pieces.

The workers moved around this structure, carrying and
fetching, some of them using hooked iron rods to pull out the

trays or push them deeper into the roaring heat. Some wore makeshift eye protectors which had the appearance of having been fashioned from odds and ends by the workers themselves. But most simply kept their heads turned away from the intense heat as much as they could.

Those rooms are terrible places. They are filled with fire and yet they are somehow dark, as if the fire has severed day from night, and sucked the light from the forgotten sun—

No, those are not indelicate remarks, they are quotations from two of our greatest writers and poets, Shakespeare and Tennyson. Have you never read the great works of our men of genius, Sir George, or wandered amidst the groves of their imaginations? Well, I suppose I am not surprised to hear you have not, and yes, I do want that written down, if you please, for it is as much a part of what happened that morning as anything else.

One of the dreadful things I discovered about the kiln room inside Salamander House that morning was the extreme youth of most of the workers. They were little more than children – perhaps ten- and twelve-year-olds, most of them boys, but there were also one or two girls. They ran about, obediently doing the bidding of the four overseers, who directed and controlled everything. It was a terrible thing to see small children cowed into such docility.

Every few moments molten gobbets and splinters of glass flew outwards from the kiln, as if demons were spitting their anger and venom from within its depths and, as a particularly fierce shower of splinters cascaded out, an order was rapped out for one of the trays to be repositioned. One of the boys went towards the kiln, clutching a hooked iron pole – I now know him to be Douglas Wilger, but at the time I did not realize who he was. As he went forward, a worker from the far end of the room set off across the room, carrying a large iron tray, on which were a number of glinting shapes – ornaments and suchlike, intended for firing.

Douglas Wilger was intent on obeying the order given to move the firing trays. He was also clearly intent on trying to avoid the scorching heat. For that reason, he was not aware of the man with the iron tray, and the man was concentrating on balancing the heavy tray.

The two of them collided. The tray fell clattering to the ground, sending the glassware flying, splintering into glinting shards. Wilger gasped and instinctively threw up his hands to shield his face and his eyes from the showering fragments. In doing so, he half fell against one of the stone plinths, knocking his head against it, and slumping to the ground. I started forward to help him, but it was already clear he was no more than slightly stunned, for he sat up almost immediately, brushing off the shards of glass, but looking fearfully at it, clearly expecting punishment.

There was a movement behind me, and I saw Augustus Breadspear standing in the doorway. I don't think he saw me; he strode forward to where Wilger half-lay. It was, I suppose, stupid to expect him to help the boy to get up, to make sure that neither he nor anyone else was cut from the glass. He did no such thing. His concern was all for the damage to his precious glass, intended for customers.

His large face was suffused with purple, and he shook his fists at the hapless boy, shouting that he was a clumsy oaf, fit for nothing but the most menial work, and that an entire tray of expensive materials had been smashed to splinters because of his inattention.

Before anyone could intervene – not that I think anyone would have dared, because even I was hesitating – Breadspear had kicked the boy hard in the ribs. Now, I am an honest and a fair man and I would have to say Breadspear's intention was almost certainly to simply remove from his path the boy who had ruined a batch of glassware, and then to see if anything might be salvaged from the wreckage. But the kick sent Wilger – still partly stunned – skidding and toppling towards the stone pillars enclosing the open kiln. There was a moment when he fought to stop himself, flailing at the air with his arms, but the force of the kick was too strong. He fell between two of the pillars, half into the kiln itself. The fires roared upwards, and the sudden glow reflected on the trays, causing the glass to glint redly like the eyes of watching devils.

Wilger was silhouetted blackly against the fire, writhing and struggling like a spitted worm on a pin, and screaming like a trapped hare. The sounds were only partly smothered by the frantic rush of the others towards him – I was among them, of course – and amidst confusion and panic we managed to pull the boy clear. His clothes were smouldering, and we had to beat at them to quench the sparks. I shouted over my shoulder for a doctor to be fetched, and when I saw Breadspear hesitate, I yelled furiously at him to damn the expense; I would pay.

By then someone had fetched a servant of some kind, for a stout woman, flushed and puffing with agitation, arrived with a bowl of something and cotton cloths.

'Soda bicarbonate, sir,' she said. 'Helpful for burns.'

They slathered the mixture over the boy's skin – I helped by cutting away some of his clothing, but two of the overseers had to hold him down. And even then I think it was clear to all of us that the burns were far beyond the help of the mild domestic remedy. Almost the whole of one side of Douglas Wilger's upper body was burned – in places the skin was *charred* for pity's sake – and although most of his face had escaped, angry weals and blisters showed down one side, down his jaw and neck. Mercifully his eyes seemed to have been spared, but this was a very small mercy indeed.

I intend to place this information and evidence before the appropriate authorities, representing that Salamander House in general and Augustus Breadspear in particular be thoroughly investigated. There are several Acts of Parliament in existence, protecting workers and young people, and all workshops and factories who employ more than fifty people have to be inspected regularly by government inspectors. I cannot tell yet if Salamander House comes into this category, having no information as to the number of people employed there. Possibly, the jurisdiction will still be with the local authority. However, whoever is responsible is fulfilling the task very poorly, and I intend to see to it that Augustus Breadspear pays for his brutality. He has certainly ruined Douglas Wilger's life, and very likely a number of other lives, as well.

There is one final fact I wish to be set down, and it is this: the frantic promise I threw out to pay a doctor's expenses for attending on young Wilger was taken up by Augustus Breadspear. Three days after the incident, he sent me the doctor's note of fee. It was half a guinea for attendance and 2s.9d for potions and dressings. I paid it the same day.

SIXTEEN

There were only a few sheets left in the parcel, and they all looked somewhat official and a bit dry. The first page was simply a medical report by the doctor who had attended Douglas Wilger.

Statement made by Doctor Ian Maguire, General Practitioner of Medicine.

I was called to Salamander House by Mr John Hurst, to tend to Douglas Wilger, who had, I was told, slipped, and fallen partly into the open kiln. When I arrived the boy was in great pain and in deep shock. The lower side of his face had suffered moderate burns, but the cause for real concern came from the other injuries. Almost the entire left half of his upper trunk was severely burned. It was not possible to determine the thickness of the burns, but they were extreme. The housekeeper had applied soda bicarbonate paste to the affected areas at once, which had afforded some slight relief. However, I used a solution of picric acid, which is a recognized cure for burns, and is sovereign in the reducing of pain and infection. Properly applied, and covered with gauze, it then allows for the formation of a scab, under which healing can take place.

Sad to report, when removing the boy's dressings three days later, as I feared, the burns had been too deep to respond well to the treatment. There is severe shrinkage of tissue on the chest wall, which has drawn the flesh of the chest inwards, and in time will pull one, and possibly both, shoulders forward. This process will be progressive and is already discernible. Eventually it will result in what will be virtually a hunchback stature – although the hunching will be due to contraction of flesh and muscle, rather than deformity of bone.

The boy's lungs are also damaged, and I think it unlikely they will heal. Coupled with the shrinkage of the upper trunk, he finds it difficult to draw in very deep breaths. Consequently, he is unable walk more than a few paces at a time.

Sadly, the lower left side of his face is somewhat disfigured from the burns. About that I can do nothing, although by God's good grace, the burns missed his eyes.

Michael reread the last couple of paragraphs. '*Shrinkage of tissue on the chest wall, which has drawn the flesh of the chest inwards, and in time will pull one, and possibly both, shoulders forward . . . Will result in what will be virtually a hunchback stature . . .*'

Was this the misshapen shadow he had seen in Deadlight Hall? A lingering memory of a sad little ghost, its body maimed, its life probably spoiled? You poor wretched little creature, he thought, then turned to the next page.

Conclusions by Sir George Buckle:

While my fellow committee members and myself are sure that Mr Breadspear's glass manufactory is run on proper and humane lines, in order to alleviate concern in the minds of several local people, a full and official inspection will be made of Salamander House.

I would make the point that such inspections are intended to bring about a moral climate of observance, rather than to supervise the general running of any industry. It is believed – indeed, it is recommended – that inspectors should not take from employers the ultimate responsibility for operating decent establishments.

Across the foot of this last page, in what Michael thought was the unknown Rosa's handwriting, were the words: 'What a cruel and unpleasant bunch of people! I am ashamed to think I have an ancestor among them!'

He wondered briefly which of the players in the long-ago drama had been Rosa's ancestor, but could not see that it mattered. He reached for the other package, disentangled the string, and began to read the contents. The first was a letter from the ubiquitous Maria.

Deadlight Hall
November 1882
My dear Mr Breadspear

I was very glad to hear from you that the inspection of Salamander House concluded that no blame could be attached to you. I was also pleased to hear that the inspectors enjoyed the lunch you arranged for them. I dare say such people do not often have the chance of sampling grouse, and it was generous of you to serve your best wines, as well.

It cannot be easy for you to arrange such occasions in your house, after the terrible tragedy, and I am glad to think that much of the unpleasantness about that is dying down. Perhaps 'unpleasantness' is rather a mild word to use, but you will know what I mean.

What is not dying down, however, is the annoyance caused to me by that man, John Hurst, with his visits to the Hall and the books he brings for the children. I always look at the books very sharply before allowing them into the house, for on his own shelves at Willow Bank Farm, Mr Hurst has a number of very questionable volumes (some are even in French), which he brazenly says are great literature. There are paintings on the walls of the farm which Hurst calls Art, but which to my mind are nothing better than shameful flaunting hussies. During the lunch he gave for the ladies of St Bertelin's Church charitable committee I did not know where to look. The lunch itself was what I can only call ostentatious.

It is a pity that the likes of Sir George Buckle take such notice of Mr Hurst's opinions, although I dare say Hurst's contributions to the Parish coffers will have much to do with that. But then Sir George seldom knows what goes on in his own household, never mind the wider world beyond. I know for a fact that one of his maidservants has regular assignations with young men whom she meets in the buttery at Buckle House, and is acquiring a very undesirable reputation among the drinkers at the King's Head. Sir George would be shocked to his toes if he knew he was employing such a hussy in his house, although he will probably find out eventually, on account of it becoming common gossip not only in the King's Head, but also the Coach and Horses. Not that I have ever frequented either place.

I dare say you will recompense me for the cost of sending the carrier to Salamander House to bring Douglas Wilger back to Deadlight Hall after the accident in your kiln room. A matter of one shilling and sixpence, which I feel is not excessive since the carter lifted the boy on and off. I am sending the note of fee with this letter.

Respectfully yours,
Maria Porringer (Mrs)

Deadlight Hall
November 1882
My dear Mr Breadspear

Regarding your enquiry about Douglas Wilger's injuries, he is recovering, although his behaviour leaves much to be desired. I have pointed out to him how fortunate he is to have been saved a worse fate, and how he might well have lost an eye in the accident, but he is disobedient and ill-mannered. The two Mabbley girls are his constant companions. I do not care for particular friendships at Deadlight Hall as these can lead to all kinds of trouble among the older ones (I will not give further details of the kind of troubles these might be, being one as was brought up to consider reference to such things indelicate, but you will take my meaning). However, at least Rosie and Daisy Mabbley push Wilger's wheeled chair around, which is fortunate, since I have no time for it.

I intend to send the Mabbley girls to you, as Wilger's replacement in the kiln room. It will separate those three, and it is high time those girls started to earn their keep. I must warn you that both have a rebellious streak and will need a firm hand.

Very truly yours,
Maria Porringer.

Deadlight Hall
December 1882
Dear Mr Breadspear,

During the last few days, the children have been behaving rather strangely, and I am becoming somewhat uneasy. I will write to you with more details, being a touch hurried at the present, since the kitchens are awaiting a delivery of dried goods, and I like to oversee such things. Mr Porringer always held that a good master (in this case mistress) ensures honesty at all levels of the establishment, and most especially in the consignment of supplies. To my mind this is true whether it is laudanum and mercury for the apothecary's shelves, or lentils and pudding rice for the larder.

Very truly yours,

Maria Porringer.

Deadlight Hall

December 1882

Dear Mr Breadspear

The children's behaviour is becoming very worrying indeed. I hesitate to use the word sinister, but it is the word that comes to my mind. They have taken to gathering in small groups, in the darker corners of the Hall, whispering together. I have tried to overhear what they are saying, but so far I have not managed it.

Last night I was wakeful, which is not a thing as normally happens to me, having a clear conscience and a healthy mind, not to mention a very good draught which was Mr Porringer's own mixture, and which I usually take on retiring. I heard some of the children tiptoe past my room and go quietly down the stairs, so I wrapped a shawl around my shoulders and crept out to see what they were about. There they were, huddled together in the hall below. The Wilger boy was with them, of course – he would have been carried down by two of the other boys, since he is no longer able to walk up or down stairs for himself.

Now, I am not a great believer in poetry and such – although Mr Porringer sometimes read a volume of poems and was inclined to quote a verse over supper if one had taken his attention – but seeing those children last night brought back the line I had heard John Hurst read – you may remember I wrote to you about it. Milton's *Paradise Lost*, so I believe. The line stayed with me, and I thought of it, seeing the children:

'When night darkens the streets, then wander forth the Sons of Belial, flown with insolence and wine . . .'

There was no wine involved, of course, but insolence – my word, there was insolence in those children's manner, and there was sly, cunning devilry in their faces. A terrible thing it was, and very frightening, to see such bitter hatred in the faces of children. Indeed, it was so strong that this morning I can almost believe the hatred still lies on the air like greasy smoke.

I shall lock my bedroom door each night, and I keep a large bread knife to hand during the daytime. If you could come to the Hall as soon as possible to discuss this, I should take that very kindly.

Yours very truly,

Maria Porringer.

Michael sat down for a moment, slightly puzzled, because it was surprising to find Maria Porringer – surely a severe and even a cruel woman – had been so frightened by a group of children whispering in a dark old house.

But whatever else she was, it had to be said that the old girl had a fine line in rhetoric when she got going, while as for John Hurst, Michael was inclined to think kindly of a man who had tried to teach Shakespeare and Milton to orphans.

He delved into the package again, to see what else it might contain, and drew out what looked like a local newspaper cutting of around the same date.

MYSTERY AT DEADLIGHT HALL: Disappearance of two girls.

Police were yesterday called to Deadlight Hall, the local Orphanage and Apprentice House owned and run by the Deadlight Hall Trust (Chairman Mr Augustus Breadspear), to investigate the whereabouts of two of the girls, Rosie and Daisy Mabbley.

The girls, who are sisters and have been in the care of the Hall for most of their lives, were discovered to be missing by Mr John Hurst of Willow Bank Farm, who visited Deadlight Hall to give his weekly reading and writing lesson to the younger children.

[Readers will be aware that Mr Hurst, something of a local philanthropist and benefactor, was active in creating the local school a few years ago.]

Mr Hurst told us that as a rule there were around eight children at his Saturday afternoon classes at the Hall, with the Mabbley sisters always present.

'They enjoyed the lessons and were keen to learn,' he said. 'I was interesting them in poetry and plays – in fact we were planning to stage a small nativity play as part of the Christmas celebrations at St Bertelin's Church. The Mabbley girls were enjoying that, very much, so the fact that they were not there that afternoon and that no explanation could be found for their absence caused me considerable concern.'

Mr Hurst had asked Mrs Maria Porringer, Deadlight Hall's superintendent, to assist him in a search of the house and the grounds. When no trace of the sisters could be found, Mr Hurst reported the girls' absence to local police and then to our newspaper, asking if we would advertise their disappearance. This, of course, we are very pleased to do, for it is a shocking thing if some tragedy has befallen two young girls, particularly so near to Christmas.

[We draw readers' attention to our weather report on Page 6, which gives a doomful warning of thick snow and blizzards over Christmas.]

Mrs Maria Porringer also spoke to our reporter when he called at Deadlight Hall, and expressed herself as very concerned for Rosie and Daisy's whereabouts.

'A very thorough search I made of the Hall,' she said. 'Mr John Hurst along with two of the older children helped me. Cellars to attics we searched, and between us we looked into every nook and cranny. There was no trace of the girls anywhere. And after Mr Hurst left, the police came in, and a young police constable helped me to go over the house again. A most helpful young man he was.'

Asked about Rosie and Daisy, she told our reporter they were very well-behaved girls.

'And only two weeks ago I was able to find them places in the employment of Mr Augustus Breadspear at Salamander House. It was a good place for them; they would have learned a trade, and also been able to work together, which I thought a very fortunate circumstance.' Here, Mrs Porringer had to break off, being overcome with emotion.

She revived sufficiently, however, to tell our reporter that the girls had seemed to like the work in Salamander House's kiln room, and had been keen to do well.

'They went off on Tuesday morning, exactly as usual,' she said. 'After eating a good breakfast, of course, for it's always been my pride to send my young people out to their work with good nourishing food inside them, particularly of a cold winter's morning. I watched them go myself, from the front door of this very house.'

This time Mrs Porringer succumbed completely to distress, and was unable to continue the interview.

Mr Augustus Breadspear admitted he had been annoyed when the girls had failed to appear on Tuesday morning. He had thought there might be some illness, and it was only much later that he had been told they had vanished.

'I am very concerned for them,' he said.

Anyone having any information that might assist in the search for the girls is asked to go at once to the local police station or come to our offices.

Rosie and Daisy Mabbley are ten and eight respectively, but are both of small build so could be taken for younger. Both have long chestnut hair. It is likely they are wearing the cotton frocks issued to all Deadlight Hall children, which are bluish grey.

Deadlight Hall
December 1882
My dear Mr Breadspear

You will have read the local newspaper, I am sure, so you will know what I have told the reporters about the Mabbley girls.

The Hall has been searched twice – once by myself and John Hurst, and a second time by a local police constable. You will be relieved to know that on both occasions I was able to arrange things so that I was the one who appeared to be searching the upper floors – and that I did so alone. I gave you my word at the outset that no one but myself would ever go up to that part of the Hall, and I have kept that promise.

I made the real search early in the morning of the following day, since I do not care to go up to those upper floors after dark. I will admit that I was anxious about what I might find up there – I suppose the same anxiety was in your mind, as well. It is a terrible secret we share.

It was a difficult search to make, but it had to be done, and without the children knowing. I made my way there at daybreak, and in the cold, bleak December light everywhere was shrouded in a clinging greyness. That is a light I dislike very much, as do you yourself. We both remember what happened in another cold cruel daybreak.

Suffice it to say that I found no trace of the missing Mabbley girls.

Since having made the search, I am no longer disposed to be very concerned about them. They are sharp girls, who know how to look after themselves. Wherever they have gone, it is not to their mother, for I visited the shameless hussy's cottage myself. A ramshackle place it is, disgracefully unkempt, and the woman herself no better. She was a kitchen maid in Sir George Buckle's house, and one who did not learn by her misfortune, but returned to sinning like the sow that was washed will wallow again in the mire. She later became notorious in the taproom of the King's Head – which is to say the kitchen maid became notorious, not the sow. It is a pity that Sir George does not take more care in the hiring of his maidservants.

However, whatever the children were plotting may now vanish. Rosie and Daisy were certainly at the heart of that, if not the actual ringleaders. Douglas Wilger I can deal with – he is too frail to pose any real threat.

As you know, I do my best to run the Hall properly, but lately it has been very difficult. The money allowed for the upkeep of the place is no longer sufficient, especially if there is to be all this conniving and contriving. I do not care to deceive the police, and I hope I shall not have to do so again. With that in mind, perhaps you will look into the current level of payments, with a view to increasing them.

Very truly yours,

Maria Porringer (Mrs).

SEVENTEEN

'**A**nd that,' said Michael, that evening in Nell's house, 'was all there was.'

'That's infuriating.' Nell was in her favourite armchair, opposite him, her hands curled around a mug of coffee.

'I went through the entire box. I read everything – old account books, seed catalogues, writing on the backs of old photographs—'

'Photographs?'

'Don't sound so eager. Church outings and self-conscious groups in gardens, mostly. Some school groups – probably of the professor as a small, solemn boy. I think there were one or two shots of Mildred and Simeon Hurst as well.'

'What were they like?'

'He looked a bit stern, and she was thin and severe. Hair pulled back in a bun, and lisle stockings. But in a strange way they looked kind,' said Michael. 'Other than that, though, I found nothing. Well, nothing that gets us any further.'

'Is the professor going to read it all for himself?'

'He said he would. I'm not sure if he will, though. He flinches from the past.'

Nell said, 'It's interesting, isn't it, that one person's name keeps recurring in all this.'

'Maria Porringer. Yes. And what intrigues me are those references she makes to some kind of secret.' Michael opened his notebook again, and flipped the pages. 'Here it is. After the Mabbley girls disappeared, Maria stressed to Breadspear that no one except herself went into the upper part of the Hall, and she said, "I gave you my word . . . It is a terrible secret we share".'

'And something about "what happened in another cold cruel daybreak",' said Nell, thoughtfully. 'Michael, you do realize this is starting to sound like the ultimate classic Victorian gothic story?'

'Yes, I do, and I wish I could think Mrs Porringer was simply making notes for a novel,' said Michael. 'But those letters are real.'

'Could we track down the egregious Maria?'

'I wonder if we could. She refers to her husband being an

apothecary,' said Michael, consulting his notes again. 'With his own business. That might give us a lead. I should think there are societies and associations that list pharmacists, although it's anybody's guess how far such lists would go back. Oh, wait, when I drove out to Deadlight Hall, I did see a pharmacy in the village street. And Maria seems to have been a local girl. It's stretching it a bit to think it's the same shop, but it's worth a try.' He put out a hand to Nell. 'You're good at that kind of thing. If I go out to look at that shop tomorrow, could you come with me?'

'Is that my cue for quoting the line about following you to the ends of the earth?'

'Well, just at the moment I was thinking about following me upstairs. Or does that sound as if I'm taking things for granted?'

'Never,' she said, smiling and taking his hand.

'Michael?'

'Nell?' He was sitting in the window seat of Nell's bedroom, where he sometimes liked to sit after they had made love. The window looked between Nell's shop and Godfrey's, straight through to part of the old Court, and Michael liked Court at this hour.

'Do you ever feel this place is a bit small?' asked Nell from the drowsy warmth of the bed.

'The shop or this house?'

'Both.'

He came back to the bed. 'The shop is fine,' he said. 'Although I suppose a bit more space would be good. You'd be able to have more stock, wouldn't you? And maybe do more renovation work. Why? Have you got some kind of project in mind?'

'Well, I have, but I'm not sure yet if it can be done.'

'Do you want to talk about it?'

Nell had decided she would not talk about it at all, until she had decided what to do. But Michael was looking at her with that intent gaze that made him so very dear and so very endearing, and his hair was tumbled so that she wanted to reach up to smooth it . . . And a very short while ago they had been locked together and there had been the feeling not just of their bodies fusing, but also of their minds flowing seamlessly back and forth. Marriage used to be referred to as being one, and when things were like this with Michael – when there was no longer any sense that they were two separate beings – Nell understood exactly what that meant.

Without knowing she had been going to speak, she said, 'Godfrey's leaving Quire Court. He's going to Stratford. And he's given me first refusal of the lease of his shop.'

Michael's eyes registered surprise, then he said, 'Instead of this one, or in addition?'

'In addition.'

'With the idea of knocking both units into one?'

'Yes.'

'And you'd live over Godfrey's shop?'

'Over it and behind it. There's masses of space.'

'And this place? Oh, but you'd make this into a workshop, wouldn't you? Like you had in Shropshire.'

Nell said, 'Exactly.'

'It sounds a tremendous idea,' he said, sliding back into bed. 'What's wrong with it?'

'The money.'

'Ah. Godfrey's asking too much? I wouldn't have thought he was particularly venal.'

'He isn't,' said Nell. 'It's the company who own the freehold. They're asking a high figure for assigning the lease to me. Well – higher than Godfrey thought.'

'How much higher?'

Nell shot him a cautious look. 'I'd be between fifteen and twenty thousand pounds short. I can raise the rest, I think.'

'Ah. Yes, I see.' He leaned back on the pillows, one arm around her shoulders. 'Nell, I'd like to hear about this, but I don't want to push in and you don't have to tell me anything you want to keep private—'

'I've just realized that I do want to tell you. It's odd, isn't it,' said Nell, 'how reserved people can be about money. Here we are, you and I, and we've just made exquisite love—'

'Thanks for the "exquisite"—'

'Well, it was. And we're so close, so intimate on every level, until it comes to—'

'The sordid subject of coinage.'

'Yes. But here's the picture. I can cash in some bonds and things that I bought after Brad died,' said Nell. 'And there's one of the insurance payouts I had when he died, which is on long deposit or something like that. That's the largest sum. Only there's a penalty for cashing it before the expiry date, so there wouldn't be nearly as much as I thought. The bank say they could most likely work out a business loan, but it would be a bit of a millstone. And if the business slumped – even if there were a couple of poor years . . .'

'Yes, I see all that.' Michael was not looking at her. In a voice that Nell thought was deliberately offhand, he said, 'Have you thought about having an investor in the business?'

'You mean a partner?'

'Not exactly. But someone with an interest. Financially, I mean. Would that solve the shortfall?'

Nell stared at him. 'You mean you?'

'I think I do.'

'But that's quite a large amount. Fifteen thousand pounds at least.'

'I know. It mightn't be possible to do it, but there are some shares and stuff from my grandfather. I've never touched them – I just let the bank sort them into suitable accounts, and some interest accrues. I'd have to find out exactly how much they'd realize, but I think there could be enough.'

'Would you cash in things like that, though? A family legacy?'

'I'd be doing it for you,' he said. 'For you and Beth. So of course I would. Only I don't know if you'd want me to do it. I don't know if you'd want such a definite commitment.'

'Would you want it?'

'Yes,' he said.

'It would have to be properly drawn up. Legally drawn up.'

'Certainly.'

'We'd have to agree on what share you'd get of the profits, and all sorts of things. But,' said Nell, thinking hard, 'if we agree we'll do it – and if the money's there . . . Yes, I think I'd want to take your offer up.' She turned on the pillows to look at him. 'I can't believe I've just said that,' she said. 'I've been so determined to be independent.'

'I know you have. It's one of the things I love about you. But you still would be independent. I wouldn't even expect "West and Flint" over the door.'

'I expect we could have that if you wanted.'

'For the moment,' said Michael, speaking slowly, as if he was choosing his words with infinite care, 'I think this is as far as you'd want to go. But I think it's something we might find would – well, it would give an extra layer to our relationship, wouldn't it?'

'Yes,' said Nell. 'Yes, it would.'

'It feels as if we've made a decision.'

'It does rather, doesn't it?' Nell reached up to trace the lines of his face. 'Ought we to celebrate that?'

'What a good idea,' said Michael, pulling her against him.

Some considerable time later, Michael said, 'Did we establish if you're coming on the Porringer hunt with me tomorrow?'

Nell had been sliding into a warm, deeply contented sleep, but she came out of it slightly. 'I'd like to. It's half-day closing, so I could shut the shop at midday.'

'Half-day closing. What a quaint old-fashioned custom.'

'I suppose if you become an investor, you'll demand a twelve-hour day and no holidays. Wasn't it Scrooge who said, "It's Christmas – take the day off"?'

'I'll install a system of clocking in and piece work,' promised Michael.

'And wear one of those sexy Victorian frock-coats, and glower over the ledgers?'

'Yes, but I draw the line at a stovepipe hat.'

'Pity. Even so, I'd like to Porringer hunt with you,' said Nell.

'In that case I'll cancel the order for the time sheets. Are you going back to sleep now, or what?'

'Is there anything else on offer?'

'There might be,' said Michael. 'Yes, I believe there might be.'

'Oh, good . . .'

As Michael drove them out of Oxford the following day, a thin soft rain was falling. Everywhere smelled fresh and new, and despite the rain Nell's spirits rose.

'I remember seeing quite a nice village pub,' said Michael, 'so we'll have some lunch there, shall we?'

'I do like the way you always incorporate eating into ghost-hunting.'

'It can be a hungry occupation.'

'Is that the sign for Willow Bank Farm?' asked Nell, a little while later.

'Yes. You can just see it across the fields. I noticed it the first time I was here, although I didn't know it was relevant then.' He pulled the car on to a grass verge for a moment. 'It's over there – it's a bit misty through this rain, but you can make out the shape of the buildings.'

'The rain makes it look slightly unreal,' said Nell, after a moment. 'Veiled and blurry, and as if it really does belong to the past.'

'Do you ever feel that this kind of rain has a sort of immortality about it?' said Michael, starting the car again. 'As if it might be the same rain that fell a hundred years ago or a thousand years ago? Or even as near as yesterday.'

'You're such a romantic. But I know what you mean. That if you only knew the exact right place to reach through that rain, you might find you were touching another era.'

'Except that with my sense of direction I'd probably miss the twentieth century altogether,' said Michael, glancing in the driving mirror as they left Willow Bank Farm behind. 'I wonder who lives there now? If it's still the Hurst family.'

'It's probably being enthusiastically chopped up into flats or single dwellings by Jack Hurst, even as we speak,' said Nell. 'And speaking of Hursts, Godfrey suggested I ask Jack to provide some figures for knocking the two shops into one.'

She sounded slightly diffident, and Michael said, 'That's a good idea. It looked as if he was making a very nice job of Deadlight Hall. If anyone could make a nice job of such a monstrosity.'

'I was going to phone him later to ask him to come in. You could be there as well. I'd tell you what he said in any case.'

'I'd quite like to be there for the meeting,' said Michael. 'But you don't have to think you've got to – to consult me or anything.'

'I know, but I'd like to. Actually though,' said Nell, 'something did occur to me. Is being part-owner of a business likely to be against Oxford's rules for its dons?'

Michael sent her a surprised look. 'I shouldn't think so,' he said. 'I don't suppose they'd look very kindly on a part-share in a brothel or a porn-film shop, but antiques are very respectable, and what I do with my money is up to me. Why on earth did you think there might be a problem? Oh – you didn't think that at all, did you? You're giving me a polite way out in case I've changed my mind.'

'Well, yes, all right, I am.'

'If I change my mind I'll tell you,' he said. 'But I'm liking the idea more and more.'

'I'm glad. Actually, I'm liking it more and more as well.'

'Would my name go on the lease of the new premises?'

'Would you want it to?'

'Yes,' he said, with unexpected firmness.

'Good. So would I.'

He did not take his eyes from the road, but he smiled. 'We understand each other, don't we?'

'As much as one person ever can understand another. Here's the village now. Pity it hasn't stopped raining.'

'Never mind the rain, can you see anywhere to park? Oh, yes – over there by the war memorial. I hope I'm remembering this place accurately. I know I said there was a pharmacist's shop, but now we're here I'm not so sure.'

'You did remember it accurately,' said Nell, producing a 1920s-style hat from her bag and jamming it over her head against the rain. 'The shop's over there.'

EIGHTEEN

The shop was not, of course, called Porringer's. Michael knew they had not expected that, and he reminded himself that it was stretching optimism anyway to think it might even be the shop that Maria Porringer's husband had owned.

The sign over the main window said: 'Trussell's – dispensing pharmacist. Est.1860.'

'Eighteen sixty. Would that fit for Porringer?' asked Nell.

'I think so.' Michael fished out the untidy notebook which accompanied him wherever he went. 'Maria's letters start in 1878, when she was appointed as trustee or warden, or whatever she was, at Deadlight Hall. She refers to the death of Porringer then.'

'And this shop was set up eighteen years before that,' said Nell. 'It sounds all right. What now? Do we just go in and ask if they've got any records we could see?'

'I don't see why not. We're on a perfectly legitimate errand – research into the area in general. And this is Oxford, so they're probably used to writers and academics researching all kinds of things.'

The shop had a pleasingly old-fashioned facade, but, as Nell said, it was not determinedly so. The displays inside were bright and clean, with familiar brand names strewn around, and there were placards about blood pressure checks and influenza jabs. At the far end were two large glass-fronted display cases with several old-fashioned scales and instruments, and a carefully arranged selection of old glass bottles inside.

'Green for poison, I think,' said Nell, pointing them out. 'Oh, and look at this!'

'What . . .?'

'It's an old Poison Book. If you wanted to buy an ounce of ratbane you had to leave your name and a signature. I don't think it was a very foolproof system, though, because presumably there was nothing to stop you going to a shop where you weren't known, and signing as John Smith or U.N. Owen, like the island murderer in the Agatha Christie book.'

The poison book was in good condition. The ink of most of the entries was faded, but the writing was legible. There was, though, the feeling that the light which fell over the pages was tinged with the flickering radiance of candlelight, wax-scented and dim, or even the bad-smelling gaslight that came later. Michael stared at it, and felt the elusive memory stir again, a little more definitely this time. Somewhere recently he had seen other books, strongly similar to this one – something about the writing, was it? But again, it would not come fully into focus.

Nell was leaning forward to study the entries more closely, when a small rotund gentleman bustled over to them, and asked if he could help.

'I'm sure you can,' said Michael, producing a card. 'We're interested in the history of your shop, and we wondered if we could have a closer look at this book you've got on display.'

The rotund gentleman, who wore a neat name badge proclaiming him to be W. Trussell, M. Pharm., studied Michael's card, then beamed with delight.

'People do like to see that display,' he said. 'How things were done in the old days. I change it every so often, of course, so as it won't get too familiar, not to say dusty.' He looked back at Michael's card. 'Well, now, Dr Flint, and . . .'

'Nell West,' supplied Nell.

'You're more than welcome to take a look at the book. We don't leave it on open display, you understand, because it's a bit fragile. But people like to see it there, and I like the reminder of the shop's past. We're one of the few independent pharmacists left in the county, you know. It's always been in private ownership, this shop, right from the start. Of course, we've had offers from the big companies,' he said, proudly, 'and probably one day we'll have to accept. But not quite yet.' He produced a small set of keys, unlocked the display cabinet, and lifted the book out with care. 'If I can't trust a senior member of an Oxford University I don't know who I can trust,' he said, and Nell caught the ghost of a half-wink from Michael at this. 'Is it for a thesis, Dr Flint? A paper?'

This was said hopefully, and Michael said, 'It might be both in the end. It might not work out, of course – we might meet dead ends. But if it does come to something, I'd make sure you got an acknowledgement.'

'Well, that would be very nice, although not at all necessary. I'll leave you to it,' said Mr Trussell. 'It's a fairly quiet time of day for us, so you'll probably be undisturbed. There're a couple of chairs over there – we keep them for people waiting for prescriptions to be made up. Feel free to use them. I'll be around if you need any help.'

He took himself off, and Nell and Michael carried the book over to the chairs.

Nell opened it with care. The entries began on a page headed *April 1870.*

ITEM: *6d worth of arsenic, purchased by Mrs Trubb, housekeeper to Sir George Buckle.*
PURPOSE OF PURCHASE: *to get rid of rats at Boundary Hall, such being a pesky nuisance, and not fitting to a gentleman's residence. Also for whitening solution for Lady Buckle's hands.*

ITEM: *Belladonna and opium, one quarter teaspoonful, purchased by Mrs Trubb.*
PURPOSE OF PURCHASE: *to cure Sir George Buckle's costiveness, it being a great trouble to him and everyone else, and not helped even by liquorice and rhubarb infusion or brimstone and treacle mixture.*
Note by Mrs Maria Porringer: *Mrs Trubb advised to allow Mr Porringer to make up a suppository from belladonna (*atropa belladonna*) and opium, by the addition of glycerin and theobroma oil, this method being a preferable method to a draught. Mr Trubb (butler to Sir George) shd be able to administer suppository, although must wash his hands very thoroughly both before and after the procedure. One bar lye soap added to order for this purpose.*

'Porringer,' said Michael, staring at the page. 'My God, we've found them. We really have. This was their shop.'

'And,' said Nell, 'it sounds as if Maria was very much part of the set-up.' She read the entry again. 'What always fascinates me about the Victorians is their contradictions,' she said. 'That bizarre blend of extreme reticence – covering up chair legs and all the euphemisms they used for childbirth and sex – and then the robust way they'd describe what they used to call ailments. Poor old Sir George, though.'

'Poor old Sir George's butler,' said Michael, grinning, and continued reading the book's entries.

ITEM: *pinch of hyssop* (hyssopus officinalis), *purchased by Ada Brittle.*

PURPOSE OF PURCHASE: *children's cough, which is something chronic at this time of year, no one getting a wink of sleep, and Brittle having to be off to his work at Salamander House at half-past six of a morning.*

Note by J. Porringer: *Mrs Brittle advised to use only one small drop for each child, since hyssop known to cause convulsions or epileptic seizures if administered in larger quantities.*

Note by Mrs Maria Porringer: *Mrs Brittle told she would do better to feed her children on good wholesome food, not rubbishing pies from cookshop, with no nourishment in them, not to mention filling probably being made from all the unwholesome parts of the animal.*

'She doesn't flinch from dishing out advice, does she?' murmured Nell. 'I'll bet the customers in this shop used to pray she wasn't around when they went in.'

'It's in her writing,' said Michael, touching the page with a fingertip. 'I recognize it from the letters in the Archives Office – and the papers Professor Rosendale had from Willow Bank Farm. The odd thing is that each time I've seen it, I've had a half-memory of having seen the same writing somewhere else.'

'In Maria's day most people would have written in very similar kinds of hands,' said Nell. 'All those pot-hooks and hangers they had to practise in copybooks. You've probably seen this style of writing quite often.'

'I know. I wish I could pin down the precise memory, though.'

ITEM: *Valve pump syringe purchased by Mrs Trubb.*

PURPOSE OF PURCHASE: *Administration of enema for Sir George Buckle (glycerin solution also purchased).*

ITEM: *Half teaspoon of ergot and rye, purchased by Polly Mabbley.*

PURPOSE OF PURCHASE: *Miss Mabbley refused to state the purpose, saying it was nothing to do with interfering old besoms, since her private life was her own affair, and what folks chose to write down in some silly book was up to them.*

'Ergot?' said Michael, looking questioningly at Nell.

'It was used to bring on a miscarriage, I think. Agonizingly painful though, and not necessarily effective. And it could be dangerous.'

'There were a couple of girls called Mabbley mentioned in those statements,' said Michael, opening his notebook again. 'I remember the name. Yes, here it is – it's the two girls who vanished from Deadlight Hall. Polly's daughters?'

'They might have been. Maybe she didn't take the ergot and rye, or it wasn't successful,' said Nell. 'And she produced a couple of bastards who were placed in Deadlight Hall. As for vanishing, it sounded more to me as if they'd simply run away. But whatever happened, this is a remarkable thumbnail sketch of village life, isn't it? And I see Maria's contributed to flighty Polly's predicament again.' She pointed to a further entry on the page.

'That sounds like the title of a girls' school story from the 1930s,' said Michael. '"The Predicament of Promiscuous Polly – A Cautionary Tale".'

'Whatever she was, Maria seems to have given her short shrift.'

'I wonder if Mr Porringer ever had a say in anything,' said Michael. 'Maria seems to have dispensed advice and disapproval in about equal measure, and she's made sure it's all recorded, as well.'

'She's even noted down some arsenic she had for her own use,' said Nell, pointing to an entry on the next page.

'"Half grain of arsenic for proprietor's use. Purpose: rats and mice in cellars." Half a grain sounds quite a lot,' said Michael.

'We can check on quantities – we might even ask Mr Trussell. Oh, look at this,' said Nell eagerly, and read the next entry. '"November 1877. To supply tincture of opium for use as soporific. Quantities: opium, two ounces." A few other ingredients, as well – oh, and a half pint of sherry wine, "if permitted", and a note about macerating and filtering. Then it says, "Account presented to H M Prison, The Governor." Probably Porringer had a standing arrangement with some local gaol to supply sedatives for the poor condemned wretches destined for the noose,' said Nell. 'Are we at the end of the book? Oh, yes, what a pity – no, wait, there's a loose sheet of paper tucked between the last two pages.'

'It's probably a receipt for the supply of the opium.'

But it was not a receipt at all. It was a handwritten letter, addressed to Mrs Thaddeus Porringer, and it was headed *Governor's Wing, H.M. Gaol*, followed by the name of the village. The date was November 1877.

Dear Madam

I am in receipt of your letter of 10th inst. and would express my gratitude that you have accepted our request to attend at the prison on Wednesday, 16th, to accompany the prisoner in her last hours. As explained to you, our female wardresses would normally undertake the task as part of their regular duties. However, both are unable to do so, one being very unwell following an inflammation of the lung, and the other declaring herself so unwilling to attend this particular prisoner, she has given notice of her intention to leave.

In addition, the prison – by which I mean all inmates and staff – will shortly be transferred to the new gaol on the other side of the county. This, while it will provide better quarters and facilities, is already causing much disruption.

You will appreciate, I know, that this has been a most difficult and distressing situation for us all, particularly with this being a local case, and with so much unfortunate publicity in the newspapers.

The execution date is Wednesday 16th, and I suggest that you and Mr Porringer spend the previous night (Tuesday 15th) as my guests here in the governor's apartments. I fear the prisoner will need much patience and understanding during those hours. She is already in a very distressed state, and has had to be restrained several times. I should therefore wish, very particularly, that she has a lady at her side during her last hours.

In regard to your suggestion that you keep your own record of the event, I would have no objection. We have our own official records, of course, and two doctors will be in attendance, who will make medical records. However, a further and objective account will not come amiss.

Very truly yours,
E. M. Glaister.

'So,' said Nell, 'Maria was called in to attend a condemned female. To see her through execution – keep her calm prior to being hanged. But that isn't likely to help us, is it?'

'I wouldn't have thought so.'

Nell was rereading the letter. 'It conjures up a bizarre scenario, doesn't it?' she said. 'I can't somehow see Maria providing what Glaister calls "patience and understanding". You'd think she'd be the last person they'd call in.'

'No, I think it's understandable,' said Michael. 'Porringer was the local chemist, remember. Not a doctor, but a man of some medical knowledge. He'd have had a modest standing in the community. Maria would have shared that, even if she does come over to us as a bossy do-gooder. I think if E. M. Glaister had to cast around for someone – a female – to take care of that condemned woman, Maria would have seemed a very good choice.'

'I wonder, though, how she got from this shop to running Deadlight Hall,' said Nell, thoughtfully.

'No idea. Is there any more?'

'Just this,' said Nell. 'Folded into the end papers.'

There were two small newspaper cuttings, creased and yellowing. The first said:

> Suddenly at his home, Mr Thaddeus Porringer (60), dearly loved husband of Mrs Maria Porringer. Funeral service at St Bertelin's Church on Monday next, at midday. Friends welcome at church and at Wotherbridge's Tea Rooms afterwards.

'Death notice,' said Nell. 'Poor old Thaddeus.'

'Living with Maria probably blighted his life.'

'Or,' said Nell, 'Maria deliberately blighted it for him. Let's not lose sight of the arsenic she booked out to herself.'

'You think she might have helped him on his way?'

'I wouldn't put it past her. She's a curious character, isn't she? A mix of dutiful and disapproving. Archetype Victorian.'

The other cutting was more formal.

> NOTICE OF CLOSURE.
> The undersigned wishes to advise all customers to Porringer's Chemist and Druggist (purveyor of perfumes, essences, soaps, spices, and all medicinal provisions since 1860), that she is under the necessity of closing the premises since the sad demise of Mr Thaddeus Porringer.
> Inquiries as to reopening of the establishment can be made

with Messrs Hollinsdale & Sons, Solicitors. Inquiries as to fiscal and credit matters should be addressed to Chubbs Bank.

'So they closed down,' said Nell. 'Was that because Maria couldn't – or wasn't allowed to – run it on her own, I wonder?'

'Or because she couldn't keep it afloat. Let's go to the pub and consider,' said Michael.

They sought out Mr Trussell, explained that they had made some very useful notes, and would be in touch if any more information was needed.

'By all means,' he said. 'This shop has been a pharmacy for more than a hundred and fifty years, you know. It was owned by a family called Porringer for three, if not more, generations. Father to son, usually. They nearly lost it once – in the mid-1800s, I believe – but then a cousin or something turned up and the name continued. The family died out during the Second World War, though.'

Nell said it was sad when family businesses did not continue within a family, and they walked across the square to the pub.

'Do you think,' she said, as their food was served, 'that we're any further on?'

'Not really. And I still don't know whether the professor's right about Deadlight Hall being haunted,' said Michael. 'There's no way of telling.' He glanced at her. 'Short of spending the night in the house.'

Nell had been eating moussaka with enjoyment, but she looked at him in disbelief. 'You aren't serious, are you?' she said.

'No. For one thing I can't think how I'd get into the place,' said Michael. 'And yet, I can't help wondering what would happen if I was there. "Once upon a midnight dreary" and all that.'

'You're starting to enjoy this,' she said, half accusingly.

'I'm not. But I'd like to know a bit more about Maria and the rest.'

'So would I. And,' said Nell, 'I'd like to know what the professor's not telling us about that house, because, sure as taxes, there's something. Are you ready to go? I ought to get back to the shop. And if you've got time to come in, I've had an email from Ashby's that you might want to see.'

The email was from Nell's contact in the sale rooms.

Hi Nell,

As you know, we've placed a preliminary ad for the upcoming sale, with the silver golem as lead item. (You should have had the page proofs, so you know how terrific the photos look!) This morning a letter came in from a Polish buyer, expressing what sounds like definite interest. See attached – although I have, of course, had to delete the address for client confidentiality. I've left the sender's name though (bit of a breach of the rules, but as it's you . . .) Also, it seems to link up with the archive stuff I sent you recently – the gentleman who wrote to us back in the 1940s. So I thought on all counts you'd like to see it.

Looking forward to seeing you soon. If you deliver the silver figure to us yourself, let me know beforehand, and we could have lunch.

The letter, scanned and sent as an attachment, had a slightly more formal note.

Dear Sirs

I see with interest that you are advertising a forthcoming Auction Sale of a silver golem, believed to date to the 18th century, and thought to have been brought to England in the early 1940s.

My great-uncle, Maurice Bensimon, spent many months trying to find a silver golem that I believe could be the one you are selling. The story of his search for it has long been a part of my family's folklore.

It may not be possible for me to actually purchase the figure – my means may not allow it – but I should be grateful if you could let me know the reserve figure when it is set.

I hope to travel to England to be present at the auction. If the golem should be sold by a private arrangement before the date, I would be very grateful if you would let me know.

Kind regards,

David Bensimon.

'I think Ashby's are right that David is the descendant of the man who wrote to Ashby's in the 1940s about finding the figure,' said Nell, as Michael laid down the printouts. 'Bensimon is probably a fairly common

Jewish name, but it's a bit of a coincidence if there were two people of that name both trying to trace the golem in the same year.'

'Maurice Bensimon wrote to Ashby's and all the other auction houses, didn't he?' said Michael, frowning in an effort of memory.

'Yes, and there was some shady character doing the same thing around the same time,' said Nell. 'Ashby's reported that one to the police. They seemed to think Bensimon's enquiry was genuine, though. It's interesting, isn't it? Part of the golem figure's background in a way. Would you like another cup of tea?'

'I'd better not. I've got to be back in College for half-past four. That photographer – Rafe – is going to make a second attempt to photograph Wilberforce for the publishers' website.'

'God help him,' said Nell.

The photo shoot for the website turned into quite a lively session.

Wilberforce regarded the photographer with thoughtful malevolence, before ensconcing himself out of reach on a top bookshelf, where he succeeded in dislodging a set of Ruskins, an early edition of George Borrow's *Romany Rye*, Michael's DVDs of *Inspector Morse*, and a folder containing notes for a lecture about the metaphysical poets, which had unaccountably found its way on to that particular shelf. The whole lot tumbled to the floor, with Wilberforce watching with pleased triumph.

Rafe helped tidy up most of the debris, agreeing that the broken DVD cases would probably not affect the actual playing of the discs and that the leather covers of the Ruskin volumes could certainly be rebound, after which Wilberforce retired to the top of the window ledge, and had to be tempted down by a dish of his favourite tinned herring. He regarded this with contempt, then tipped up the dish with a paw, sending the contents over Rafe's light meter and splattering it on to Michael's lecture notes into the bargain.

'I'm terribly sorry,' said Michael, grabbing a cloth, while Rafe surveyed the light meter, whose screen was completely obscured by tomato sauce, with dismay. 'He isn't usually this disruptive. No, that's a lie, he's always this disruptive.'

In the end, Rafe managed to clean the light meter sufficiently to get several shots of Wilberforce scowling at the camera. The best shot, Rafe thought, would be the one where Wilberforce's whiskers and front paws were covered in tomato sauce from the herring. It was a pity the publicist would probably not use it, on account of it looking as if Wilberforce had just killed something in a particularly gruesome fashion.

After Rafe had gone, Michael threw away the remains of the herring, sponged the carpet, and sat down to write a chapter for the Wilberforce Histories, in which the Tudor Wilberforce was mistaken for the Royal executioner, and found himself on Tower Hill, complete with headsman's axe and block. The publishers would not be able to use that either, but writing it made him feel better, and he then embarked on a more moderate episode in which Wilberforce, adorned with gold earring and bandanna, sailed the seven seas, braving a tempestuous storm and discovering an unknown island, on which he planted a flag. Michael followed this up with a lively scene in which Elizabeth Tudor announced the island would henceforth be known as Wilberforce Island. He rifled the atlas to make sure there was not actually a real Wilberforce Island somewhere, then described the Queen presenting the intrepid explorer (now richly clad in doublet and hose) with a casket of doubloons (which would make for a good illustration), and a churn of best dairy cream. Or was cream a bit too lush in today's cholesterol-conscious, five-a-day climate? Michael deleted the cream, and then, with the idea of imparting a few vaguely educational facts to his youthful readers, allowed Wilberforce to be borne off to The Globe, where he met luminaries of the era, one of whom was a certain Master Will Shakespeare. Master Shakespeare was so entranced with the tale of Wilberforce's exploits on the high seas that he declared his intention to one day write a play in which a massive storm – 'A veritable tempest!' exclaimed Master Will with enthusiasm – caused a group of people to be shipwrecked on just such an island as Wilberforce had found.

Michael emailed the pirate/playhouse version to his editor, added the Tower Hill one just in case, and pressed Send before he could change his mind.

He then turned his attention to the lecture on the metaphysical poets which he had been trying to compile for the last three days. The melancholic allegories and intensities came as something of a rest cure after the brooding darknesses of Deadlight Hall and Salamander House.

NINETEEN

I t was not until Friday afternoon that the elusive memory attached to the handwriting – the memory that had been nudging at Michael's mind – suddenly clicked into place.

Books – old books – that was at the centre of it. Children's books in the main, with the exception of one. That one was not a printed book at all; it was leather-bound, the edges worn and one edge very slightly split. He concentrated, and the image came properly into focus. The shelf of books in the attic at Deadlight Hall. That was what he had been trying to remember – he had seen them through that blur of migraine, but he was sure there had been a small book among them – a book whose pages had slightly uneven edges. Beneath the split cover he had glimpsed handwriting – the same kind of handwriting he had seen in the old Poison Book and in Maria's letters.

How reliable was the memory, though? Even if it was accurate, it was too much to hope that the book could be a diary. It could be an old household account book, or even a cookery book left behind by some long-ago cook. Nothing to do with Maria Porringer's story at all. But Michael would not be able to rest until he had found out.

It was just on four o'clock. He had no more tutorials until Monday, and the rest of the day was free. If he drove out to Deadlight Hall now he should be able to get there before Jack Hurst's men finished for the day. Hurst would not think it odd that Michael wanted to take a second look round.

It was not quite dark by the time he turned into the drive leading to the Hall. The builders' rubble and machinery were still in evidence, and Michael saw Jack Hurst's van. The main doors were open, and as he went up the stone steps and stepped inside, the remembered scents closed about him – clean new timbers and freshly applied paint. But underneath was the same whiff of something unwholesome, something old and troubled.

There was no sign of Jack or any of his men, but they must be around. Michael called out, hoping for a response, but there was nothing. Very well, he would go openly up to the attic floor, and take a quick look for the book. Now he was here he did not relish the prospect, but he had been perfectly all right last time. Nothing had come boiling out of the woodwork to gibber at him, or clank its chains in his face. There had just been a few whispering voices and eerie shadows, all of which could have been a product of his headache. As for the thuddings from the attic, Jack Hurst had said they were something to do with an airlock in the pipes.

No lights were on, but it was reasonably easy to see the way. The first floor was silent and still, but as he went up to the second floor, Michael had the impression of something moving somewhere in the house.

The attic floor was dark, but there was enough daylight left to see everything. As he had remembered, the rooms had certainly been partitioned at some earlier stage, but one thing he had not noticed last time was that the door of the inner room had had a padlock on it – part of it was still attached to the frame. It seemed odd to have a padlock on the outside of an attic, but perhaps valuables had been stored up here. Or, said his mind, perhaps it had something to do with the secret that Maria promised Augustus Breadspear she would keep.

He pushed the door back and went inside. His memory had been right, after all. There were the books on a low shelf, and they were indeed children's books. Could this have been a nursery floor once? But not even the grimmest of the Victorians would have stowed children away in an attic and padlocked the door.

'Children . . .'

The word came lightly and with a struggle, like dried insect wings or the tapping of tattered finger bones, and Michael turned sharply round. Had something moved near the door? Something that walked awkwardly, and that had the hunched gait of the shadow he had seen here last time? No, there was nothing.

He turned back to the shelves. There were several Rudyard Kipling volumes and some Rider Haggards; also a copy of *Treasure Island* and the Charlotte M. Yonge classic *The Daisy Chain*, which rubbed shoulders with *Lorna Doone*. Perhaps these were the books that the ungodly and irrepressible John Hurst had brought for those long-ago children. That poor wretched little Douglas Wilger, and the Mabbley girls who had vanished – probably because they had run away to find golden pavements and fortunes.

Michael knelt down to see the rest of the small collection. And there it was. A small, leather-bound book, exactly as his mind had presented it to him. The pages were uneven, as if they had worked loose or never been firmly anchored in the first place – or as if extra loose pages or notes had been thrust into them.

Michael drew it out from its place, and very carefully opened it. Yes, it was handwritten – had he actually looked inside it last time? He did not think he had, but he could not remember very clearly; he could only remember the sick blur of his vision, and the storm raging overhead.

But the writing was clear and firm, and Michael knew it was the writing he had seen in Maria Porringer's letters, and in the old Poison Book.

It was completely reprehensible to put the book into his jacket pocket – it was certainly not in keeping with conduct expected of a senior member of Oriel College, and it was undoubtedly committing a felony, albeit a minor one. Michael did not care if he was committing all the crimes in the Newgate Calendar; he could not have left this book on its unobtrusive shelf if it had been guarded by the three-headed Cerberus on temporary secondment from the entrance to the underworld.

With the book firmly in his pocket, he went back down the stairs, hoping he would encounter Jack Hurst so he could explain his presence here.

The two lower floors were still deserted, and when he reached the main hall that, too, was silent and empty. As Michael went across to the big double doors, he saw a large dusty van going down the drive, away from the house. Jack Hurst's van.

Apprehension clutched him, and he reached for the door handles. Neither one moved. Jack Hurst, conscientious and responsible builder, having finished work for the day – presumably for the weekend – had secured the house before driving away.

Michael was locked in.

There was no need for panic, of course. He had only to phone Jack Hurst and explain, and Hurst would come back to let him out. There was even a display board on the drive, displaying Hurst's phone number. Michael sat down on the window seat and dialled it. He was greeted by a recorded message, saying Hurst's were closed until Monday at 8.30 a.m., but please to leave a message. Not very hopefully, Michael left a message.

There was still no need to panic. Estate agents were handling the actual selling of the flats, and they would certainly have a key – or they would know where one could be reached. Michael tried to remember who the agents were. There had certainly been a large For Sale board at the head of the drive, by the turning to the main road. He peered through both windows, and although he could just see the board, it was turned towards the road, and there was nothing on the back of it. But phone numbers could be obtained, and he rang one of the directory enquiry services. They were helpful and efficient, and said there were nineteen estate agents in the immediate vicinity. Michael wrote them all down, then asked if they had a number for Hurst's Builders. They had, but it was the mobile number he had already tried. How about a home number? They were very sorry, but no other number was listed.

Michael rang off, and saw with some concern that it was ten-past five. All those nineteen offices probably closed at half-past, in which case it would probably be quicker to phone Nell and ask her to look the name up in the local paper.

He dialled the shop, which went to voicemail. Then he dialled her mobile, which did the same thing. Michael swore, realizing that at this time of the day Nell would be collecting Beth from school. She did not have a hands-free attachment for the phone in the car, so the mobile would be switched off. No matter, he would leave a message, explaining briefly what had happened, and asking her to call him as soon as possible. She would get back pretty soon; she was very good about returning calls.

Was there anyone else he could contact? What about the professor, who might know the name of the estate agents? But the professor's phone also went to voicemail, and Michael remembered he was giving another of his lectures at the Radcliffe – one of a series on Philosophy.

It was twenty-past five, and he had better at least make a start on the nineteen estate agents. The first four on the list said no, they were not handling the Deadlight Hall flats. No, they were sorry, they did not know who was. The fifth firm said, rather sharply, that it was not the business of estate agents to give out information about other companies. Michael rang off, chastened, and ploughed on. But the seventh firm he rang answered with a recording saying they were closed until 9.a.m tomorrow. The eighth and ninth had similar messages.

Michael cursed, and thought he would simply have to sit here and wait for Nell to call back. She might have Jack Hurst's address or a home phone number for him – she had mentioned contacting him for a quote for the shop. He hoped he would not end up phoning the police to get him out. If it came to it, he would have to break a ground-floor window and climb out.

Deadlight Hall was not the ideal place to be on your own, but it would not be for long. In the meantime, he remembered that he had what might be interesting company in the form of Maria Porringer. Positioning himself more comfortably on the window seat, checking to make sure his phone was still switched on, he opened the small book and began to read.

It appeared to be a kind of continuation of the notes he and Nell had found in Porringer's shop, and it began with Maria's record of the visit she made to the gaol to be with a condemned prisoner.

Tuesday 15th: 4.00 p.m.
A short while ago Mr Porringer and I arrived at the gaol, and were shown to a very pleasant bedroom in the governor's own wing. (Glazed chintz curtains and *very* superior bedroom china.)

5.00 p.m.
Mr Glaister conducted a short interview with me, which I thought considerate of him. He is a most gentlemanly person (more so than I had expected, considering that he consorts with murderers and all manner of felons each day), and thanked me when I expressed my appreciation of our rooms. 'Although we shall not be here for much longer, as you know,' he said. 'The remove to the new prison is imminent.'

He explained to me that I would be required to remain in the condemned cell with the prisoner through the night.

'And to be present at the execution itself, if we think it would help her,' he said.

When I did not speak, Mr Glaister said, 'It is a swift method of death. We use what is called the long drop – the suspension drop – which is calculated very carefully and precisely. It is far preferable to the old "short drop", which was often little better than slow strangulation. With this method complete unconsciousness occurs within a second or two, and actual death is some fifteen or twenty minutes after that. It is ugly, but surprisingly humane. And, of course, it is the law of the land.'

'Also the law of God. "An eye for an eye, a tooth for a tooth."'

'Just so.'

I hesitated, then I put the question that had been in my mind for some time.

'I suppose,' I said, 'there is no question as to her guilt?'

'None whatsoever,' said Mr Glaister at once. 'The evidence was clear, and there can be no doubt.'

'Thank you.'

6.00 p.m.

An hour ago I was taken to the condemned cell. It is one of a row of cells opening off a stone-walled passageway. All the doors are strong and fitted with heavy locks, and most have a small hatch near the top.

A male attendant conducted me there – a plump person with unattractive red pimples spattering across his face. Bad diet is my opinion of the cause of that, and I told the man so, recommending Mr Porringer's compound of sulphur as an ointment. But he is a person of surly nature, for he only grunted, and unlocked the door of the cell.

It is a very terrible place, that condemned cell, and even though I trust I am not a fanciful woman I was aware of a feeling of such fear and despair that it was as if it lay on the air, like the stench of curdled milk.

At first I thought the prisoner did not recognize me, so I sat on the single hard chair provided and introduced myself, reminding her how we had met on several occasions when she came into the shop for purchases. (Mostly items of adornment they were: creams and lotions for the face, and softening ointments for hands. A vain creature I always thought her.)

She did not reply, and I was about to speak again when she turned her head very slowly and stared at me. As God is my judge, there was something very frightening in that blank, mad stare. I had been prepared to encounter madness though; there is surely no sanity in the mind of a woman who has killed – and the killing so shocking.

'Mrs Porringer,' she said at last, as if trying the words out, and seeing if they could be arranged in a recognizable pattern. Then, 'Yes, I do remember you.'

She has a soft voice, educated I suppose it could be called, and although she did not actually say, 'Oh, yes, you're the shop-woman,' I heard it in her tone, and charitable as I was resolved to be, a deep resentful anger churned up for a moment. I dare say we could all have nice gentle voices and money for creams and scented oils for smooth white skin if only we had been born into comfort and married into money.

(I had intended this to be a formal account of the event, but do not see why I should not incorporate a few thoughts and opinions of my own, since it is unlikely anyone will ever read it, aside from Mr Porringer, who does not count and knows better than to gossip anyway.)

As for gossip – I do not, myself, listen to it, but it is not always possible to avoid it, and the word is that this woman came from a good, but impoverished family, and that the marriage to Mr Breadspear was arranged to mend the family fortunes.

So the prisoner whom Maria had been summoned to care for had been Augustus Breadspear's wife. Michael had not expected this; there had been no mention in any of the letters of Breadspear having a wife – although that was probably not surprising, if she had been hanged for murder.

But the murder of whom? He continued reading.

The pimpled man remained outside the cell, but he did not close the door completely, and he watched as I gave Esther Breadspear the draught Mr Porringer had mixed. A tincture of opium it was, as detailed in the Poison Book kept at Mr Porringer's shop. Mr Porringer had added a spoonful of honey to sweeten it a little. Myself, I should not have bothered with such a refinement (and honey so expensive), but he was ever susceptible to a soft manner and a doe-eyed prettiness. If I did not keep a firm eye on Mr Porringer, he would certainly be handing out credit to all and sundry, and plunging us into poverty.

7.30 p.m.
Supper in governor's private dining room. He has rooms adjoining the gaol, and he is an unmarried man which is a pity, although I suppose there are very few women who would care to have their home within prison walls. Perhaps, though, he will have more conventional quarters in the new gaol building. And as it is, he seems well served by his household.

The prison chaplain was there, and Mr Porringer had thought

that the hangman himself might also be present, which was not something I viewed with equanimity. To sit at table with the hangman cannot be regarded as a comfortable situation for anyone. Also, Mr Porringer is apt to suffer from acidity if he is upset, and if dining with the Queen's executioner is not upsetting I do not know what is. (I discovered shortly before supper that Mr Porringer had not brought his bismuth mixture. I was not best pleased, for I had reminded him of it before leaving, but it is typical of him to forget despite the reminder.)

However, the hangman did not appear and the chaplain murmured something about there being a tradition of him, along with his assistant, taking his supper at some local pub.

The meal was most agreeable, with linen table napkins, and four courses – soup, roast chicken, a dessert of syllabub, and sardines on toast for the savoury. Mr Porringer, after a warning frown from me, declined the syllabub, but partook of everything else.

9.00 p.m.

I am about to go along to the condemned cell, where I am to spend the greater part of the night.

I am unhappy about Esther Breadspear's behaviour in the coming hours, but I cannot think I shall have to deal with any actual violence – she can have no animosity towards me personally. When I put this point to Mr Glaister, he said that condemned prisoners generally have animosity towards the whole world in their final hours, and I must be prepared for all eventualities.

However, the pimpled man will be immediately outside the door, the chaplain will be nearby, and I have more of Mr Porringer's opium draught if needed.

It will be difficult to fill the hours until the morning. Sleep is clearly impossible, except perhaps in short snatches. The chaplain will visit us during the night, and has promised to leave a Bible with us. I feel, though, that we should not read any of that, for it will be read aloud in the morning, as the woman is taken to the execution shed. There is a door from this part of the prison leading on to a small courtyard, in which is situated the execution shed.

I had thought I might take in my needlework, but of course needles or anything sharp cannot be allowed. However, I believe we are permitted to play simple games – backgammon and perhaps piquet.

I shall also take writing paper with me, in case the woman wishes to record any last thoughts. A pen and inkstand will not be allowed, but several charcoal sticks, of the kind used by artists for sketching, have been brought, which will do perfectly well, and I shall make some entries in this book.

10.00 p.m.

I should like to record that everywhere is quiet and calm, but it is not. As I write this there is a kind of uneasy murmuring – almost as the very stones and bricks are humming with anger and resentment at what lies ahead.

They have kept the oil lights burning in the passage outside – a very low light it is, and it casts strange shadows everywhere.

Mr Glaister told me earlier that the other prisoners will know of the forthcoming hanging – they try to keep executions a secret, but the information always leaks out.

'They become restless on the night beforehand,' he said. 'Sometimes they begin banging on their cell walls, or chanting protests. Occasionally prayers or hymns. It is accepted by anyone who has worked in this kind of gaol that the night before a hanging is always a strange one. And it may be particularly so tonight, since this is probably the last hanging that will take place here.' He hesitated, then said, 'I cannot explain it to you, that strangeness, but it is a feeling of dark suffocation.'

I had thought this a fanciful remark for a man in his position to make, but as I sit here I understand what he meant.

Mr Glaister said something else to me over supper, and I could wish he had not done so, for with night closing around the prison, his words keep whispering in my brain.

'At some time during the night you may have the impression that someone is creeping along the corridor outside the cell,' he said. 'And you may think someone has come to stand outside the condemned cell and is looking in at you through the hatch. If you should hear such a sound, do not let it alarm you, for it will be the hangman.'

We had reached the savoury course, and I was about to accept a helping of sardines, but at this I paused.

'The hangman?'

'Yes. He will have to study the prisoner in advance of the morning,' said Mr Glaister. 'To assess how best – how smoothly – to carry out his work. To make his calculations for the drop. But he always makes such an inspection discreetly, so as not to cause undue distress.'

Beside me, Mr Porringer gulped down his glass of port with a speed that will certainly provoke one of his acidity attacks.

'So if you should hear such sounds,' went on Mr Glaister, 'you should try to ignore them. In no circumstances draw the prisoner's attention to them.'

And now I am indeed hearing stealthy footsteps beyond the door of the cell. It will be the hangman, of course, making his quiet inspection, and yet . . .

And yet I would have thought the hangman would have known his way around this place – indeed, around many such places – and I would certainly have thought he would know the way to the condemned cell, even along the dimly lit passages . . .

I find I constantly look towards the door. The small hatch near the top is not quite closed; I can see the dull faint glow of the oil lights in the passage beyond. They have just flickered wildly as if a current of air has disturbed them, or as if someone has walked past. Is it the hangman? Does he stand there now, even as I write this? Will he have the noose already in his hands? They say he wears gloves to do his deed – I visualize them as thick and black. How would it feel to have those thick black hands slide the rope around your neck?

'The long drop,' Mr Glaister called it. 'The victim stands on the trapdoor, the bolt is drawn, and in the abrupt descent, the neck is broken. It is a quick death.'

A quick death.

It was not a very quick death that Esther Breadspear gave her two children. They were eight and six years old when she butchered them, slitting their throats. They found her, crouched over their bodies, still clutching the dripping knife, her night-gown wet with their blood. There can be no doubt about her guilt, of course. But does anyone know why she killed them? Could she give a sane answer to the question? When they tried to restrain her (for Mr Breadspear had called for Dr Maguire), she broke away from them, and ran through the house, sobbing and screaming, calling for the children to come back to her, opening doors of rooms as if trying to find them. Mr Breadspear and the doctor eventually cornered her in the dark gardens, and Dr Maguire administered a bromide.

If Esther Breadspear was not insane that night, I believe she is certainly insane now.

11.00 p.m.
Earlier I had perforce to help Esther to the commode – she has vomited profusely and there are other bodily functions she now seems unable to control. Mr Glaister, a gentleman, had not mentioned that likelihood, but the pimpled warder, called to assist, said it was a common occurrence.

'It's the fear,' he said. 'Turns their bowels to water, the fear.'

I told him I was not accustomed to hearing such terms used so casually, and he was please to empty the receptacle, and sluice and replace it. He has done so, but the small enclosed room still stinks.

Esther is huddled on the narrow bed, and is pressing herself against the wall behind it. Her hair hangs down over her face, and she presents an unkempt appearance. Earlier I tried to tie back her hair and button up her gown, but she threw me off, and she has surprising and rather frightening strength for all she is such a thin frail creature.

A few moments ago she began calling out for her children, exactly as she is said to have done on the night she murdered them. I do not think I have ever heard anything quite so eerie as that cracked, faltering voice, calling for her children.

11.30 p.m.
Esther has sunk into an uneasy slumber, having had a further dose of Mr Porringer's opium mixture, which he brought to the door of the cell. Even so, there is a line of white under her eyelids, as if she is still watching everything.

I heard the fumbling footsteps outside again a short time ago, and when I looked towards the door, I believe a shadow showed through the small hatch, as if someone stood there.

The hangman, peering in at his prey . . .

TWENTY

Michael came out of Maria's journal to the realization that Deadlight Hall was no longer as silent as it had been. Soft footsteps were walking about overhead – slow, dragging steps, as if their owner was crippled. He looked across at the stairs, trying to quell his racing heartbeat. Had something moved there – had something shuffled in an ungainly way across the top landing, casting a blurred, misshapen shadow as it went? Surely it was only the shifting light outside? His watch showed it to be six o'clock. He dialled Nell's numbers again, but both were still on voicemail. But he would give it until half-past, then he would see if there was another way out. There was sure to be a kitchen door – a former tradesman's entrance. The conscientious Jack Hurst would no doubt have locked that as well, but it would be worth trying. But Nell would have phoned back long before then. In the meantime, there was the rest of Maria's journal.

Wednesday 15th
3.00 a.m. Remarkably I have slept for a brief time. Esther does not seem to have stirred. She has six hours of life left.

5.00 a.m. A grey light is trickling in, and there are sounds beyond the room, suggesting people are abroad. Even so, they are moving quietly, and I remember that Mr Glaister said they try to keep an execution secret from the other prisoners.

7.00 a.m. A mug of tea and a wedge of bread and butter has just been brought to us. I have eaten and drunk gratefully, but Esther shook her head and refused to eat or drink.

The pimpled attendant glanced at me, as if for help, but I could find nothing to say. The normal remarks such as 'You must eat to keep up your strength' or 'You will feel better for some food' scarcely apply. It does not matter if she feels better, for soon she will be dead.

8.30 a.m. A few moments ago Mr Glaister himself looked in to ask if there was anything I needed. I thanked him, and said not. Indeed, I have been able to wash and tidy myself in a small washroom, to which the attendant took me after my own breakfast. I feel better and fresher for doing so – better armoured against what is ahead.

People are gathering in the passage outside the cell. Mr Porringer is with them – I can just see him. He has the pale cheeks and flushed nose that indicates he is, or is about to be, bilious. This is unfortunate and also annoying, because we cannot be coping with biliousness at such a time.

Esther has refused to get dressed, despite all my efforts to persuade her. She will not even wear shoes or stockings. I have tried again to tie back her hair, but she fought me off, clawing at my face, then retreated into a corner, wrapping thick coils of her hair around her neck. For a moment I feared she was trying to strangle herself with her own hair, in order to cheat the hangman, but then she stopped, and fell back on the bed.

Several times she has called for the children again, and I cannot find it in my heart to tell her that her children will never come to her again. For how can we know what may happen to the soul in its last moments, and how can I know if those two little ones may not be waiting for her, ready to forgive her?

It is ten minutes to nine o'clock, and the cell door is being unlocked. The time has come.

Governor's house: midday.
I write this still in a state of considerable shock, but it seems important to record it while it is still clear in my mind. Clear! May God help me, I do not think it will ever be anything other than clear to me for the rest of my life.

This is what happened.

With the clock showing ten minutes before nine, a small sad procession assembled immediately outside the condemned cell, in the narrow passageway

Two male warders took Esther Breadspear's arms, and bound them behind her back, using leather pinions. She submitted docilely enough, but she was barely able to stand – whether from terror or the opium draught, I have no idea – and they had to hold her up.

The chaplain was wearing plain black vestments, and he carried the Book of Common Prayer. Behind him was Mr Glaister, and two male warders, and there were three other gentlemen. One was clearly a doctor for he had a medical bag, and I heard later that another was from the newspapers, since it is customary for an official notice to appear in the newspapers of an execution, and that must be written from an actual witness's account. The other, I believe, was some official who was present in order to make a report of the proceedings. As they began to walk forward, I hesitated, not knowing quite what was expected of me at this stage. I did not want to interrupt the grim solemnity of the occasion, so I stepped quietly into line behind them.

Mr Glaister unlocked a door and a dull grey light filtered in. Esther seemed to flinch, whether from being faced with light after so many weeks in the windowless cell, or simply from fear, I could not tell.

The courtyard outside was stone-paved and rather ill-kept. Weeds grew through cracks in the stones. The execution block was some ten or twelve yards away – the short walk. The door of what Mr Glaister had called the execution shed was already open, and I could not help thinking that the word 'shed' was inappropriate, for it is a stone-built place, the stonework carved and weathered. Above the door were two of those carved stone faces – blow-cheeked cherubs with sculptured curls. I suppose they had originally been designed as benign – as serene, happy faces. But time had worn them, distorting their features. The lips of one had broken away, so that it appeared to be screaming silently through a lipless mouth, while the other one's eyes had chipped, making it seem as if the eyes had been partly removed. As we walked towards the open door, I could not help staring at these two faces – the screaming and the blind – and thinking that the twisted faces of two children were the last things Esther Breadspear should see as she walked to her execution.

The chaplain was intoning the words of the funeral service as we went – and no matter the crime, it must be a terrible thing to hear your own funeral service read.

At the words 'Ashes to ashes and dust to dust', Esther looked up and saw the stone creatures, and that was when she swooned in earnest. She had to be lifted and carried the rest of the way, and between them, the warders got her through the door. And there inside, waiting for her, was the sturdy figure of the hangman, his hands gloved – black and thick, exactly as I had imagined. His eyes displayed no emotion, although I suppose he has had to school himself not to do so. His assistant – a runty-looking youth – stood nearby.

The hangman – I dislike referring to him in such terms, but I never heard his name, and in fact would rather not know it – held a white canvas hood, rather like a large sugar bag. As he stepped forward I saw that immediately behind him was the outline of the trapdoor in the floor, with a massive lever rising up from it. I have always prided myself on my phlegmatic nature, but my heart began to beat uncomfortably fast, and when I glanced at Mr Porringer I saw he was the colour of a tallow candle.

A white line was painted on the trapdoor, and the warders carried Esther across and positioned her exactly on it. She was still barely able to stand, and someone murmured something about a chair. But as the hangman pulled the hood over her head, she seemed to straighten up, as if accepting what was to come, and squaring her shoulders to meet it. Moving quickly and smoothly, the hangman slid the thick rope over her head and adjusted it around her neck, paying particular attention to the placing of the massive knot.

The first chime of nine o'clock sounded, and Mr Glaister, standing next to me, said, very softly, 'It will be over by the last chime of nine.'

But it was not.

As the hangman threw the massive lever, the screech of the mechanism tore through that small room like the rasp of a nail on slate, and even from where I stood I felt the floor shiver.

The trapdoor moved slightly, as if something immensely heavy had jumped on to it. But it did not open. That is the thought that etched itself on my mind, and those are the words that have stayed with me. *It did not open.*

The woman on the trap raised her head slightly, as if trying to understand, or as if trying to see through the thick hood. The hangman shook his head as if angry or bewildered or both, dragged the lever back to its original place, and pressed hard, this time using both hands.

Again there was the shiver of movement, and a faint creak of old wood. But again the trapdoor remained closed.

Mr Glaister and the doctor both stepped forward then – there was some kind of hasty murmured discussion, which I could not hear. Behind me, Mr Porringer swayed slightly and pressed a hand to his lips, and I remember feeling a spurt of anger towards him, because it was scarcely the moment to display weakness. In a low, furious whisper, I said, 'If you are about to be ill, you had best go outside.'

He gulped and nodded, and I stepped back to open the door for him. He rushed out, his handkerchief to his mouth.

When I returned to the room, they had moved Esther off the trapdoor, and the men seemed to be conducting some kind of test. A thick plank had been lain across the trap, and the assistant was crawling around the edges, examining the hinges, tapping at the thick oak. The wood resonated slightly, with a dull hollow sound. The hangman himself was poring over what looked like a chart with weights and calculations on it. And all the while, the woman waiting to die stood between two warders, still blinded by the dreadful hood, but turning her head from side to side like an uncomprehending animal being led to the slaughterhouse. I am not an emotional woman, but I felt a deep pity for Esther Breadspear.

Then the executioner stepped back and nodded, and said something about 'Deeply regret' or 'Deeply distressed' and added, 'All is now in order.'

Mr Glaister, that good, kind gentleman, reached out to pat Esther's shoulder, and said, 'Soon you will be beyond all this, my dear.'

But she was not.

When they made the third attempt, something even more terrible happened. The trapdoor opened, and there was a dreadful cracking sound – the kind of crack that makes you wince and feel as if something deep and agonizing has wrenched at the base of your neck. Esther Breadspear gave a moan of pain, and it was then that I saw only half of the trap had opened. It had jerked the doomed woman into an ugly, uneven position, so that part of her was dangling over the execution pit, but the left side of her body was resting on the half of the door – the half that had not moved. She struggled and writhed frantically.

The hangman dragged at the lever again, but the remaining door refused to open. Even from where I stood I saw sweat break

out on his brow, then the assistant ran over to him, and they put
their combined weight behind the task. Still the half of the door
did not move, and still Esther Breadspear writhed and moaned.

The hangman turned to the watchers, and put up his hands
in a gesture of panic, as if saying, 'Help me – I don't know
what to do.' He was visibly shaken, and his hands – those
dreadful gloved hands – were trembling. The assistant looked
as if he was about to faint.

Mr Glaister took over. He rapped out an order to the two
warders, who at once dropped a thick plank over the gaping
pit. By dint of standing on that and stretching out their arms,
they could reach Esther.

'Cut her down,' said Mr Glaister very sharply. 'Quickly now.'

The hangman said, uncertainly, 'Perhaps if she's left long
enough . . .'

'She isn't strangling,' put in the doctor. 'But she's badly
injured. Glaister is right. You must get her down.' He produced
some sort of surgical implement from his bag, and the warders
seized it and sawed through the thick rope. As the strands
parted, Esther fell prone, but even lying all anyhow on the
floor we could all see that her neck had been impossibly twisted
by the lopsided fall, and that one of her shoulders had been
wrenched askew, giving her body a warped, hunched shape.

Under the doctor's guidance, the warders carried her out,
and Mr Glaister looked towards me and said, 'Please to go
with her, if you would be so kind.'

And so we sat, Esther Breadspear and I, in that dreadful
cell, the pinions and the hood removed, and we waited to be
told what would happen next. Esther did not speak, and I could
think of nothing to say. The doctor spent a long time examining
her, and when he finally stepped back from the bed, he told
me that her spine had been severely twisted.

'Fatally?' asked the chaplain, who had followed us in, and
had tried to say a few ineffectual words about trusting in the
Lord's mercy until I glared at him and he relapsed into silence.

'No, not fatally, but I do not think it can be put right,' said
the doctor, frowning. He bent over the figure on the bed again,
then shook his head. 'It is beyond my medical knowledge to
pronounce exactly. As for her mind . . .' A shrug. 'I do not
think she has a mind any longer.'

He scarcely needed to say this. Esther was staring ahead of her with empty eyes, rinsed of all emotion and comprehension.

I have no idea how long it was before Mr Glaister came to us, because time no longer had any meaning in that room. When he appeared, the official gentleman was with him, and also Mr Augustus Breadspear, Esther's husband. To see Mr Breadspear was a shock, for it was said he had had nothing to do with his wife since the tragedy. I looked at Esther for a reaction, but there was only that dreadful blank stare.

Mr Glaister said, in a very gentle voice, 'We are faced with an extraordinarily difficult situation. This is something that happens so rarely, the law is not entirely clear as to the procedure we have to follow. And in light of the prisoner's severe injuries . . .' He frowned, then appeared to collect himself. 'This gentleman is from the Home Office,' he said. 'He is helping us to make a decision.'

The Home Office gentleman said, 'There is not exactly provision in the law for this kind of unfortunate eventuality, but there is something referred to as an Act of God. That is regarded as being the case when there have been three unsuccessful attempts at execution. It seems to me that this may apply here, although I should have to consult my superiors, of course.'

'If what has just happened is not an Act of God, I do not know what is,' put in the chaplain.

'And the prisoner is now clearly mad,' said the doctor.

'Mad people have been hanged before now,' said the Home Office gentleman. 'But . . .'

He looked at the doctor who, as if responding to a signal, said, 'She has certain injuries to the spine and neck.' He went on to use terms I had never heard, and although there was something about the vertebrae (I believe this to mean the spine) and something about damage – a fracture or dislocation – I am not recording any of what he said, since I may not have understood correctly.

What I do understand, however, is what the doctor said next.

'You may seek other opinions,' he said. 'Indeed, I think you should do so. But I believe any authorities you consult will agree with my findings.' He paused, and then said, 'It is my opinion that in view of the injuries caused during the bungled execution, it will no longer be physically possible to hang Esther Breadspear.'

TWENTY-ONE

Michael paused again. This was an appalling story to read in any situation or setting. Reading it in the semi-darkness, in this eerie old house, it was terrifying.

Maria's description of Esther, after the bungled hanging, having that warped, hunched shape fitted eerily with the image of the figure he had glimpsed on his first visit. But there could not be any connection between Esther and Deadlight Hall – or could there? What about the secret that Augustus Breadspear had laid on Maria Porringer?

He looked back at the doctor's statement. Had Maria got that right? Could a key vertebra have been so severely dislocated or fractured or misaligned that it really had made hanging impossible?

Darkness was creeping out from the corners of the hall, and the narrow windows on each side of the door showed hardly any light. Decisively, Michael jammed the small book into his pocket and set off on an exploration of the ground floor. He was not yet seriously considering breaking a window to get out, but he would at least see if there were any breakable windows – or even another door where he might snap the lock. Paying for the replacement of a window was beginning to look infinitely preferable to remaining here for a night.

The ground-floor windows could all be ruled out as escape routes. Even if Michael smashed one, the thin lead strips of lattice on all of them would make climbing out virtually impossible. What about the rear of the house though? Where were the sculleries, the larders? How did you get to the back of the house, for heaven's sake?

He had just made out a door at the far end, partly hidden by the curve of the stairs, when another sound disturbed the uneasy silence. Tapping – almost thudding. Michael froze, listening intently, trying to identify the source. The sounds were certainly coming from overhead – quite far overhead, he thought, because they were muffled and distant. He remembered that Jack Hurst had referred to something he had called water hammer – a large airlock in the pipes that made them judder. But would pipes judder unless someone had turned on a tap or flushed a cistern? Wild images of the resident ghosts reminding each other to nip along to the loo before setting out on their nightly haunting went through his mind – 'Because it's a cold night, and a long stretch of spooking ahead of us.' But for all he knew pipes might have a life of their own, and not require any human intervention to start banging and juddering by themselves.

But water hammer or not, he would see about getting out of here without any more delay, and the best place to start was the door at the back of the hall, which could lead to servants' quarters or sculleries. Michael tried the handle, and although it screeched like a tortured soul, the door swung inwards.

There was a tiny stone landing immediately beyond, and then a flight of worn stone steps leading down. Michael went down the first two steps, but the darkness was so thick he could not see anything, and there was no handrail of any kind. Even if he could get to the foot of these steps without breaking his ankle or worse, he certainly would not be able to find his way around down there. He swore, and came back into the hall and the window seat, and he was just thinking he would try Nell again when his phone rang. He had been hoping to hear it, but it was startlingly loud in the quiet house, and Michael jumped.

It was Nell.

'Thank God to hear your voice,' said Michael.

'What on earth's happened? I was collecting Beth from an after-school music lesson, so I've only just got your message. It was a bit fuzzy – something about being stuck at Deadlight Hall.'

'I am stuck,' said Michael. 'I'm bloody locked in. I'll explain properly later, but Nell, can you possibly track down Jack Hurst and get a key to let me out? I've tried his number, and it's on voicemail until Monday.'

'I think I've got a home number for him,' said Nell. 'Godfrey gave it to me for the work on the shop. Hold on—' There was a rustle of papers and Michael visualized her sitting at her desk in Quire Court, rifling her notes.

'Here it is,' she said. 'It's a landline – is that the one you tried?'

'No, a mobile.'

'OK, ring off and I'll try to get him on this number now. No point in wasting your phone battery. I'll call straight back.'

She rang off and Michael sat in the hall. The bouts of thudding were coming in batches now – a run of them, then a break. But nothing else seemed to be happening. He began to work out how long it would take for Nell to reach Jack Hurst, and for Hurst to drive out here with the keys. Supposing Hurst was not at home? Supposing the keys had to be collected from somewhere on the other side of the county? Supposing . . .

The phone rang again, and Nell said, 'Sorry it took so long, but it's all fixed. I got Jack's wife – he's had to go out to an emergency job, but she rang the house where he'd gone and explained, and he'll be here as soon as he can with the keys.'

'Well, thank goodness for that.'

'She was very apologetic and so was he, apparently. He's usually very careful about checking the house before they lock up, but he got this call about somebody's leaking water tank, so he went off in a bit of a scramble.'

'And to be fair, he didn't realize I was here,' said Michael.

'No. He's still at the emergency though, so he'll be at least forty minutes. He'll have to go back home to actually get the keys first. Will you be all right?'

Michael, closing his mind to the thuds and the drifting shadow, said he would be fine.

'But,' said Nell, 'I'll bet Jack Hurst's forty minutes is more likely to be nearer an hour.' She named a village on the other side of Oxford.

'At least an hour,' said Michael, trying not to sound dismayed.

'Yes, so listen, I'll drive out there now and see if there's any way in from outside.'

'There isn't. Nell, there's no need for you to drag yourself all the way out here.'

'No, but I'd be company. I can wave through a window to you, or sit on the front step and make rude gestures,' said Nell.

The thought of having Nell on the other side of the door was almost irresistible, but Michael did not want her coming out here. He said, 'What about Beth? You can't leave her on her own, and I don't think you should bring her. It's not a very good place for a child.'

He did not say it was probably not a very good place for Nell either, but Nell said, 'Beth can spend an hour with Godfrey Purbles. He's got some Victorian children's games in, which he's just found, and he wants her to see them. Beth's keen to see them, as well, so they'll both be pleased. Stay put, Michael darling, and I'll be with you before you know it.'

It felt abruptly lonely after Nell rang off. Michael looked at his watch, and tried to think that she would be here before it reached half-past seven, and that Jack Hurst would probably be here with the keys before it was showing quarter to eight. Once home, he and Nell might have supper at Quire Court – they could pick up some food – and he would show her Maria's journal.

The journal was still in his pocket. Would it be better or worse to finish reading it while he waited? It might prove so interesting he would not notice the time or hear any strange sounds. On the other hand, it might kick-start his imagination into conjuring up a whole new raft of macabre visions.

Instead he opened his own notebook with the idea of scribbling down a few ideas for the Wilberforce Histories. Having dealt with the Elizabethan Wilberforce, it might be as well to skip over the complex and often gruesome religious brangles of the next few decades, and move on to the Civil War, although Michael thought he would leapfrog over Charles I's beheading. But there was no reason why the seventeenth-century Wilberforce could not don a dashing Royalist outfit, and even partake in one or two roistering adventures with the exiled Charles II. Michael wrote this down, then sketched out a scene in which Wilberforce rode into London with the restored King and had a popular song written, detailing his brave exploits. He considered this last possibility, then crossed it out, because his energetic editor would probably leap on the idea and demand the song itself, complete with the music, and might even harry the publicity department into putting out a CD. Michael did not think he was equal to writing a semi-pop, semi-Restoration jingle, so instead he drafted a later scene depicting the Fire of London, which Wilberforce was instrumental in helping to subdue. 'And Master Wilberforce organized chains of men with buckets of water from the River Thames itself.'

Having dealt with this, Wilberforce next assisted Samuel Pepys to disinter the cheeses Pepys had buried in his garden to preserve them from the fire's ravagings, after which the two of them went on to eat oranges with Nell Gwynne. Re-reading this, Michael deleted Nell Gwynne, whose robust way of life might be thought a bit too colourful for seven- and eight-year-olds.

He closed the notebook. It was just on seven. Would it hurt to glance at Maria's journal again? It might even provide one or two answers to the Hall's strangeness, and those answers might be reassuring. He would scan a few more pages, and if anything started to be eerie – if Maria Porringer showed signs of developing a taste for lacing her narrative with the macabre – he would close the book and return to Wilberforce.

The journal resumed its tale two days after the macabre attempts to execute Esther, and the first pages had been written in Porringer's shop.

Friday 18th
11.00. a.m.

This has been a difficult time for everyone, and I think it will continue to be.

I had intended this to be a record of the execution of Esther Breadspear, and of my own part in the event. (Also, of course, of Mr Porringer.)

However, in light of the bizarre and macabre happenings in the condemned cell, I now feel it would be prudent to set down a proper account of the aftermath. People gossip, tongues wag, and although I do not intend this report to be made known in any general way, I think it prudent to have an honest record of everything, against any future accusations.

Mr Porringer and I returned to our own house yesterday. As he said, business was business, and we had our customers to consider. As I write this, he is in the shop, weighing out pills and potions. He is not bustling around quite as briskly as usual, and his nose has the strawberry hue which is always an indication that his digestion is severely upset. Not that it can be wondered. He has eaten nothing save a little bread and milk for the last twenty-four hours.

I am in the parlour, awaiting a visit from Mr Augustus Breadspear, who has requested a private interview.

3.30 p.m.

I do not know what I had expected from Mr Breadspear's visit, but it was certainly not the proposal he outlined to me.

He admitted that his plan would not have been possible if the prison were not being transferred to a larger, more modern building on the other side of the county.

'And I don't object to telling you, Mrs Porringer, that I have made substantial contributions to the Prison Reform Society,' he said, linking his fat fingers together and regarding me. He has a pudgy face and small, rather mean eyes, but he is a well-respected businessman, and his company at Salamander House thought most prosperous. 'As a consequence of which, the prison authorities – including the good Mr Glaister – are inclined to look favourably on any request I make.'

In short, it seems that Mr Breadspear is to purchase Deadlight Hall. I suppose a very large sum of money must be involved, but Esther Breadspear's fortune will now be completely in his control. Everyone knows that Esther's father, a shrewd gentleman, tied up his daughter's money in some kind of Trust, with a great many restrictions written into it. I imagine none of those apply any longer.

Mr Breadspear intends to turn Deadlight Hall into a small orphanage, which I dare say is a very praiseworthy thing, and in addition will create what he calls an Apprentice House – a place where young people learning their trade can live. This, too, is worthy and will be useful, for Mr Breadspear himself takes a good many young apprentices into Salamander House, and there are other manufactories and organizations in this area that do the same.

He has asked me if I will take on the post of housekeeper and general manager at Deadlight Hall. He feels I would be reliable and efficient.

'And discreet,' he said, looking at me very intently.

Not betraying my surprise, I said, 'I believe I could be interested. If circumstances were favourable.'

'I should make them favourable,' said Mr Breadspear. 'You would not be the loser, Mrs Porringer. But there is one extremely important condition, and it would be a private – a very private – arrangement between us.'

'Well?'

'Within the household of Deadlight Hall I want a locked room – a completely private place of security set as far apart from the household as possible. No one must know of its existence. That means that whoever undertakes the post of manager and housekeeper will be responsible for overseeing the creation of such a room.'

'And who would it be intended for, this room?' I asked.

He took a moment to answer, and I had the impression that he was choosing his words very carefully. He is not what I would call an educated man, but he has learned most of the trappings of gentlemanly behaviour and speech along the way.

He said, 'An order has been made for my wife to be deported. The colonies – Australia, I think. But I'm not prepared to let that happen.'

Now, in most men those words would have indicated a protectiveness – a determination to shield a loved one from a dreadful future. In Augustus Breadspear they indicated something very different indeed. His whole expression shifted and altered, so that it was as if someone else looked out through his eyes. Someone who was cruel and vindictive and bent on a very particular kind of revenge.

'But surely you can't do anything to stop it,' I said.

'Oh, can't I indeed?' He made the gesture of rubbing his thumb and forefinger together. 'Wheels can be oiled,' he said. 'People in certain positions can be persuaded to bend rules.'

I stared at him. 'You are saying you could – you would – pay people to ensure that instead of Mrs Breadspear being deported, she is released into your care.'

Even as I said it I could hear how incredible it sounded, but he instantly said, 'Yes, exactly that. She will not be put on board that convict ship. As for where she goes when she is placed in my hands – well, I can't keep her in my own house, of course. For one thing the arrangement of the rooms makes it impossible to provide the necessary accommodation for her. She would be seen – and heard. For another thing – to be frank with you, I can't bear the prospect of having her under my own roof.' He made a gesture of repulsion. 'She is the woman who brutally killed her two children and mine. But her wits are in shreds, as we both know. And,' he said, assuming an air of piety, 'she is my wife, and I feel an obligation.'

'And so you want to put her in Deadlight Hall?' I said, bluntly. 'As a hidden prisoner?'

'I do.' His eyes gleamed and he said, 'I prefer to have her under my own control.' His lips twisted in an unpleasant smile, and again that other person showed. 'A hidden prisoner,' he said, half to himself.

'But you referred to young people being at Deadlight Hall. Children with no parents – or parents who did not want them. Young apprentices from the various manufactories.'

'Yes?'

'Wouldn't there be danger?' I said, in a lowered voice. 'From – from your wife?'

'Not if she were kept properly secured.' Again I heard and sensed the 'otherness' behind the words. In that moment I believe I understood him, and I saw that he actually wanted his wife to be within tantalizing reach of children – not because he wanted the children hurt in any way, but because he believed it would add another layer of cruelty and punishment to his wife's captivity.

Then, in an ordinary voice, he said, 'Such an arrangement would have to be reliant on certain things. As I said, I need to employ some suitable person as a keeper – ideally someone with a little medical knowledge—'

'It would be a residential post, I take it?' I asked.

'It would have to be,' he said. 'And I appreciate that as a married lady that might pose a difficulty. But for the right person, I am prepared to pay very handsomely.'

We looked at one another. Then I said, 'I think something might be arranged.'

But this is a situation that requires careful thought. I will certainly accept that Mr Breadspear can, as he calls it, oil the wheels and that he has – or will – persuade certain people to let his wife go. I suppose there will be some sort of plan by which it will appear she has been put on to a convict ship. In reality, though, she will never go aboard. She will remain here.

It is Breadspear's own behaviour and manner that disturbs me. In particular, that moment when he said, 'I prefer to have her under my control.'

I am convinced that Augustus Breadspear wants to witness as much as possible of his wife's captivity and her suffering. What is worse, I believe he will enjoy witnessing it.

But in his own words he is prepared to pay handsomely.

Michael leaned his head back against the latticed window, his mind tumbling with images. So they had brought Esther to Deadlight

Hall, and they had imprisoned her in the attics. It had been a twisted punishment on Breadspear's part, and on Maria's . . .

On Maria's part, what? Greed, most likely.

He glanced back at some of the entries, and it occurred to him that Thaddeus Porringer had died rather conveniently. Had Maria been behind that? She had certainly recorded buying half a grain of arsenic in the Poison Book.

He flipped over to the next page. Here, indeed, was a note of Thaddeus Porringer's death, with Maria writing that in view of the sad demise of her beloved husband and the looming loss of the shop that had been his life's work – which she feared was inevitable and imminent – she was accepting Mr Breadspear's offer of work, and glad to do so. There were cousins who might take on the business, she wrote, but it was no longer her concern what happened to the place.

Most of her entries were undated, other than an occasional reference to it being Thursday 12th, or Monday 16th, or sometimes the time of day, but a brief time appeared to have elapsed before her next entry.

This was a list of work done by various tradesmen in Deadlight Hall, along with the costs, and dates the accounts were paid. Had that all been for rooms in the attics for Esther? Yes, of course.

A later page had details of the children placed in the Hall – the majority seemed to have been bastards of the local gentry, which Michael had already picked up from the material in the Archives Offices. He hoped the journal was not going to degenerate into a dry account book. He did not much like what he knew of Maria Porringer, but it could not be denied that she had an energetic way of setting down her exploits, and she sounded very organized and efficient.

He was glad to see she seemed to have thought it prudent to set down some of the daily routines she had instigated at the Hall. For, as she wrote:

> People are not always to be trusted, and at some time in the future I may find it valuable to have a record of my work.
>
> So, for that reason, I will detail how I take the prisoner's meals to her myself – collecting a tray from the kitchen, and carrying it up to the attic floor. Breakfast, midday dinner, and a light supper. It is plain fare we have here – such children as

are being housed do not, I consider, require anything more. The prisoner has the same.

Twice a day I collect the tray and each morning I leave a jug of warm water and a towel for washing purposes. I am firm about this last, cleanliness being next to Godliness, but despite that a sickly, stale smell is starting to pervade the room.

Each morning I also deal with the commode. It is menial work, even degrading, but Mr Breadspear is paying, as he promised, handsomely, and I make no doubt that I shall find other ways to increase the sums he pays.

I often write in this journal in the small room adjoining the prisoner's. I leave her door slightly open at these times. Mr Breadspear had wanted chains at the onset, but I had stood firm against that, not wanting to chain up any human creature as if a wild animal. But twice now the prisoner has somehow managed to break out, and has roamed the upper rooms, calling for the children to come to her. That was not something that could be allowed or risked, so I agreed to Mr Breadspear's demand – although I suggested an extra payment for all the trouble and inconvenience. I did so perfectly politely, since it is not necessary to bludgeon people with demands. He paid, albeit grudgingly.

However, he was right to suggest chains, for the prisoner is now clearly completely insane. There are times when a wild look comes into her eyes, and when she glares at me and tries to claw at me. I am very glad of the chains at those times – they are of carefully judged length, and she cannot reach me. If she starts howling I simply close the door and go down to my own room on the second floor. If it were not for my sleeping mixture I should be kept awake for hours by her mewlings on those nights.

The children are not permitted past the first floor, and they know that severe punishments will be meted out to those who disobey. So I have no real worries that they will venture up to the attics, or that anyone will hear anything.

Other than the occasional bout of frenzy, the prisoner sits with her hands folded in her lap – sometimes she stands in one corner of the attic room, in that dreadful hunched-over position caused by the bungled execution. I have taken up a few old books for her – simple ones, even children's books, which she might be able to understand – but she is uninterested in them. She stares at nothing, or at her own hands. If I am in the adjoining room, she watches me. It is unnerving, that unblinking stare. At other times she calls for her children, wanting to find them, telling them she will do so in the end.

At those times I close my journal, put it in the pocket of my gown, and lock the attic rooms and go downstairs.

Michael was just thinking Nell would be here any minute – it was half-past seven – when his phone rang again.

'I'm not far away,' said Nell. 'But there's a bit of a hold-up just outside Oxford – some idiot's run into the back of another car, and it's created a bottleneck. We've been crawling along at five miles an hour, and now the traffic's stopped altogether. Are you all right?'

'Never better.'

'Good. I left Beth immersed in Animal Grab and a jigsaw puzzle of Queen Victoria's coronation – both circa 1840, and in beautiful condition.'

'Nell, you really don't need to struggle through all that traffic, and if there's a hold-up—'

'No, it's fine – the road blocks are still in place, but the police are starting to wave cars through in single file, so they must have cleared part of the road. It looks a bit of a squeeze, but the cars in front seem to be managing. I'd better ring off – I'm fourth in line for the squeeze. After this I'd better get one of those hands-free phone kits for the car, hadn't I?'

Michael smiled, rang off, and returned to Maria Porringer.

TWENTY-TWO

The next entry seemed to have been written much later, and Michael saw at once that it was in an entirely different vein to the businesslike lists of costings and tradesmen's accounts. The writing was less careful, as well, as if some strong emotion had driven the writer. And yet it was difficult to associate Maria Porringer with any strong emotion.

He glanced through the tall window behind him. It was almost dark now, but there was still enough light to read. Nell would not be much longer, and Jack Hurst was on the way with the keys.

Earlier this evening I became aware of the children grouping together in the hall, as they have done several times lately. I went quietly along to the upper landing, and, taking care to keep to the shadows, but leaning over the banister as far as I dared, I listened. It is not a very appealing picture – that of the eavesdropper – but it is necessary to know what goes on.

The Wilger boy was there, of course – even crippled and maimed, he is still at the heart of any trouble – and several of the others were with him. It is still strange not to see the Mabbley girls among the children, and there has been no news of them. It is my belief they are bound for London, where I suppose they will eventually succumb to the lure of the disgraceful trade of the streets. Like mother, like daughters, and what is in the meat comes out in the gravy.

It was exactly the scene I had overlooked a few nights ago, but this time there seemed to be more purpose to it. I heard the Wilger boy say, 'Does everyone understand? At eleven o'clock we will meet here in the hall.'

They all nodded, then Douglas Wilger said, 'And we wait for the Silent Minute. If we do that, we shall be safe. We can't be caught or punished for anything done in those seconds of the Silent Minute.'

Something cold seemed to brush against my whole body, because I knew what the Silent Minute was. It's an old country superstition I was told as a girl. I thought it had been long since forgotten and lost, but here were these children knowing it – more than knowing it; making use of it against something they were planning to do.

The Silent Minute, the very stroke of midnight when the night hands over to the day – when the world takes a step from one realm of existence into another – when there is a gap between darkness and light, and when God walks the ragged edges of that strange place, to protect the soul from all evil . . .

'Remember,' Wilger was saying, 'in that minute we'll be protected from all evil. Nothing can hurt us.'

I do not believe the old superstition, of course. But the children believe it. They are planning something, and whatever it is, it is something so serious they are going to wait for the Silent Minute so it will protect them from the consequences.

10.55 p.m.

I am writing this in my own room. I have left the door slightly open so as to hear if anything happens. Perhaps nothing will, and it is all no more than some childish adventure or game. If so, there will have to be a punishment, for I cannot allow the children to rampage around the house during the night. Quite aside from it being bad for them to behave in such an unruly manner, there is the prisoner to be thought of. Secrecy must be preserved.

11.05 p.m.

I was wrong to write that nothing would happen. Doors are being furtively opened, and I can hear stealthy footsteps and the faint creak of a floorboard. I think the children are creeping down the stairs to the main hall. So I shall put this journal in my pocket and go downstairs. I shall not immediately confront them, though. I shall try to find out what they are about.

2.00 a.m.

I am not sure if I will be able to properly set down what has happened tonight. But I think I must try.

The hall, when I reached it, was in darkness. There are

gaslights in most of the house, and oil lamps in some places, but at this hour no lights were burning anywhere, of course.

The children were clustered together at the back of the hall, grouped around Douglas Wilger's wheelchair. They did not see me, and by keeping to the shadows, I was able to tiptoe to the front of the hall, and step into the concealment of the deep window by the front doors. Then one of them moved slightly, and I received a real shock, because there, bold as brass, were the two Mabbley girls.

Before I could recover from the surprise, they, along with four of the others, went up the stairs, moving as lightly and as swiftly as shadows. The remaining two boys lifted Wilger from his wheelchair, and carried him between them. He cannot walk up or down stairs for himself since he was injured in the fire, so the others take it in turns to carry him, and push the chair. As they went up, he was clutching their shoulders and his eyes shone like a malevolent imp.

I waited until I heard them reach the first floor and start the ascent to the second. I shall not say fear seized me at that point, but I was aware of growing concern. The prisoner had been restless earlier, murmuring about her children again, pacing the floor so that the chains slithered coldly on the bare boards. If the children were to hear her . . .

I crept up the stairs after them, pausing just before reaching the second floor. There is a curve in the stair, and by dint of standing there I could look through the banister posts and watch them. Douglas Wilger was set down and left half-sitting against the wall, while the others went along the corridor to my own room. I was glad to remember I had locked it, and that the key hung on the ring, clipped to my waist.

They did not need a key, though, because they had no intention of going into the room. Three of them seized a big blanket chest standing by the wall, and dragged it across the floor, positioning it across the door of my room. Rosie and Daisy Mabbley, working together, pulled out a large court cupboard that stands a little further along, and between them they pushed this against the blanket chest.

A barricade. They thought they had barricaded me into my room, and it was only by the purest good luck they had not done so.

By now I was more than concerned, I was frightened. And minutes later I knew it did not matter whether the prisoner howled like a banshee, because it was startlingly apparent that they knew she was there. How they knew, I have no idea, for I had taken such care, but know they did, and they were bounding up the attic stair, carrying young Wilger with them, and then hammering on the door of the inner attic room to get to her. The floor was reverberating with the sounds and the force of the blows, and through it the prisoner was screaming – terrible, trapped-hare screams that shivered throughout the whole house.

Then the children themselves began to shout, loudly and angrily, as if they no longer cared about being heard. And why should they? They believed I was safely behind the barricade, and unable to get out to them.

I heard one shout, 'You are a murderess.'

'We know what you did,' cried another.

'And we know what you still want to do.'

Douglas Wilger's voice rose above the rest. 'We're doing this to stop you doing to Rosie and Daisy what you did to your own children,' he screamed. 'We've all heard you, you murdering bitch. All those nights, calling to us to come to you – did you think we didn't know what you wanted!'

'You wanted us,' cried Rosie Mabbley. 'Daisy and me! You thought we were your own daughters come back from the dead. You wanted to kill us all over again.'

'We heard you – we know how you got out of your room when *she* was asleep,' shouted Daisy.

'When she's gin sodden,' said another of the girls.

'That's when you come prowling through the house looking for us,' cried Rosie.

This all came as an unpleasant shock, for I had no idea that the prisoner had ever done any such thing. (As for the accusation of gin, I should like it understood I only ever take a little nip last thing at night, and then as medicinal, and to sweeten the sleeping draught.)

There was one final massive blow, and the sound of wood splintering. Something fell on to the floor with a clang, and I realized they had smashed the padlock and they were in the prisoner's room.

You will admit, you who may one day be reading this, that

the only thing I could do was fetch help. I did not dare confront the children on my own – they were in the grip of something wild and savage, and they would have turned on me as greedily as they were turning on Esther Breadspear.

I crept back down the stairs, across the hall, and out through the main door. It had been locked and bolted for the night, but the keys were on the ring. I was as quiet as I could be in opening it. Once outside, I locked it again – perhaps I had some idea of making sure the children did not get out.

And now I had two choices – two people to whom I could go for help. One was Augustus Breadspear, who would certainly come out to the Hall and would most likely bring some of his household with him. But Salamander House was a fair distance – I am not a young woman and I did not think I could reach it before midnight.

What, then, of the other possibility?

I hesitated, glancing back at the house. A light flickered in the tiny attic window – the light of candles or an oil lamp, and as I looked, two small figures moved across it. It was God's guess and the devil's mercy as to what they intended to do to Esther Breadspear. But whatever it was, they would wait until midnight – until the twelfth chime, the Silent Minute – which meant I had perhaps half an hour.

There was really only one choice. Summoning up my energy, I set off as fast as I could towards the old carriage path. Towards Willow Bank Farm and John Hurst.

It was a terrible walk. There was very little light – thick clouds hid the moon, and there were flurries of thin, spiteful rain that whipped into my face. Twice I walked blindly into a hedge, and once I stumbled on an uneven piece of ground and almost went headlong, which is a shocking thing for a woman of my years.

As I ran through that bitter, stinging darkness, alongside the fear something ran with me – a knowledge so dreadful I hesitate to write it. But I will write it and I will write it here because it belongs to that part of the story. It was with me throughout that night.

Esther Breadspear was innocent of the murders. That is the knowledge that overshadowed everything as I ran towards Willow Bank Farm for help. She did not slaughter her two small daughters as everyone believed. She found their bodies

– she heard them cry out, and when she ran to their bedroom, they were already dead. But she did not kill them. I think she tried to revive them and when she failed, her mind splintered, and she ran screaming for help through the house, her night-gown soaked in blood.

When I learned of her innocence it was too late to help her, because by that time she was not just half mad, but completely so. What the discovery of her daughters' bodies began, the ordeal of the bungled execution completed.

I should never have known the truth if it had it not been for the gossipy tongue of the constable who came to the Hall to search for Rosie and Daisy Mabbley. He was more interested in lossicking in the kitchen and drinking tea than in making a search for the girls. I added a goodly slug of gin to his tea, I will admit, for I did not want him too alert during his search of the house. Perhaps it loosened his tongue that little bit more, because he boasted of the important arrests he had made – and of one in particular. That of a drunken vagrant, caught poaching on Sir George Buckle's land.

'Nasty, vicious piece of work,' said the constable. 'And will you believe this – he told me he was the one who had killed the two Breadspear children. Ah, I thought that would shock you.' He slurped more of his tea in drunken triumph. 'Perfectly true, though. Brazen as you like, he was, telling how he'd been angry at old man Breadspear for laying him off a month or so earlier and intended to have his revenge. Meant to kill Breadspear himself is my guess, but was so drunk he got into the wrong bedroom.' He took another swig. 'I never told anyone,' he said, righteously. 'The man was roaring drunk – he'd have denied the whole thing later, and I'd have been called a liar. Kind of thing that could ruin a man's career. And Esther Breadspear's long since gone – swung on the end of a rope, although there's some as say her old man got her away – money talks, don't it? – and that she was sent off to Australy. Can't bring her back whichever it was, so I shan't say anything.'

I had never said anything, either. The world believed Esther either hanged or deported to a penal colony, and for her to be brought back would have exposed the devil's pact I had entered into with Augustus Breadspear, and damned us both.

But the knowledge that she was innocent clamped itself

painfully around my mind that night as I struggled through the darkness to John Hurst. With it was the memory of Mr Glaister and the Home Office gentleman, on that bleak morning, talking about an Act of God intervening in the execution.

As I reached the end of the carriage path, the old church clock at St Bertelin's sounded the half-hour chime. Thirty minutes to midnight. I redoubled my efforts, and saw, with gratitude, the gates of Willow Bank Farm ahead of me.

I had not expected to see any lights burning, but there was an oblong of amber warmth in a downstairs room. When I hammered on the door he opened it almost at once, and I all but fell across the threshold.

I will say one thing for him – profligate and reprobate he may be, but he grasped the situation almost immediately, and was reaching for his jacket and a shotgun almost before I finished speaking. Then we were going back along the lanes, along the way I had come. He rapped out a few questions as we went; I answered them as best I could, but between fear and being out of breath, I was almost incoherent. But John Hurst nodded, and in the darkness I saw his jaw set firmly and angrily. As we reached the carriage road, the nearby church clock of St Berlin's began to chime midnight. Like a death knell ringing out in the lonely night.

Midnight. The Silent Minute.

'We're going to be too late,' I said, and he shook his head, although whether in anger or in refute of my words, I could not tell.

The chimes had died away by the time we reached the Hall. John Hurst was ahead of me, running up the stone steps. He swore when he realized the doors were locked, but I was already fumbling for the keys. We lost precious seconds, but finally the door swung open and Hurst bounded across the hall and up the stairs. I followed him, going as fast as I could, but I had to pause twice to regain my breath. I was not far behind him, though.

But long before either of us reached the attic floor we heard the sounds. Terrible sounds. A gasping wet choking. And a drumming, tapping sound. I struggled the rest of the way, and finally reached the top floor.

The inner door, the door to the prisoner's room, was open, and the heavy padlock lay on the ground. The flickering light from the candles lit by the children leapt and danced on the walls.

Esther Breadspear was hanging from a roof beam, a thick rope around her neck. The children had tried to do to her what the hangman had not managed. They had tried to hang this woman whom they believed was a killer of children. They must have wound the rope around her neck, looped it over the beam, then simply pulled on it to hoist her aloft.

And she was still alive. In those sickening, horror-filled minutes my conversation with Mr Glaister flashed back into my mind. The long drop, he had said, was used these days. Carefully calculated to bring about a quick, merciful snapping of the neck. So much kinder than the old 'short drop', which was little better than slow strangulation.

What was happening in the attic room was no merciful long drop. This was the old method, the ugly, protracted strangulation, with the victim struggling and writhing, gasping for air, and kicking frenziedly. Esther was fighting for air, her heels banging against the wall behind her, over and over again, as desperately as if she could kick her way back into life. One of the children had scraped back her hair, so that her face was exposed, and it was a terrible sight – suffused with crimson, the eyes bulging. Froth appeared on her lips and ran down her chin. Her shadow behind her, grossly magnified and grotesque, twisted and writhed along with her.

John Hurst pushed the children aside and reached up to the rope – there was a horrid echo of the scene I had witnessed in the execution shed.

Behind me, one of the children – a younger one – said in a scared voice, 'We thought she'd die at once.'

'In the Silent Minute,' said another.

'And so long as she died then, we couldn't be punished for killing her,' added Douglas.

'Get her down,' I said, trying to get free of the small hands that still held me. 'For pity's sake get her down.' The words *she is innocent* hovered on my lips, but I did not say them.

'Damn you, woman, I'm trying,' said Hurst, and added another oath. 'You,' he said to one of the boys, 'drag that table across so I can stand on it and reach her. Quickly.'

The boy, with a scared glance at me, did as he was bidden,

and Hurst climbed on to the table. Precious minutes ticked past, and Esther's struggles grew weaker.

Hurst reached up for the rope, and fought to free it from the beam. 'I can't do it,' he said. 'And the knot's too tight round her neck . . . Hell and damnation.' The fury and frustration in his voice was plain. 'How long has she been like this?' he said sharply.

'Since midnight,' said Douglas Wilger. He was trying to remain rebellious, but most of the defiance had drained away.

'And it's now . . .?'

'A quarter past,' I said.

'Dear God, she's slowly strangling to death. We'll have to cut her down. Get a knife, someone.'

I turned to the children, who would certainly be faster than I would. 'A good stout knife from the kitchens,' I said. 'A large bread knife – quick as you can.'

'Take one of the oil lamps,' said Hurst. 'You'll see your way better.'

One of the girls grabbed the nearer of the two lamps and scurried away.

With the loss of one of the lamps, the candle flames threw even more grotesque shapes across the attics. As they flickered, Esther gave a last convulsive jerk, knocking over one of the candles. A thin line of flame ran across the floor, and licked at the window. The wisp of curtain I had hung there to give the room a less cell-like appearance, flared up, lighting the attic to vivid life, but before I could get to it, Rosie Mabbley snatched the cloth from Esther's small table, and smothered the fire with it. One of the other girls stamped the tiny flames out on the floor. There was a smell of burnt cloth, and there were scorch marks across the floor, but nothing more.

It was then that Hurst said, 'I think it's too late,' and as he spoke, a wet bubbling sound came from Esther Breadspear's throat.

'Death rattle,' said Hurst, half to himself. 'But we'll keep trying.'

The girl who had run downstairs returned then, proffering two knives, both with sharp edges.

But again valuable minutes ticked away as John Hurst sawed at the thick tough rope constricting her neck. The strands parted reluctantly, but Esther was limp and still by that time.

'She's gone,' said Hurst, briefly. 'God have mercy on her soul.'

He caught her as she fell from the cut rope, and laid her on the ground, covering her with his own coat. Only then did he turn to the children.

Most of the mutinous anger had drained away, but when Hurst said, 'Between you, you have just committed murder. And I think at least two of you might be judged old enough to hang for it,' a spark of rebellion flared in one or two faces.

'We executed a murderer,' said Douglas Wilger, and again I had to fight not to speak out. 'And we shan't hang,' he said, thrusting out his lower lip stubbornly.

'The Silent Minute won't protect you, stupid boy!' said Hurst. 'It's nothing but a superstition, fit for credulous old women!'

'Not that. We shan't hang because you'll never tell anyone what happened here tonight.'

For a bad moment I thought the children were about to launch an attack on Hurst – and perhaps then turn on me – but they remained where they were.

'You had better explain that,' said Hurst. 'And you can do it here, within a few feet of that woman's body. I have no intention of shielding you from the ugliness – the brutality – of what you've done.'

'Yes, you will shield us,' said Douglas.

'Mind your manners,' I said at once, but Wilger was still looking at John Hurst.

'Of course you'll shield us,' he said, softly.

And in that moment, seeing them both staring at one another, I saw what I should have seen at the start. Douglas Wilger was John Hurst's son. The likeness was remarkable. Even the name was a clue – Wilger, or perhaps *wilge*, an old country word for willow – originally foreign, I believe. Mr Porringer had liked to know the old words for herbs and plants and suchlike, and I had learned some of them from him.

Hurst clearly knew who Douglas was. He had probably known all along, and that was behind his frequent visits to the Hall – and his help with the children's schooling. I remembered, as well, how vehement he had been against Mr Breadspear when Douglas was burned.

But clearly Hurst had not been aware that Douglas himself knew, and equally clearly the discovery disconcerted him. Then he made the gesture of squaring his shoulders as if to bear a sudden and very heavy weight.

'Very well,' he said. 'We both know who – and what – we are. But the immediate problem is with us in this room. Had you a plan in mind? For after the deed?'

'We had.'

'Also,' I put in, for I had no mind to be kept out of any of this, 'I should like to know about the presence of Rosie and Daisy Mabbley.'

'It's because of Rosie and Daisy that we did this,' said Douglas.

'Explain that,' said Hurst.

'She was after us,' said Rosie, with a glance towards Esther's body. 'She wanted to kill us like she killed her own children.'

'That's nonsense,' I said, sharply.

'We looked like them, you see,' put in Daisy. 'We had the same kind of hair as her little girls.'

'We used to lie in our beds and hear her,' said Rosie.

'You can't have done.' But I remembered how Esther would call incessantly for her murdered children.

'We all heard her,' put in another of the girls, and Douglas nodded.

'*Children, where are you?* That's what she used to whisper,' said Rosie. '*Children, I'll find you in the end* . . . So we ran away before she could catch us.'

'In stories, children always run away from the wicked old witch who wants to eat them up,' said the small Daisy.

'Or the giant who wants to kill them,' said another girl, and I sent an angry look to John Hurst, because this was what came of filling up children's heads with fairy tales and nonsense.

'Where did you go?' asked Hurst.

'To our mother's cottage,' said Rosie. 'She let us hide there. She didn't know why we ran away – we said it was because of *her*.' This time the gesture was towards me. 'We said she was unkind and she made us work hard all day. Our mother said she could believe it,' said Rosie. 'And she thought we were hiding until we could go to London to make our fortune.'

'Where,' murmured John Hurst, 'the streets are, of course, paved with gold. Earth has not anything to show more fair.'

'That's what you told us,' nodded Daisy. 'That's why we

thought we'd go. Our mother's going to come with us. We're
going to make our fortunes.'

'May God pity me for what I said,' remarked Hurst.

'When you came looking for us, we hid in the loft of the
cottage,' said Daisy, looking at me again. 'You never guessed,
did you?'

'No.'

'None of us guessed anything,' said Hurst, getting to his
feet. 'But now we have to deal with what's happened tonight.'

Wilger said, with almost eagerness, 'You'll help us?'

Hurst looked at the boy who was his son for what seemed
to be a very long time. Then he said, 'You give me no
alternative.'

'And her?' Wilger sent me another of the spiky looks. 'We
can't risk her telling.'

John Hurst spoke slowly, as if he was considering each
word. 'I believe Mrs Porringer will not wish for a scandal,' he
said. 'It could, after all, ruin her future. No one would employ
her, of course. She might even face prison. Well, Mrs Porringer?'

I said, 'I shall keep your secrets.' I thought: may God forgive
me for the secret about Esther I already have to keep.

It was Hurst who carried Esther Breadspear's body down the
stairs, down to the hall. The children followed, Douglas Wilger
being carried, as usual. They were all silent – not exactly cowed,
for any group containing young Wilger would never be that, but
certainly prepared to do whatever they were told. I have to say
here that John Hurst was mainly responsible for that. I do not
approve of the man, but there is no denying he has an authority.

They laid Esther on the ground, near the window, still
covered with Hurst's jacket, then he and two of the boys went
down the steps to those grim underground rooms – the rooms
that once were cells, used for housing condemned prisoners,
including Esther herself.

St Bertelin's was chiming one o'clock when at last we heard
the dull roar of the furnace.

TWENTY-THREE

The sweep of car headlights outside the house pulled Michael out of Maria Porringer's grim, candlelit midnight, and into the present.

He knelt on the window seat and waved, and the headlights flashed, then Nell parked the car so that the lights shone on to the window. She got out, then went back into the car to switch to sidelights, and came up to the window.

'Can you hear me through all that glass and bits of lead?'

'Loud and clear,' said Michael. 'And I'm selfishly glad to see you.'

'So this is the nightmare mansion,' said Nell. 'It's a grim old place, isn't it? I feel like something out of one of those old horror films. The face at the window. Tod Slaughter?'

'Yes. It's a good film, but I could wish you hadn't reminded me of it at this minute. Thanks for tracking down Jack Hurst,' said Michael.

'He should be here with the keys soon. But,' observed Nell, stepping back to look up at the Hall's facade, 'this house looks as if it needs more than just keys to open its doors. Are you sure we don't need to chant a dark spell or read runic symbols? Or even dance round the bonfire reciting from Dr Dee's occult language?'

'What on earth . . .?'

'Elizabethan occultist,' said Nell, grinning. 'One of Elizabeth Tudor's favourites.'

'I know who he is, I just didn't know he had an occult language.'

'According to his journal he talked with angels. Although I believe that the original angelic language was lost when Adam was booted out of Paradise.'

Michael said, 'You know, you are still a constant source of surprise to me.'

'Oh good,' said Nell. She was still staring up at the house. 'Whatever language you use, it's still the nightmare mansion or the ogre's castle, isn't it? As if it might have been made from the ground-up blood and bones of an Englishman.'

'If so, we'd better forget Dee's angelic language, and recite one of those ancient High German things instead. "Bone to bone, marrow to marrow, flesh to flesh . . ."'

'Never mind ancient High German, I'm going to stand in the shelter of the main doors, because it's starting to rain,' said Nell. 'So—'

'What?' said Michael, as she broke off.

'I'm not sure, but . . . Michael, I can see a light right at the top of the house.'

'That's impossible,' said Michael, but he felt suddenly icy cold. They lit candles that night, he thought. The flames flickered on the walls as Esther Breadspear strangled to death – she kicked one over, and it burned part of the attic. But he said firmly, 'There can't be any lights. There's no electricity on – I've tried the switches. And there's no one else in the house.'

'Did you go up to the top floor?' said Nell.

'Yes, because I wanted to find a book I remembered seeing. It's quite a find as well – Maria Porringer's journal, and you'll be—'

'Did you light anything while you were there?' Nell interrupted. 'A lamp or candles?'

'There was nothing to light,' said Michael. 'And if there had been, there wouldn't have been anything to light it with. Why – what are you seeing?'

'I can't be sure,' she said, narrowing her eyes and looking up. 'But it looks like candlelight.' Her voice wavered suddenly. 'And Michael, it's getting stronger.'

'Stronger how?'

Nell said, 'As if something's caught fire.'

The next moments were blurred. Both Michael and Nell snatched their phones to tap out 999.

'The fire engine's on its way,' said Michael, who had got the call in first. 'Only—'

'Only it's got to come through the road block that held me up,' said Nell.

'Yes. And if there really is a fire—'

'Michael, don't go up there to investigate,' she said at once.

'That's the last thing I'm going to do. What I am going to do,' said Michael, 'is find something to smash a window and get out.'

He paused, as Nell's phone rang. She waved to him to wait, spoke for a moment, then said, 'It's Jack Hurst. His wife gave him my mobile number, and he's ringing to say he's about fifteen minutes away. I've told him we think there might be a bit of a fire.'

'What did he say?' Michael was watching the stair, praying not to see any wisps of smoke.

'He said, "Sodding duff electricals," and something about dismembering Darren on Monday morning. But I've given him your number and he's going to phone you and see if he can guide you through the basement to where you might be able to smash open a kitchen window or something.'

Michael's phone rang almost at once, and Jack Hurst's voice, horrified and slightly panic-stricken, fired questions. Was Dr Flint sure he was safe? That there was no smoke reaching the ground floor? No crackle of flames or smell of burning?'

'No,' said Michael. 'It might be nothing at all, but—'

'But we can't take the chance,' said Hurst.

'The fire brigade's on its way, but—'

'That bloody roadblock. Yes, I know. I'm stuck in it at the moment – they're letting single-file traffic through, but I'm in the big van so I might have trouble getting round. But the fire engine will find a way through, be sure of that.'

'Yes,' said Michael, who was not sure at all.

'And we can get you out. What I'll do, I'll guide you down to the basement – there's a garden door down there. It'll be locked – in fact we've never opened it because we've never needed to and we haven't got keys to it. But the top half is plain glass and if you can break that you should be able to climb through. Can you find a hammer or something? Those boys are sure to have left stuff lying around. I tell them time after time – "Tidy up as you go," I tell them, but do they take any notice? Do they buggery, excuse my swearing, Dr Flint.'

'Swear away,' said Michael. 'Hold on, I'll see if there's something I can use on the window. There's a bit more light now – Nell's parked so that her headlights are shining in.' He walked into the main downstairs rooms. 'Nothing yet,' he said. 'Paint brushes – they wouldn't be heavy enough . . . Oh, wait, there's a big old broom here. The handle should do it.'

'Good enough. Back to the hall, and there's a door set a bit back, near the stairs.'

'I tried that a while ago,' said Michael, 'but it was as dark as the devil's forehead, so I didn't dare investigate. But if Nell can move the car a bit more . . . Wait a minute, I'll tell her what we want.'

Nell was still at the window, and Michael explained, pointing towards the door.

'That sounds fine,' said Nell. 'Once I've got the car's lights lined up, I'll try to make my way round to the back so I can help you climb out.'

'Nell, it'll be pitch dark!'

'Michael, my love, did you think I'd drive out to a dark old house without a torch in the car?' She brandished a large torch.

'Well, all right. I'll go down the steps,' said Michael. 'I don't know if it's straight down the rabbit hole, though, or whether it's more a case of "Down, down, to hell, and say I sent thee thither".'

'No one but you would find an apt quotation at a moment like this.'

'I don't know about quotations, but I'm going to feel utterly ridiculous descending to hell clutching a broom.'

'They'd probably let you sweep it out,' said Nell. 'Michael . . .'

'Yes?'

'Be careful.'

Before he could respond, she had gone back to the car. The engine fired, and Nell reversed and then drove the car back towards the house. Michael waved and indicated to her to move slightly to the left. This time the lights fell directly across the door.

He waved again, and sent a thumbs-up sign. 'We're all set,' he said into the phone. 'I'm about to plumb the depths.'

The door opened again, with only a small protesting creak, and a smell of damp and decay breathed out.

'There's a flight of stone steps inside,' said Jack. 'And at the bottom are several small rooms, with the furnace room at the far end.'

The furnace room, thought Michael. They fired the furnace that night to burn Esther Breadspear's body.

He said, 'Yes, I can see the steps.'

'Go past the furnace room – you'll recognize it because it's got strips of iron over it and a round window. Then you should see the garden door. It leads to a small courtyard on the left of the house.'

The car headlights were doing a reasonable job of lighting the stone steps, and Michael, still clutching the broom, reached the foot without mishap.

'So far so good,' he said to Hurst. 'Are you still hearing me?'

'Yes, but you're a bit crackly. Listen, if the signal goes – and you're underground remember – all you've got to do is go along the passage as far as you can.'

'All right.'

A thick smell of damp and decay hung everywhere, but Michael would rather grope his way through this bad-smelling darkness than remain trapped in the hall with the threat of fire.

At the foot of the stairs was a narrow passageway with brackets along the wall where gaslights might once have been. It was a dismal place; the stones were leprous-looking, and there were puddles of oily condensation on the ground. Thick cobwebs trailed from the ceiling; Michael tried to avoid them, but several times they brushed his face, and he shuddered and swiped them away.

'Can you see the row of doors yet?' asked Hurst.

'Not yet . . . Oh, yes, I can now,' said Michael after a moment.

'Six rooms,' said Hurst. 'The furnace room's the seventh.'

Michael said, half to himself, 'It would be the seventh chamber. of course. The one containing Bluebeard's butchered wives.'

'Sorry? You're breaking up—'

'I think the signal's going,' said Michael, snapping back to reality. 'But I should be almost there now. Is there any sign of the fire engine yet?'

'No, but—' Hurst's friendly voice cut off and a thin whine emitted from the phone.

'Hell and damnation,' said Michael, and the enclosed space picked up his last words and spun them eerily around him. He cursed under his breath, thrust the phone into his pocket, and went cautiously along the stone passage.

Here were the six doors. Despite the need to get out, he was aware of a sudden compulsion to open each one. Why? his mind demanded. To see if there are any more sad, twisted wraiths wandering around? Or were you expecting to find a calendar scratched into the stones by some forgotten, unjustly incarcerated prisoner? Still, if the Count of Monte Cristo had been here, at least he would have been company for Bluebeard's wives.

He began to feel as if he had been groping his way through this bad-smelling darkness for a very long time – and clutching a broom, said his mind, wryly. But it was no longer quite as dark as it had been. Michael registered this with relief, because if light was trickling in it must mean he was almost at the door with the window.

Except there was something odd about the light. It was not the thin bluish light of outdoors; it was not moonlight or even the electrical beam from Nell's torch. It was a flickering light – dull and tinged with red as if something had bled into it . . .

For several panic-filled seconds Michael thought it was the fire – that it had spread down here – then logic kicked in, because the fire Nell had seen had been two – no, three – floors up. If it had somehow found its way down here, he would have heard it – smelled smoke at the very least.

Here was the furnace room. The seventh chamber. This was where that other Hurst had carried Esther's body, so that all evidence of his son's murder could be destroyed. It was extraordinarily sinister. Black and secret – banded by the thick strips of iron, and with the unblinking eye of the circular window set into the top half. The dull light seemed to be coming from inside it.

Michael stood up against the door, peering through the thick glass. The light was coming from inside – he could see a faint red haze. And a movement – two small figures with long hair . . .? Imagination surely. He tried the handle, but it did not move, and he was about to continue along the stone passage when he became aware of other sounds. Footsteps? No, the sounds were too rhythmic; they were more like water dripping, or even someone tapping lightly with a hammer. He listened, and with a dawning horror realized what he was hearing.

It was the slow, inexorable ticking of machinery heating up. After a moment, a new sound began: a slow, deep, grating noise, as if an old, forgotten mechanism was struggling into life. Michael could see the shape of the furnace now – black and massive. There was a gaping hole where there must once have been a round door. Inside, threads of scarlet were thickening into solid blocks of fierce heat. There was a dull roar from the corroded pipes, and a smell of hot iron. The furnace was firing. It could not be happening, but it was. In another moment it would roar into life.

Michael went swiftly down the passage, and with immense thankfulness saw ahead of him the door Jack Hurst had described. A triangle of torchlight showed beyond it, with Nell's face peering anxiously through the window.

The dull roaring was getting louder, and the scent of hot metal was filling up the passageway. Michael grabbed the broom firmly, and waved to Nell to stand clear. He brought the blunt handle of the broom smashing against the glass. It splintered at once, but nothing more, and he dealt it a second blow, then a third. Still the glass would not break completely, and by now he could hear the fire burning up, and the sound of something heavy crashing over. Pipework caving in?

He returned to the window and at the next attempt large splinters began to fall out. Michael plied the broom again, and this time most of the glass fell away. Behind him he could hear the fire roaring up, and the stone walls were flickering and glowing. Beating down panic, Michael knocked out the remaining shards, and Nell stepped back to the door, unwinding the thick woollen scarf she was wearing, and folding it over the rim, to pad any remaining fragments.

'Can you climb out?' she said, a bit breathlessly.

'It might have to be head-first, and you'll have to catch me. And it'll have to be quick – I think the fire's getting a stronger hold.'

It was not as easy as he had thought to get through the opening, but it was not as difficult as it might have been. He slithered to the ground, and took several grateful breaths of the clean cold night air. As he did so, there was a louder crash from the direction of the furnace room.

Nell grabbed his arm. 'Let's get clear of this. The fire engines are on the way – I heard the siren a few moments ago.'

As she spoke, Michael heard them, as well. 'I think the fire spread through the pipes or something,' he said, brushing splinters of glass off his jacket as they crossed a small courtyard. 'It's fired up an old furnace, and—' He stopped abruptly, staring at a little straggle of buildings on the other side of the small courtyard.

'Michael, come *on.*'

'No, wait. Look there. Those stone outbuildings.'

'What? Where?'

'The carvings over that door,' said Michael. 'Can I have the torch a moment?'

'Two downspouts carved as faces,' said Nell, as Michael directed the torch. 'A bit chipped and sort of sly and leery. Is it significant?'

'Oh yes,' said Michael, and half to himself, he said, '"Blow-cheeked cherubs. The lips of one had broken away, so that it appeared to be screaming silently through a lipless mouth, while the other one's eyes had chipped, making it seem as if the eyes had been partly removed. The screaming and the blind . . ." That's what she called them.'

'Who? Michael, what on earth . . .?'

'Maria Porringer,' he said, still staring at the carved stone faces. 'She was here. This was once a murderers' prison.' Seeing her expression, he said, 'It's all right, I'm not delirious or anything. I found Maria's journal, and it's all there. And,' he said, as they made their way back to the front of the house, 'if ever this house was going to be haunted, it would have to be haunted by Esther Breadspear. This is where they tried three times to hang her.'

Nell looked at him, but before she could say anything, the flashing lights of the fire engine sirens cut through the darkness.

They stood with Jack Hurst as the massive hoses directed powerful jets of water on to Deadlight Hall's upper floors.

Three more firefighters had snaked hoses around the side of the house, and had broken down the door through which Michael had made his exit.

'Everything's safe now, sir,' said the most senior of the men, coming up to give Jack Hurst an interim report. 'The fire was in the attic as you thought, but it had – well, in layman's terms, it had whooshed through some old pipes and burst into an old furnace room. That's pretty much ruined now. Burnt out almost entirely, I'm afraid – half of one wall's fallen in, and most of what's in there is charred to cinders. There'll be a more detailed investigation about the cause when everything's cooled – particularly if the owners are claiming on the insurance.'

'The owners won't do that,' said Jack Hurst.

'Are you sure?'

'Yes, I am sure. I'm the owner,' he said.

Michael glanced at Nell, and saw his own surprise mirrored in her expression.

Hurst said, 'What's your best guess on the cause of the fire?'

'Difficult to be exact,' said the fire officer. 'You've never had any kind of flame up there, have you?'

'Of course I haven't. No one but a complete idiot would have a naked flame up there.'

No one, thought Michael, but a group of frightened and bitter children, who lit candles so they could execute a murderess . . . Candles which were overturned as she fought for life . . .

'Dr Flint, I don't suppose you even went up there?' said the fire officer.

'No,' said Michael, unhesitatingly.

'There was that storm a couple of days back,' said the man, thoughtfully. 'Lightning can give an electrical charge to metal, so old plumbing can sometimes be vulnerable. It doesn't happen much nowadays, but in a house of this age . . . It's just about possible the lightning caused a small fire up there, and the fire smouldered for a couple of days. At the moment that's the best solution I can see. But we'll send a report to you. Everyone else all right? We can call the paramedics to get you checked out if need be?'

He glanced at Michael and Nell, and Michael said, 'No need for paramedics. I'm fine, thanks, and I'm very grateful to be safely outside. Thanks very much – to all of you.'

'All part of the service, sir,' said the man, who then sketched a mock salute, and went off to the waiting fire engine.

Michael said to Jack Hurst, 'I didn't realize you owned the place.'

'Yes. And I can't tell you how sorry I am about this.'

'I'm sorry about the house. I escaped unscathed, but it doesn't look as if Deadlight Hall has.' He glanced at the drenched facade.

'Oh, don't be sorry about the house,' said Hurst. 'This is the final straw if I'm honest. I'm abandoning the whole project.'

'You are?'

'I scraped and scrimped to buy this ugly old pile,' he said, staring up at it. 'I was sentimental about it, see. There's some connection to an ancestor of mine – bit of a wild boy from all the family stories. They vary a bit, those tales – some say he owned the place, some say he only lived in it, or that he used it for his bastards. Some versions even say he was part of some sort of murder scandal, about a century and a half ago. I don't know the truth and it's all a long time ago anyway, but I always felt an attachment to the place, and we're an acquisitive lot, us Hursts. Buying it became a bit of an ambition for me. I worked and saved, and worked some more, until I managed it. I got it for a song, and I thought I could make money out of turning it into posh apartments. Bad idea and very bad decision. It's an unlucky house – and it's not often you hear a builder say that. But there've been a few bad incidents there over the years – probably all hearsay again, but people have long memories.'

'What will you do with it?' asked Michael.

'Demolish it,' said Jack Hurst at once. 'Raze it to the ground and crunch it all up beneath the diggers and the bulldozers.'

'And then?'

'Develop the land,' he said, with a sudden grin. 'Standing here,

I've been thinking. I reckon I'd get half a dozen luxury bungalows on this site, each with a third of an acre of ground. And very nice too. You might like to take a look when they're done.'

'We might indeed,' said Michael.

As they walked over to their cars, Nell suddenly said, 'Michael – I think there's someone over there – in that bit of garden on the left.'

Michael looked to where she indicated. 'I can't see anything. Probably the firefighters are still around.'

'It isn't the firefighters,' said Nell. 'They're all round the vehicle, packing up their equipment. Whatever I saw was blurred, like one of those photographs when someone's moved as the shutters clicked, so I can't be sure I saw anything at all. It might only have been the trees moving in the wind.'

'Let's walk to the side of the house and see. We'll have to wait for the fire engine to move anyway before we can get the cars out.'

The house cast dense shadows on this side, but there was still an overspill from the fire engine's lights, and it was possible to see that tall weeds grew up between the cracks of what might once have been a terrace. There was the outline of what had been a large lawn on two levels, with moss-covered steps between the two, and a cracked sundial, covered with lichen. On a bright summer's afternoon, with cheerful voices, this could have been a lively, happy place. A family place, where children would have run free and enjoyed playing.

Children.

The two figures were indistinct – so much so that they could have been scribbled on the darkness by a child's pencil. It was not entirely certain if they were even there.

'It looks like two small girls,' said Nell, almost in a whisper. 'I can see their long hair.'

The girls could have been anywhere between six and ten years old, and they were moving away from the house, hand in hand, not exactly running, but not walking slowly. One of them looked back over her shoulder, and put up a hand. The gesture was so indistinct it could have been anything. But it could have been a gesture of farewell. Michael drew in a sharp breath, then sketched a similar gesture.

Behind them, the fire engine revved, its lights swung round, and the figures vanished.

'We did see that, didn't we?' said Nell, sounding slightly shaken.

'Yes.'

'They weren't . . . real children, were they?'

'No.'

'Who were they?'

'I could make a guess, but it'll be easier to tell you after you've read Maria's journal,' said Michael.

The fire engine was trundling down the drive, towards the main road, and as they went over to their cars, he said, 'Nell – about that journal I found. How would you feel about having the professor in on it? He started all this, so I think he'd like to know what we've found.'

'I'd like that. D'you think he'd be free to come to supper?' said Nell. 'But it's half-past eight already, so it'll have to be takeaway.'

'Bless you,' said Michael, smiling. 'I'll phone him now.'

Leo, listening to Michael's brief explanation, expressed himself as horrified to hear about the fire. Invited to Quire Court, he said he had not dined yet – he had been working on his Radcliffe lecture, and he had not noticed the time.

'But after what's happened tonight I don't want to cause Nell any trouble—'

'She'd like you to come. And,' said Michael, 'we're picking up supper on the way home so it won't be any trouble at all. Can you meet us at Quire Court in about an hour?'

'Yes, certainly.'

'And can you eat Chinese food?'

'I can indeed,' said Leo.

TWENTY-FOUR

They opted for Cantonese food in the end, and reached Quire Court laden with foil cartons. Leo arrived ten minutes later, bearing two bottles of wine – a Chablis and a good claret. There was also a bottle of some bright pink concoction which the professor had spotted in the wine shop and which he thought Beth might like.

'I love pink concoctions,' said Beth, who was being allowed an extra half hour before going off to bed, and who had no idea what the bottle contained. 'Thank you very much.'

'Don't spill any of it on Michael's notes,' said Nell.

But the Cantonese restaurant, with its customary attention to customers' comfort, had provided small, moist, sweet-scented paper napkins, which they shared out.

'It's beautifully hygienic,' said Michael. 'Pass me the crispy duck, Beth. We're going to provide Professor Rosendale with some information after you've gone to bed, so we're going to stoke up with food now. Then we'll tell him the tale, and we'll begin at the beginning—'

'And go on until you reach the end, then stop,' chanted Beth, delightedly.

'What an intelligent daughter you have,' said Leo, smiling at Nell. 'I didn't think anyone read *Alice in Wonderland* any longer.'

'Beth practically knows it by heart.'

'We'll have a competition on it one day, Beth, but I'll have to reread it beforehand, so I can keep up with you. Are there any more chicken wings? Let's divide them up, shall we?'

It was not until Beth, who Nell could see was entranced by Professor Rosendale, had been scooted up to bed, and Michael had refilled the wine glasses, that he commenced the story of Maria Porringer.

He had made some notes while they were eating, and he now gave Nell and Leo a précis of the journal.

'Extraordinary,' said Leo, when Michael reached the part where Esther's body had been cut down, and John Hurst had agreed to conceal the evidence.

'That's as far as I got,' said Michael. 'Then Nell turned up and the fire started, and everything was chaotic. I thought we'd read the last few pages now, but I think we'll simply find they burned her body in the old furnace.'

'You brought the journal with you?' said Leo.

'I did. I wasn't going to leave it there. And,' said Michael, taking the journal from his jacket pocket and setting it down on the table, 'it's a good thing I did, because it would either have been destroyed by fire or drenched to sodden illegibility by the firefighters.' He looked at Nell. 'It's written by a woman,' he said. 'So it's a woman's "voice".'

Nell stared at him, not immediately comprehending.

'I suspect Michael thinks it would sound better if you read it,' said Leo. 'I agree.'

'Well . . .'

'Please.'

Nell made a gesture of acceptance, and reached for the book.

'Her writing's very clear,' she said, after a moment. 'All right, here goes.' She reached out to tilt a small table lamp slightly nearer, then began to read the closing pages of Maria Porringer's journal.

It was John Hurst who carried Esther down to the stone corridors beneath the Hall, and along to the furnace room. I went with him, of course.

We had told the children to stay in the hall, and most of them did so. It was only as we went down the steps that I saw two small shadows behind me, and realized that Rosie and Daisy Mabbley had followed us.

'You are to go back upstairs at once,' I said, sharply.

'No,' said Rosie with defiance, and Daisy shook her head. 'We want to see that she's gone. We want to make sure she can't come back.'

'She was evil,' said Rosie. 'She killed her own children.'

'She chopped them up with a knife,' put in Daisy, her voice trembling.

'Dead people don't come back,' said Hurst, in an unexpectedly gentle voice. 'And although she did that wicked thing, her mind was sick – very sick.'

'Now do as you're told,' I said.

'You can't tell us what to do any longer.' Rosie again, of course, very mutinous. 'We don't live here now.'

'We're going to live in London with our mother,' affirmed Daisy.

'Let them come with us,' said Hurst, impatiently. 'It'll teach them a lesson if nothing else.'

So they came with us, walking down the steps and along the stone corridor. I had the oil lamp, and in fact it was useful to have the two girls with us, for Rosie was able to carry the second of the lamps.

We went past those silent rooms where condemned prisoners were once kept until their execution. Even to me it's a bad place – I do not accept that emotions can linger in a building, but since coming to live at Deadlight Hall, there have been times, walking along that corridor for some ordinary domestic reason, when I have felt the weight of those prisoners' fear and despair.

The furnace room is a dingy, dismal place, and if there had been any other means of heating I should have insisted that the furnace be ripped out by its roots, and the room closed off. But I do not think there was any other way, and as far as I could ever make out, the furnace and all its pipes are built into the structure of the building.

Hurst had fired the furnace effectively – I suspect he would be efficient at whatever he did – and it was roaring away, heat belching out, the scent of hot iron tainting the air. Scarlet fire showed all round the edges of the door.

Hurst laid Esther's body on the ground, then turned to face us. 'When I open that door, you two, Rosie and Daisy – and you, as well, Mrs Porringer – must stand well clear. The heat will be immense. You understand?'

We all nodded, and indeed I had already moved well away from the furnace, and was standing on one side of the door of the room, up against the wall. Hurst levered back the front cover, using the long hooked rod kept for the purpose. As it came open, heat poured out, blisteringly hot, so that my eyes felt scorched and my skin prickled.

'Quickly now,' said Hurst, bending to lift Esther. He glanced across at me. 'Mrs Porringer, we have no clergyman to speak the funeral service, but—'

I said, 'She has already had the funeral service. It was read during the procession to hang her – outside this very room, in fact. But,' I said, as his expression darkened, 'perhaps we should all say the Lord's Prayer, as a wish that the woman's soul will find repose.'

'And sanity and some peace,' said Hurst.

I began the prayer. Behind me, Rosie and Daisy drew closer together, and I saw them link hands. I cannot be sure that they joined in the prayer, but I think they did.

Hurst lifted Esther's body, and carried it to the furnace. His skin was flushed from the heat, and he was keeping his head slightly turned away from the open door.

As we reached the words 'forgive us our trespasses' he swung the body towards the furnace.

And Esther Breadspear opened her eyes.

It was too late to stop the momentum of the throw. Hurst had put all his force behind it – like a man throwing a ball at cricket – and that force had propelled Esther inexorably into the furnace. Hurst realized what was happening, and he also realized he was powerless to stop it. His face twisted with horror, but she was already tumbling into the depths of the furnace.

Someone had begun to scream, but I cannot say, even now, if it was Esther who screamed, or if I was screaming, or even if it was John Hurst.

In that moment the two girls rushed forward. They looked like small demons – lit by the flames, their hair tousled – and at first I thought they were following their earlier avowal – that they wanted to make sure she was dead and that they were now making sure she burned. Then I saw I was wrong. The reality of what was happening had hit them, and they were trying to do what neither I nor Hurst could – they were trying to save her. It was no use, of course, because they could not get near enough, but they tried to grab the woman, reaching for her with their small hands. Esther was probably dead already, from shock, if from nothing else. At least, that is what I tell myself.

John Hurst had backed into a corner, and was huddled there, his hands over his face, like a terrified child suffering from a nightmare. Somehow I managed to get him back up the stairs to my own room. I sent the children to their beds – a couple of the boys helped Douglas Wilger – telling them we would discuss this more in the morning.

Nothing I could say or do seemed to break through John Hurst's frozen horror, and I wondered if I should send for Dr Maguire – although what explanation I would have given I have no idea. I poured a glass of my own sleeping draught, and Hurst had just taken it from me when I realized that Rosie and Daisy had not been with the other children when they went off to their own rooms.

With that realization came another. Deep within the basement, the furnace was still thrumming.

I did not stop to think or reason. I ran from the room, down the main stairs, and down the narrow stone steps to the furnace room. Halfway down I heard Hurst coming after me, and I was aware of gratitude. As he caught me up, I saw that his eyes were sensible and clear, and I managed to gasp out an explanation. 'The two girls – Rosie and Daisy – I think they're still down here.'

He flinched, then said, 'Pray God you're wrong.'

But I was not wrong. They were both in there, standing up against the iron door – which was closed. They were beating on the round glass window with their small fists, and screaming for help, their faces wild with fear, their eyes wide and terrified. But they were silent screams, for the massive old door smothered their cries. That's another of the things that I believe will haunt me – those silent screams.

Behind them, the furnace was roaring up, and the black iron lid – the lid that I thought we had closed before leaving the room – was no longer in place. The fire belched out, uncontrolled and fierce, and the iron door, even from this side, was already almost too hot to touch. The open furnace was heating up the room.

John Hurst and I fought to get the door open, but it resisted all our efforts. It had jammed, or its lock had snapped – I do not know which, and it does not matter. The moment when I realized we could not reach those girls is one that will stay with me for the rest of my life.

We put everything we had into trying to get that door open, but it was all to no avail. Neither Hurst's greater strength nor my lesser, puny strength could free the lock. I remember he ran down to the scullery, and I heard him crashing into cupboards, ransacking the place for an implement that would force the door. He came back with chisels and knives and a couple of wooden mallets used for tenderizing meat. He tried everything; his hands were blistering from the heat of the door, and his hair was beaded with sweat.

'The only thing left is to try to smash the glass and help them climb through,' he said, and I nodded, and seized one of the mallets.

But the glass was fearsomely thick – intended to act as a barrier between the furnace's heat and the rest of the house – and the mallets were not designed for such a task. We barely managed to splinter the window's surface.

'They'll die,' I said, in despair. 'They'll roast alive.'

As I said the words, something seemed to huff malevolent breath on the furnace so that it roared up, like a fire will roar up inside a chimney when strong bellows are used on it.

The room became bathed in angry scarlet – I do know that sounds fantastical, but it is what happened. The screams did reach us then – but only for a few seconds. Then there was silence.

Nell laid down the journal for a moment, and reached for her wine.

'It's appalling,' said Michael, after a few moments.

'Yes. Those little girls – and that poor creature, Esther. But,' said Nell, 'did you pick up an odd crumb of actual humanity in Maria Porringer towards the end of it all?'

'Just a crumb or two,' said Michael. 'But she still kept Esther imprisoned, even when she knew she was innocent.'

'But what was the alternative by then?' said Nell. 'Esther was completely insane, poor woman. If they hadn't deported her, they'd have thrown her into one of those appalling Victorian asylums.'

'Professor?'

Leo was leaning back in his chair. His eyes were in shadow, and it was a moment before he spoke. Then he said, 'Those two girls . . .'

'I know,' said Nell at once. 'I can't bear it either.' She hesitated, then said, 'I think we saw them. As we were leaving the Hall tonight.'

'Two small girls, with long chestnut hair?' said Leo.

'Yes.' Nell looked at him in surprise. 'They were a bit blurred, but just for a moment they were there.'

'They were going away from the house,' said Michael. He was

looking at Leo, as well. 'Hand in hand – as if they were going quite freely and – well, almost happily.'

'One of them turned and put up a hand as if saying goodbye,' said Nell.

'I didn't know you'd seen that,' said Michael, turning to look at her.

'I didn't know you had, either.'

The moment lengthened. Nell thought: there's something behind this – something the professor hasn't told us. But perhaps it's something he doesn't want to tell us. With the idea of smoothing this over, she said, 'There's just a couple more pages of the journal – although I shouldn't think there's any more to tell.'

'Professor, are you all right to stay with this?' asked Michael, and Nell heard the note of concern in his voice and knew that he, too, had picked up that sudden spike of emotion when the professor had asked about the two small girls she and Michael had seen.

But Leo said, 'Of course I am. Please finish reading, Nell. But I'll have a half glass more wine, if I may?' He glanced at Michael. 'Yes, I am supposed to be driving back to College,' he said. 'But if necessary I'll call a taxi and leave the car here. I think my reputation will allow me this one gaudy night. Let's finish the journal and wind up the spell.'

Maria wrote in the last pages:

> Today I came to Deadlight Hall for the last time. I cannot say why I did so, for I am not given to sentimentality or emotional farewells. There was no reason for me to enter the house ever again. It is closed up – the children gone to different homes and different employers. Even the Wilger boy has found a home – one of John Hurst's cousins, so I hear, and Douglas will help with the writing of letters and keeping of accounts.
>
> It was strange to walk through the village again this morning, and to see our old shop. A distant cousin of Mr Porringer's took it over – the name is still over the door, which Mr Porringer would be glad to see. As to the cousin, I make no comment, but most of the men in that family were sadly weak.
>
> I had expected Deadlight Hall to be deserted and empty, but as I reached the courtyard I saw someone was ahead of me. A thin rain was falling – I had needed my umbrella – and

there were wet footprints on the steps leading up to the front door. My heart began to beat faster. The main doors were slightly ajar, and after a moment I pushed them wide and went inside.

The hall was dim and silent, but the house did not feel empty. Standing there I had the strong impression that someone watched me – someone who crouched on the stairs in a twisted, hunched-over way, and someone who had walked these rooms, calling for the children.

With the thought, a faint soft whisper formed on the silence. *'Children, are you here?'*

She's still here, I thought in horror. Esther Breadspear, who it was believed butchered her two young daughters, and who cheated the hangman – not once, but three times. No, four times in all. Thrice in the execution shed, and once again in the attics.

I do not believe in ghosts – I should like that understood by anyone who ever reads this. But if ever a soul had cause to haunt, then surely that is Esther.

The line of damp footprints went across the hall and up the main stairs. There was no reason why I should follow them. If someone was here, it was none of my business, not now, not ever.

But I went quietly up the stairs to the first floor. As I reached it, the whisper came again, and with it, the sound of someone struggling to breathe. Esther, I thought. Strangled on the end of a rope.

You will think, you who may one day read this, that a prudent woman would have gone back down the stairs, and out into the safe, rain-scented gardens. But I needed to know, you see. I needed to be reassured as to what was in here. And ghosts, surely, do not leave wet footprints.

The prints continued to the second floor, then along to the narrow attic stair. They were drying and fading, but they were leading to the attics.

It was as I approached the attic stairs that I heard the sounds, and cold fear closed round my heart, for I had heard those sounds before – I had heard them on the night the children tried to hang Esther Breadspear. It was the sound of her heels drumming against the walls as she twisted and struggled and half strangled to death.

I called out, 'Hello? Is someone here?'

The rhythmic sounds increased – they became frenzied. I said, 'Esther?' and the old house picked up the word and spun it mockingly around my head.

There was faint candlelight now, and as I stepped on to the attic floor, I saw the shadow that danced grotesquely against the wall. I knew it at once for what it was. And I knew who it was who danced and struggled. Not Esther, this time – not even a poor sad remnant of her – but a living person. A human being who could no longer live with the knowledge of what he had done – that he had burned another human creature alive and in the wake of that, two small girls had also died. A man who had come to the place where it happened, to end his own life.

John Hurst, hanging by candlelight from the same roof beam where the children had tried to hang Esther, writhing and squirming, and slowly strangling to death.

I tried to get him down – I really did. I climbed on to the table – the very table he himself had used when trying to free Esther – and I tore my fingernails to bleeding shreds in an attempt to loosen the rope.

But the rope was too thick and the knots too firm. As for lifting him – he was a well-built man, tall and muscular, and I am well beyond my youth. I climbed down and I ran all the way down to the sculleries, my heart pounding, praying to find a knife. But there was nothing. When Deadlight Hall was closed, its contents were cleared out, and there was nothing anywhere that I could use.

He is not yet dead. I am sitting here, in the small room where once I kept watch on Esther, writing in my old journal, and he still struggles and writhes in front of me.

A moment ago the momentum of his frantic struggles brought his body jerking around to face me, and the blood-flecked eyes stared into mine.

I cannot do anything for him, but I shall stay here with him until he dies. I do not know if he realizes I am here, but I shall not leave him.

Later

It is over at last. He is dead. I shall not cry, for tears are of no use to anyone.

I shall never know whether he killed himself from remorse or as atonement for what happened to Esther Breadspear and the Mabbley girls, or whether . . .

Or whether the rest of the children were watching him, and followed him out here – perhaps even lured him here with some message. And once he was here, they killed him – either to stop him from incriminating them, or because of what happened to Rosie and Daisy.

There is one more thing I can do for him, though. I can make sure that his death is regarded as suicide, and that if the children were his killers, they are not suspected. This, I know, is what he would want, especially for his son, Douglas, who will live on in the area.

There is so much shame surrounding a suicide, but I do not think that John – I will call him by the name I always used for him in my mind – I do not think that John will care for that.

So I have written a note purporting to come from him – I think I have made a fair job of forging his hand, and I do not think it will be questioned.

I have not referred to any of the deaths, of course – Polly Mabbley's cottage is shut up, and as far as anyone hereabouts knows, she and her two daughters went off to London one night, as she had so often said they would. People can continue to believe that.

In the note I have simply said it is impossible to face the burden of debt any longer, and for that reason, he is ending his life. I have no idea of his financial situation, but I feel this is as acceptable a reason as any. I shall place the note in the pocket of his coat. It may be a while before the body is found, but I cannot help that. It will be found in the end, and the note with it.

I want no involvement in any of it, though. I know the truth and the secrets, but cannot see that revealing them will do any good to anyone.

It is all done. And now I have given way to the stupid painful tears for the man who had been irrepressible and ungodly and whom I shall never forget.

Signed, *Maria Porringer.*

TWENTY-FIVE

'So,' said Nell at last, 'that's what happened. It's a remarkable story.'

'Yes.' Michael was looking at Leo.

Leo's eyes were still in shadow, but at Michael's words, he seemed to recollect his surroundings.

He said, 'I think this is the time when I tell you my own part in Deadlight Hall's history.'

'If you felt you could do that, it wouldn't go any further,' said Nell, and he smiled at her.

'I know that.' A small frown of concentration touched his brow, as if he was assembling his thoughts, then he said, 'It's a long story, though, so I shall have to begin right at the beginning.' He smiled at Nell. 'And follow Beth's maxim to go on until I reach the end.'

'Good enough.'

'It began when I came to England, when I was six,' said Leo. 'When I and a group of other children were smuggled out of Poland by a man we knew as Schönbrunn.'

Nell, listening to him, watching the play of expressions and emotions on his face as he spoke, heard – and knew Michael would be hearing – the deep sadness behind his words. He spoke concisely and well – she supposed this was to be expected – but she still found herself fascinated by his voice.

When Leo talked of Sophie and Susannah Reiss, and described what he had seen them do in Deadlight Hall's furnace room, his voice faltered for the first time.

'I believed that what I saw that night was my dear twins wreaking a revenge on a woman they thought posed a threat,' he said. 'But now—'

'Now?'

'Now I am not so sure. But that night I made a vow to myself – and to the twins – that I would never speak of what I saw,' he said. 'It was a child's vow, but it was deeply and genuinely meant. Today is the first time I've ever spoken about it,' he said.

'A vow made out of loyalty?' Michael's tone was hesitant, but Rosendale looked at him eagerly, as if grateful for this comprehension.

'I can't be sure,' he said, 'because it was a very long time ago, and I was very young, as well as being quite seriously ill. But I think it was mostly loyalty. We – the three of us – had all been through so much, and I believed that nursing sister had been immensely cruel to the twins. I didn't understand then about the tests they had to do for meningitis.'

'Lumbar puncture,' said Nell, nodding. 'I believe it's very unpleasant and painful.'

'Yes. Probably they tried to explain it to us, but none of us had much English. And to have grasped medical terms—' He leaned forward, his thin graceful hands clasped together so tightly the knuckles showed white. 'I knew – at least, I thought then – that part of the twins' motive was to punish that woman,' he said. 'But I also thought there was more to it than that.' He looked from one to the other of his listeners, as if to be sure they wanted him to continue. Michael said, 'Please go on,' and Nell nodded.

'When we were smuggled out to this country,' said Leo, 'we were surrounded by an atmosphere of what I can only describe as extreme fear. We had spent the previous two years – perhaps longer than that – in the midst of terror and secrecy. Most of us hadn't really known any other world. And the one thing we all knew about was what the adults called the ovens. We had heard – half heard – our parents whispering – and we knew fragments of the stories. We knew people had vanished into the ovens – almost every family we knew had a tragedy, a loss.' His eyes narrowed in memory. 'It's difficult to convey to you now the absolute menace those words – *the Ovens* – held,' he said. 'For the children it was tangled up with the grisly old fairy tales. Hansel and Gretel, and the gingerbread house with the oven. Ogres who would grind men's bones to make bread. It wasn't until many years later that I understood what our parents had really feared.'

'Not ovens at all,' said Michael, softly, almost as if he was afraid to say the words too loudly. 'The gas chambers.'

'Yes. They sent us away to save us,' said Leo. 'It wasn't until much later that I understood that. But in those years – 1941, 1942 – the Nazis were combing the towns and the villages for our people. The German High Command had given orders for what they called the "resettling of Jews in the East". That was a euphemism, of course. What they were doing was interning hundreds of thousands of Jews in labour camps, and then exterminating most of them. So when we saw the old furnace in Deadlight Hall . . .' He made a brief, expressive gesture with one hand. 'We equated it with the nightmares from our home,' he said.

'I understand that,' said Nell, torn with pity for the small boy he had been.

'Go on,' said Michael.

'Sophie and Susannah thought someone was watching the house where they had been placed. Battersby, I think the name of the family was – odd how things like that come back to you, isn't it? And on that night in Deadlight Hall, they thought they were going to be dragged into the ovens. When I saw – when I thought I saw them with that nursing sister, I assumed they were acting in self-defence. But in light of that journal,' he said, 'I'm no longer sure if what I saw was real.'

'What happened to the twins?' asked Nell. 'To Sophie and Susannah?'

'I never knew. They simply vanished that night. I suppose I could have tried to find out what happened, but I was very young, and I was in a foreign country with strangers.'

'Did you ever return to your home?'

'No. But I heard – at second or third hand – that the Nazis did march in,' he said. 'So I don't think there's much doubt about what happened to my family and the people I knew there.' He said this with such humility and such acceptance that Nell's heart twisted with pity.

'Then, when I was eleven,' he said, 'I was taken to the Hall by Simeon Hurst, and I saw the twins again. I knew with my head and my brain that it wasn't the real Sophie and Susannah I was seeing – of course I did, it was five years after they vanished – but my emotions kept telling me otherwise. Perhaps I wanted them to be still there.' A pause. 'And on that day I saw it all happen again,' he said. 'Only this time it was Simeon Hurst they killed. I tried to save him, but I couldn't.' Again there was the quick expressive gesture with his hands. 'It sounds like the wildest flight of fantasy,' he said, 'but—'

'You thought you were seeing the murder of the nursing sister replayed?'

'Yes. I found I could believe that the . . . the hatred and the terror that Sophie and Susannah had felt that night had remained inside that house.'

'Printed itself on the walls,' said Nell.

'In a strange, child's way, I even thought I might be being given a second chance to stop it all happening. But tonight, listening to that journal, I have to ask whether it was a different replay altogether I was seeing.'

'A replay of a much older tragedy,' said Michael, softly. 'The burning of Esther.'

'Tomorrow I may argue against you on that,' said Leo. 'But tonight . . . yes, tonight I can believe that.'

'What happened about Simeon's death?'

'It was put down as a bizarre accident. And eventually I managed to . . . not forget it exactly, but to put it to the back of my mind. Life went along, and other things overlaid his death. School and study and then Oxford. I came here as a young man,' he said. 'And I never left. But the years have been good to me, you know. I like my work and my students. I like being part of Oxford. I enjoy the research and the friendships. Even the little feuds and power struggles that go on. But then I read that Deadlight Hall was being restored – that people would be living in it again – and I couldn't get rid of the fear that the old hatred – the twins' hatred and their terror – might somehow reactivate. So I came to you for help,' he said, looking at Michael.

There was a brief silence, then Michael said, 'There's something more, isn't there? Something you haven't told us. Is it to do with the twins?'

Leo hesitated, then said, 'A long-standing nightmare. On the night we were smuggled out of our village, we heard some of the grown-ups talking about the *Todesengel*. The Angel of Death.'

Nell looked at him questioningly, and it was Michael who said, 'Josef Mengele. That was what they called him, wasn't it? My God, yes, of course. Mengele experimented on twins in the concentration camps.'

'Yes. I didn't know at the time, of course, but I've come to know since, that Dr Mengele was deeply interested in telepathy between twins. He was hunting for case studies. Sophie and Susannah were strongly telepathic. I think he was hunting for them.'

'Did you find out what happened to them?'

'No. But that night in Deadlight Hall I heard – and the twins heard – someone prowling through the house, calling for the children.'

'*Children where are you? I will find you, you know*,' said Michael softly. 'Was it Mengele's agents, do you think, or . . . or was it the voice I heard? That the nineteenth-century children heard?'

'I don't know. But Sophie and Susannah vanished that night, as silently and as efficiently as if they had been snatched up by someone who knew exactly what he was doing and what he wanted. Someone working to very precise orders.'

'Orders from Josef Mengele?'

'That's what I've always thought,' said Leo. 'At least – until tonight.'

'Is there no one – no one at all – who might know about your twins?'

'It's too long ago,' he said.

Nell said, 'Not necessarily,' and handed him the letter Ashby's had sent from David Bensimon.

'What . . .?'

'It probably won't lead to anything,' she said. 'But read it anyway.'

Leo frowned, and began to read. As he did, Nell saw that the pupils of his eyes contracted as if he had suddenly been faced with a dazzling light.

'How extraordinary,' he said, at last. 'Maurice Bensimon.' His voice sounded faraway, as if he had retreated into the past, or as if he was trying to reach back a very long way in order to unwrap an old and fragile memory. 'I never thought I'd hear that name again. But this man – this David – says his great-uncle tried to find a silver golem during the years of the Second World War.'

'And he believes the one you're selling could be that same figure,' said Nell. 'Could it be?'

'Yes. Yes, I think it must be,' said Leo.

'Did you know Maurice Bensimon?'

'Oh, yes. He taught for a while in the village school I attended – history, it was, although very simplified history because we were all quite young. Infants' class. It's a long time ago, but I still remember him. He was a gentle, scholarly man, but beneath it there was a steely core. I think he had immense courage and resilience.'

'Ashby's knew him as a collector – something to do with jewellery and silver,' said Nell.

'I don't know what he was. I certainly don't think teaching was his profession. The conditions in Europe at that time meant people – my people in particular – had to take on jobs that weren't the norm for them. Sometimes it was camouflage for secret work against the Nazis. What I do know, though, is that Maurice Bensimon was part of some sort of resistance network in the war years,' said Leo. 'I think he was part of the escape plan that got us – myself and the other children – out to England in 1943. He worked with Schönbrunn, and Schönbrunn was the real heart of that network. He organized a great many escapes from the concentration camps, and he was a kind of legend. Even as children we knew about him. And when we met him on the night we left our homes for ever . . . We thought he was a god,' said the professor. 'He told us he would save us from the ovens and that we would be safe, and we believed him. And he did save us. He brought us to England.' The smile deepened for a moment. 'A remarkable man,' he said. 'Very charismatic.'

'Professor, if you wish, I could ask Ashby's to forward a letter to David Bensimon,' said Nell.

She had not been sure how he would react, but the light came into his eyes again at once. 'Could you do that? Would they agree?'

'Let's try,' said Nell.

TWENTY-SIX

Professor Rosendale's study was not particularly small, but as Nell and Michael waited with him for David Bensimon to arrive, Nell thought the room was filled almost to suffocation point with anticipation.

She had thought the professor was taking it very calmly, but when they heard the step on the stair, he stood up to face the door, and she saw that he grasped the back of his chair so tightly, his knuckles whitened.

David Bensimon came in quietly enough, and shook hands politely. He was around forty years of age, and Nell had the impression that although he wore casual, unobtrusive clothes, he had taken considerable care in the choosing of them. He had dark hair and eyes, and sensitive hands. He acknowledged Nell and Michael, then stood looking at the professor for a long time, before putting out his hands. As their hands met and gripped, Nell felt as if something had sizzled on the air – as if two electrical leads had been joined and become live.

'Professor Rosendale,' said David, at last. 'I feel I am meeting a part of my great-uncle's past.'

'You have a strong look of Maurice. I'm so pleased to meet you.' The words were conventional; the tone in which they were spoken was filled with emotion. 'Please sit down,' said Leo. 'There is coffee there, or whisky if you prefer.'

'Coffee, please. I shall keep a level head. Later we can get drunk.' He smiled, then said, 'I was right about the golem, wasn't I? It's the one Maurice tried to find?'

'It is. It came to England seventy years ago,' said Leo. 'I had no idea your great-uncle tried to find it.'

'He spent years in the search,' said David. 'The family legend is that he was trying to trace two girls. He hoped that if he could find the figure – if someone was trying to sell it – then that might give him a path to them.'

'But . . . he didn't find them?' Nell thought she and Michael both heard the hope in the professor's voice.

'No.'

'Did he ever mention a man called Schönbrunn?'

David Bensimon's eyes lit up at once. 'Ah, Schönbrunn,' he said. 'There were so many stories about that man. Maurice died in 1970 – I was only ten at the time, but I remember all the stories. He regarded Schönbrunn as a god, I think.'

'We all did.' Leo leaned forward. 'You said you had letters written by Maurice . . .'

'Written by him, and also to him. A number of them weren't in English, of course, but over the years my family translated them. I've brought photocopies of the translations for you.' He reached into his briefcase and brought out a manilla folder. 'Some were written to our village – to a man there who was thought to work for Schönbrunn's network. Later, the letters were found in that man's house.'

'Later?'

David Bensimon said, 'You had better read them for yourself.'

He opened the folder, and Nell and Michael saw the heading – *The Village School House, Nr Warsaw, 1942* and the opening line.

The Village School House, Nr Warsaw, 1942
Autumn
My dear M.B.

We agreed that, in the British expression, there would be 'no names, no pack drill' in these messages, so I address you by your initials only, and sign in the same way. Forgive the discourtesy, my good friend.

With great reluctance, we have agreed that despite the emotional cost to their families, the children in our village may need to be removed to safety. You mentioned a possible escape plan from the man we both know as Schönbrunn. Does such a plan actually exist? Can you give me information about it? And can it – and Schönbrunn himself – be trusted?

Affectionately,
J.W.

Leo looked up, his eyes clouded with memory.

'You should read them all,' said David. 'It won't take very long. I've put them in chronological order. In places they're harrowing, but it may answer some questions for you.'

'Let me pass them to Nell and Michael as I read,' said Leo. Then, to Nell, 'You don't mind that?'

'Professor,' said Nell, 'I'd have been devastated if you hadn't let us see them.'

For a long time there was no sound in the study, save the rustle of papers. Nell and Michael sat next to each other, reading together. David Bensimon watched, nodding occasionally as Leo looked up having read a particular section, not quite questioningly, but as if to say, *This is right?*

The clock ticked steadily on the mantelpiece, but Nell thought it was almost as if it had been wound backwards so they could be pulled into this strange, troubled fragment of the past.

When Leo picked up the last letter he recoiled slightly. Then he said, 'It's a remarkable story you've brought me, David. Your great-uncle – that gentle scholarly man – he did all that. He tried to find the twins – he came to England to search.'

'And,' said Nell, 'he and Schönbrunn went to Deadlight Hall as part of that search.'

'They heard that voice,' said Michael. *'Children, are you here?'*

'That always puzzled him, I think,' said David. 'He never found a satisfactory explanation for it.'

'I don't think there is one,' said Michael. 'How strange to see that Porringer name again.'

'Paul Porringer was a traitor to this country,' said David. 'My great-uncle found that despicable and impossible to understand. But towards the end of his life, when he became a little more talkative about those years, he said no man should have to suffer such a death as Porringer did. I believe he never forgot what he saw.'

Michael said, 'Professor, these letters – in particular the one about their visit to Deadlight Hall – give even more proof that whatever you saw and heard that night – and again on the day Simeon was killed – it wasn't your twins.'

'I know.' Leo looked at the final letter. 'One more river to cross, and I think this one is going to be the River of Jordan. Will it be distressing to read this?' he said to David.

'Yes. But you need to know.'

'Yes, I do.' He reached for his glass, and as he did so, Nell caught sight of the heading. The address was The Schoolhouse, but beneath that had been written:

To J.W. Nuremberg Prison.

The date was October 1946.

Leo suddenly said, 'Michael, we asked Nell to read Maria's journal. This was written by a man – would you read it for us?'

'If you're sure it's what you want?'

'I am.'

Michael took the letter, glanced at the heading, then began to read.

> My dear J.W.
>
> I am permitted to send you this letter following your trial. I hope it will reach you before you are led out to your death. I shall think of you on that morning, but . . .
>
> But, my dear, one-time friend, how could I have been so deceived and for so long? I am cold and sick when I remember how you seemed to help our children to escape – how you warned us that Mengele's agents were converging on our village, and how you helped with the plans – plans whose details I had given you. And all the time, it seems you were herding those children together – most particularly Sophie and Susannah Reiss – for Dr Mengele's agents. I can forgive many people many things, but I can never forgive you for that.
>
> It horrifies me to know that when I sent you all those details of our travels, and of how and where we searched for the twins, you were relaying it all to Mengele's people. That, I now see, is how Paul Porringer found us in the old house, Deadlight Hall.
>
> As you know, the twins were never found, and as far as I understand it, Mengele himself has evaded justice so far.
>
> I am sorry for your approaching execution, and bid you farewell and safe journey beyond. In time I hope I shall come to think more kindly of our years of friendship.
>
> M.B.

At the foot of the letter was written, 'Returned to sender after the execution of the recipient for war crimes.'

Michael laid the letter down as carefully as if it might fall apart. For a long time no one spoke – Nell thought none of them could find anything to say.

Then Leo said, 'So that is what happened. That is the ending.'

'Yes.'

'Did that man – Paul Porringer – really know what had happened to the twins, do you think?'

'I don't know. I don't think Maurice or Schönbrunn knew – they both talked of the "hesitation" when they asked Porringer the direct question about the twins.'

'As if he was not prepared to admit that he, or his people, had failed to take them,' said Michael.

'Yes. But I don't think either of them was prepared to take the chance,' said David. 'That's why Schönbrunn went to Auschwitz. Nothing more was heard of him.'

'And Mengele evaded justice,' said Leo, half to himself.

'Oh, yes. He left Auschwitz for a camp in Gross Rosen, but he fled from there a week before the Russian soldiers arrived. He lived most of the remainder of his life in South America. I think he died in the late 1970s. My great-uncle made several more attempts to find Sophie and Susannah Reiss, but he never did. As for Schönbrunn – no one ever knew his real name, so it was impossible to make any proper search.'

'Yes, of course. Well,' said Leo, 'it's all a long time ago, and I'll try to think that Schönbrunn probably died in a rebellious blaze of battle somewhere.'

'It's the likeliest thing.'

'Oh yes.'

But Nell, watching him, knew he had been hoping that Maurice Bensimon's letters might have told him what had happened to his beloved twins. She was filled with deep sadness that they had not done so.

*

Dear Nell

Everything is now in place for our auction next month. We have had considerable interest in the silver golem, following the PR campaign – the TV segment was particularly good, we thought – hope you caught that – and there was also a mention on *Antiques Roadshow*. The mail-out of our pre-sale catalogue has brought a number of enquiries, and we think we're in for some lively bidding on the day.

I'm looking forward to seeing you again at the sale, and it's good to hear you're bringing the owner of the golem with you. Can I take you both to dinner after the sale, please?

However, my main reason for emailing you is that yesterday we were contacted by a lady who apparently owns the 'twin' to Professor Rosendale's figure. She had seen one of the TV items, and has asked if we would deal with the sale of her own figure. It is identical in all respects, except for being engraved on the underside with the Jewish character for the letter *L* – the *Lamed*, a thick horizontal stroke with the upjutting line on the left and the downward tail on the right.

We are, of course, happy to deal with this sale, but feel very strongly that it would be far more advantageous to sell the figures as a pair. This really would be a case of the sum being greater than the component parts. The proceeds could be divided on a strict 50/50 basis between the two owners (less, of course, your commission and ours).

As Professor Rosendale's representative, could you put the proposal to him, and let me know his decision as soon as possible?

It would be a bit of a scramble to alter the present selling arrangements – amend the catalogue and do a new mail-out – but we think we could manage it, and in fact there should be some useful publicity to be got from the discovery of the second figure!

I don't think we can disclose this second seller's name at this stage, but I can tell you she is a Polish lady who escaped Nazi-occupied Warsaw as a small child in 1943 along with her sister. Apparently they were later smuggled out of England by a nursing sister who worked for Military Intelligence, and who believed the girls were in danger from Josef Mengele. It sounds as if the woman simply removed the two girls from some house in the depths of winter, and got them away before anyone realized. Another of those remarkable and unsung stories of bravery!

The girls were taken to Canada, where they both went on to study medicine. The nurse also found work there, and never returned to England, severing all connections in order to safeguard the two girls – even though she had family ties in the area, and a great-uncle or something who once owned a glass manufactory there. But she wanted to destroy all traces, in case she and the two girls could be found – although it seems she did leave some old papers with a local farmer and his sister.

The owner of the second golem is one of those girls, and she hopes very much that Professor Rosendale will agree to her request for the sale of both golems. She feels – as I and my colleagues do – that it would be the right thing for these two figures to be brought together again after so many years.

All best wishes.

*

MON PLAISIR, MONMOUTH STREET
DINNER RESERVATION
Table for seven booked for 8 p.m. this evening:
Reservation contact: Ashby's Auction House (host)
Guests: Professor Leo Rosendale
Mr David Bensimon
Dr Michael Flint
Mrs Nell West
Dr Sophia Reiss
Miss Susannah Reiss